Bairns of Bridgend

by

Cairine Caskie

ISBN No. 0-9553057-0-5

Published by
Jamieson and Munro

Printed by
The Monument Press, Riverside, Stirling FK8 1LP

*This book has been produced by Jamieson & Munro
and production costs were supported
by a grant from the
Trustees of the John Jamieson Munro Charitable Trust*

Dedicated with love to the memory of my mother,
Margaret McLeod Miller Moir.
And for the latest family members,
Thomas Alexander and Rory James Caskie.

BAIRNS OF BRIDGEND
DUNBLANE

INTRODUCTION

Each and every character named in the ten tales of Bairns of Bridgend is recorded as having lived in the area around the time that his or her tale is set. Being based in one small Scottish community from 1558 to 1945, the stories, though individually self-contained, also reflect changes in society through each child's particular experience.

The twentieth century tales are based on personal recollections of the main characters who were able to discuss their childhood days with me and indeed edited their own stories.

The other tales draw on local sources, being gleaned from local histories, local newspapers and archival material from Stirling, Perth and the Scottish Record Office, Edinburgh.

These written sources are listed after each story along with the names of local people who shared their personal memories with me. Without their invaluable input the stories would not have been written.

General historical background reading is listed at the back of the book.

The dialogue of the characters is a blend of Scots and English. Much of the Scots that is understood and spoken in the area today has its roots in the nineteenth century and I have consciously tried to avoid putting that Scots vocabulary into the mouths of sixteenth and seventeenth century characters. So instead of *clype* Bessie Broun says 'carry tales', and instead of *stramash*, Jamie in 'Andrew Kerr' simply says 'commotion'. I have also avoided using obsolete Scots words and spelling that general readers would not recognize at all.

The brief notes after each story summarise what is historically recorded about the characters and contemporary events.

The rest is 'creative' writing!

INDEX

Cover: Haymaking scene in Dunblane by John Bell circa 1860.
Some Bridgend cottages are seen between the trees on the opposite bank of Allan Water.

Photograph: 'Chuckie Row', Calderwood Place, circa 1909. The child is Mary McGregor.
All black and white sketches are by Cairine Caskie

Illustration and Map acknowledgments
Bairns of Bridgend
by Cairine Caskie

Cover, Main Picture: Haymaking scene in Dunblane. John Bell circa 1860. Reproduced by permission of the Trustees of Dunblane Museum.

Cover: 'Chuckie Row', Calderwood Place, circa 1909. Reproduced by permission of Stirling Council Library Service.

1   Helen Wilson 1945. Map Dunblane in the 1940's. O.S. Map National Library of Scotland.

4   William Hogg 1864. Map *Central Perthshire* Sheet 12 John Bartholomew & Son The Geographical Institute, Edinburgh.

5   Schulebairns 1782. Dunblane and District. From *Stobie's Map of Perth and Clackmannanshire 1783*. Reproduced by permission of Stirling Council Archives.

6   Peggy Lucas 1745. Map *Dunblane and Environs* from *The Map of Hugh Barclay circa 1830*. Journal of The Society of Friends of Dunblane Cathedral Vol II, iii.

7   John Wright 1726. *A Map of Stirlingshire from a survey of William Edgar in 1745*. Issued with Nimmo's *History of Stirlingshire 1777*. Reproduced by permission of the Trustees of the National Library of Scotland.

8   Marian Corsar 1665. Maps (a) Shielings, Cambushinnie From *A Survey of the Lands of Kinbuck 1762*. Extracted from RHP 13498 1. National Archives Scotland. (b) *Dunblane to Cambushinnie*, based on O.S. Sheet NN70 1975. National Library of Scotland.

BAIRNS OF BRIDGEND DUNBLANE

HELEN WILSON 1944 -45

We'll meet again
Don't know where
Don't know when,
But I know we'll meet again some sunny day.

Keep smiling through
Just like you always do
Till the blue skies drive the dark clouds far away.

So will you please say hello
To the folks that I know?
Tell them I won't be long –
They'll be happy to know
That as you saw me go,
I was singing this song –

We'll meet again
Don't know where
Don't know when,
But I know we'll meet again some sunny day.

Words and Music *Ross Parker & Hughie Charles.*
Sung in Britain by *Vera Lynn.*

BAIRNS OF BRIDGEND DUNBLANE

HELEN WILSON 1944 -45

There was a hubbub of excitement from the children waiting at Dunblane Cross for the fancy dress parade. The organisers trying to usher them into their age groups were not helped by the mothers fussing over the girls and boys, adjusting a skirt here and tying a bow there. Princesses and Victorian ladies were prettily adorned in costumes of taffeta and organdie created from their mothers' best dance dresses in days gone by. Among the boys some comical tramps and scarecrows or tattie-bogles were clad in their fathers' cast-offs. At last, the parade was off to a sprightly bagpipe march, led by a tiny shepherdess whose borrowed crook threatened to trip her up. As the wee ones at the front trotted along to keep up with the piper's long strides, the onlookers lining the High Street applauded the prettiest and laughed at the original costumes on display.

Helen laughed and chuckled too, half wishing that she had entered this year's competition, but it was too late now, and anyway she was too big for such nonsense. After all, she reminded herself, she had been at MacLaren High School for two years now. Still, some of her friends were in the parade and she followed them round the corner and across the bridge over Allan Water. Bringing up the rear of the procession came the decorated bicycles, bedecked with flowers and streamers, bells jangling merrily as they passed the railway station. Now the competitors and onlookers squeezed into the Victoria Hall for the judging.

Victoria Hall.

No one was surprised when the little shepherdess was awarded a prize. The applause was warm too for two girls of Helen's age, Jean Napier, the youngest of the blacksmith's big family, and Helen's close friend Grace Carmichael dressed as elegant Victorian ladies. Other popular choices were 'The most original', Margaret Morrow and her partner Isobel Wilkie, an appealing and topical pair as a 'Wounded 'Tommy' and a Red Cross Nurse'. Another ripple of applause went round the hall when the judges awarded prizes to two decorated bicycles with patriotic slogans, 'Peace', by Jemima Dowling and 'Dig for Victory', by Robert Tait. These struck a chord with everyone at the end of another successful day of Dunblane's 'Stay at Home' holiday.

Peace and victory were uppermost in everyone's thoughts, fed by reports of the progress of the war. Allied soldiers had entered Paris triumphantly, liberating the city after four years of German occupation. The newspapers and cinema newsreels were full of scenes of joy throughout France's villages where grateful villagers showered British troops and their armoured vehicles with flowers.

So the Dunblane mothers and children who scattered to their homes on that warm August evening had more than local events to be cheerful about. They were sure that by Christmas the war would be over and that the husbands, fathers, sons and brothers who had survived would be safely home. As Helen, Jean and Grace walked past the railway station on their way to Bridgend they paid little attention to the buses lined up outside.

A little later a crowd of schoolgirls and their teachers clambered from the train arriving from London. Weary after their twelve hour journey, they boarded the waiting buses that took them to the Hydro Hotel. That short run contrasted sharply with their earlier journey that morning from their Surrey convent school through the vast war torn area of London, pockmarked with bombsites. Dunblane's unscathed High Street, the solid villas of Perth Road and the panorama of mountains seen from the Hydro seemed to belong to a different world from southern England where the girls had spent days huddled in air raid shelters.

In their evening prayers the evacuees thanked God for their deliverance from the target zone of terrifying flying bombs. The schoolgirls who found refuge in Dunblane had mixed emotions, relief to be out of danger and fear for their families left behind in that other perilous world. Many a pillow was wet in the rows of hospital beds in the hotel that night.

In the remaining golden days of August while the evacuees created their separate community, Dunblane bairns returned to their own schools and the rhythm of the countryside brought harvest time around. Grain ripened in the fields and ears of oats hung heavy ready for the reaper. Apart from the shortage of men to help, it was hard to imagine that this was a country still at war as the corn was cut under peaceful blue skies.

But as farmer Millar of Hillside followed the reaper to set up the sheaves, he had a sudden sharp reminder of the times. Bending down to stook some bundles, his eye caught something round and grey nestling in the stubble. It was an unexploded hand grenade! It hardly compared with the unstoppable rockets that were still blitzing London, but the find gave Dunblane folk something to talk about.

"Well! It just shows that nowhere is safe."

"Aye, Mr Millar could have lost his foot, if he'd knocked the pin oot!"

"It must hae been lyin since yon Home Guard exercise tae capture Kippenross House last year."

From then on the harvesters at Hillside were extra cautious and luckily no more hidden dangers were revealed as the rest of the corn was gathered safely.

The harvest was not complete however. Buried in the ground lay the crop that the children helped to pick in autumn – the potatoes. While the days shortened and grew colder, the crop swelled and was ready for digging. The 'Tattie Howking' holiday began.

On the train coming home from MacLaren High in Callander, the children debated about which farmer's tatties they would pick.

"Well, we could just go to Angus's. It's the closest, just across the road from my house," suggested Grace. "That's where Anne and Isobel Wilkie are going. It's handy for them in George Street too."

"The thing is though, Grace, Angus is awful stingy. If we go a wee bit out of Dunblane, we'll get more than five shillings a day. How about trying out by Kinbuck?"

So it was agreed and on a chill autumn Monday morning the girls made their way from Bridgend to Hutchison farm north of Dunblane. They were a motley crew who gathered at the side of the potato field, tinker families travelling from one seasonal job to another, local housewives earning some extra cash for Christmas and school children answering the government's call for sixty thousand pickers throughout Scotland. They all listened to the farmer's instructions.

"Spread oot alang the side. Tak a stent each. Keep up wi the tractor and pick every tattie – no leavin the wee anes mind."

The girls looked across the furrows of greenery that stretched ahead forever like the waves of the sea. The tractor was crossing their path going up the first drill and behind it the potatoes were churned up to the surface of the soil.

"Here we go, Grace," said Helen as the pickers strung out along the length of the field each taking a stent, a marked width, to clear. "Try and get wire baskets. They're lighter, easier to drag when they get full."

And with that they were off, filling the baskets as fast as they could. Already ahead of them the tractor was re-crossing their path uprooting another row and the girls scrambled over the drills clearing the tatties from the soil. In their efforts to keep up with the digger, their crouch walk became a fast crawl on hands and knees, and before long they began to look like the tramps they'd all laughed at in the summer parade.

By noon when the dinner break came, they were more than ready for it. Thankfully they sat on the hay bales set out for them and opened up their sandwiches.

"Oh, no," said Grace, "Corned beef again! I've told my mum I don't like it but she says I need built up! What's on your pieces, Helen?"

Helen peered at her own slices of purple stained bread. "Bramble jelly – just made last week. I helped my mum to pick them myself. I've still got the scratches."

"Swop over then Helen, a bramble jelly for a corned beef. Be a pal!"

By the time the friends had finished their exchange, the farmer's wife was pouring tea from a huge urn. The girls stood in line with the other workers, their

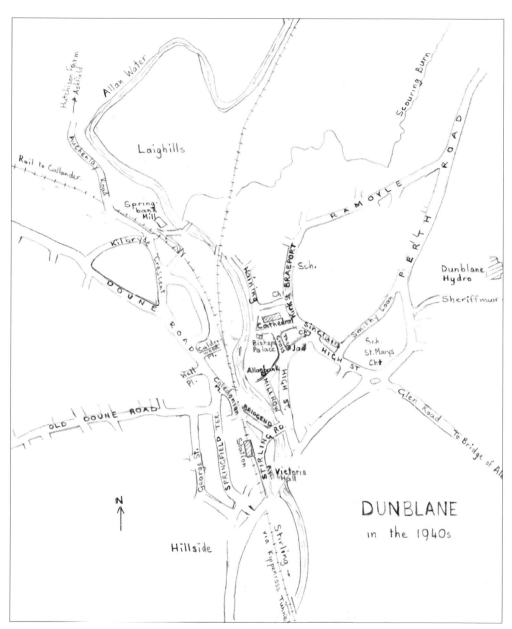

Dunblane 1940's

enamel mugs at the ready.

In front of them one lad was heard asking, "Any sugar Missus?"

"Dinna be funny, son! Where would I get extra sugar rations for a' this lot? Content yersel wi extra milk. We've mair than enough o that. Awa you go!"

The lad and those around him chuckled. It was worth a try anyway! All too soon the dinner hour was over and the pickers were back down on their hands and knees on the brown soil.

By the end of that first day the girls felt their backs and shoulders ache and they were reminded that the words, Tattie Holidays, were just a bit misleading when they actually meant days on end grubbing about in a field and humphing heavy baskets around. They consoled themselves on the way home discussing what they'd do with their well-earned cash at the end of the 'holiday'. Grace knew exactly what she wanted.

"There's a smashing pair of boots in Norwell's window. They're lovely and furry, black with suede trim. I'd love them for the winter. I can just see myself going to church in them! What are you going to get, Helen?"

"Oh, I'll be giving the money to my mum. You know she's a widow and she has to manage on what my big sisters get paid with our brother John away in the Air Force. Still, John should be back soon. The war should be over by Christmas."

"Yes, and my big brother Donald should be home too. Last time we saw him was after he'd been in hospital with his hip wound. My mum and dad worried themselves sick about him but he's fine now. I think he's somewhere in France."

"John was in North Africa, the last we heard. He's a wireless operator," Helen added proudly, as the girls parted company at Bridgend.

At number twenty, Helen's mother had her tea ready and as they ate, mother and daughter exchanged their day's news. Mrs Wilson was excited about the arrival of a parcel from friends in America.

"Everyone's rich in America, you know! That's why they can send us parcels. Jessie and Betty will be tickled pink. There's nylons for them in the parcel!"

For a moment, Helen felt a stab of envy. She'd love nylons too, but of course she was still at school and wouldn't dare ask for some. Not with her sisters going short all this time. All the same, she was fed up with being the youngest, the baby, the one who got the hand-me-downs. . . .

Her mother's chatter broke through her thoughts.

"And there's chocolate for you, Helen - Hershey bars! It's not the same as Duncan's chocolate of course but it's a rare treat anyway . . . Here, I don't think you've heard a word I've been saying!"

"Sorry, mum – Chocolate – that's great . . ."

"Yes, and dried egg, and tinned peaches. We'll keep them for John's homecoming."

"Mum, I've been thinking . . ."

"I can see that! You've not been listening to me anyway."

"Sorry – It's about my tattie picking money …"

"Well, a penny for your thoughts then, and eat up your tea before it's cold."

"It's all right, mum." Helen could not put into words the sudden longing she had for a new dress, one of her very own, that hadn't belonged to one of her sisters. But even thinking that way made her feel guilty, so she quickly changed the subject.

"What's on at the pictures this week, Mum. Maybe we could go one night."

"Maybe, pet," replied her mother. "Have a look in the papers. You could go with your sisters."

Mrs Wilson smiled, but as she cleared away the dishes she looked very thoughtfully at her youngest child.

By Saturday, the end of the first week of tattie howking, the pickers were beginning to wish that they'd never see another potato. What had begun as crisp bright autumn weather had suddenly changed with dismal grey rain lashing down. Worse, what had been back breaking but reasonably dry work, now turned into a nightmare of mud.

Try as they might to keep warm, the workers found the wet seeping through trousers, up sleeves, down necks and into wellington boots. The farmer's wife, sorry for the bairns, made kale broth for them and they shifted to the barn for their dinner break.

In the evening when Helen returned to Bridgend, her mother brought the zinc bath into the kitchen and filled it with steaming pailsful of water from the boiler. Thankfully, she peeled off the wet clothes and sank into the comforting warmth while her mother wrang out her things and hoisted them up on the pulley to dry off.

Not even the attractions of an Errol Flynn film at the Regal Cinema in Stirling could tempt Helen away from the warmth of number twenty Bridgend. Settling for an evening at home, Mrs Wilson and she tuned into BBC radio for their evening's entertainment.

The BBC orchestra played some light music and then it was time for their favourite, 'ITMA', Tommy Handley in 'It's That Man Again'. His antics made them forget the rain outside, but then it was time for the news from London. Helen paid little attention to the voice that crackled loudly and then faded alternately. The news bored her especially when it kept repeating the same thing about 'the allies meeting resistance' as they pushed through Europe. Helen preferred to lose herself in a good story while she lay curled up in bed.

"Goodnight, mum. I'm off to read my book".

"Night night, pet. I'll just listen to the play on the wireless while I finish my mending. See you in the morning."

Sunday, with its routine of church in the morning and Sunday school later, slipped by all too quickly and Monday found Helen and Grace sloshing through the mud of yet another churned up potato field. All the harvesters, from the farmer to the smallest tinker bairn, had to grit their teeth to carry on, and in spite of the damp misery there were occasional flashes of humour.

When Robert Tait slipped and fell face first to rise oozing mud someone shouted,

"Whaur's yer 'Dig for Victory' got ye noo, Rab? Covered in glaur!"

Everyone, including Rab, laughed, but it was a timely reminder to all the pickers that their efforts were indeed essential in the nationwide drive to feed Britain and somehow the quip gave them heart to carry on. If they had known that the awful weather was to last throughout the remaining days of harvesting, they might not have been so cheery. They needed every ounce of determination to keep going.

Hutchison Farm overlooking Ashfield.

By the time the crop was in, buried safely in straw lined pits to protect the potatoes from winter frosts, the girls were almost numb with fatigue. Grace clutched her purse with her well-earned cash as they made their weary way back to Dunblane. She confided in her friend.

"I know we were 'digging for victory' and all that," she said, "but I was picking for these furry black boots. Every basket I filled, I said to myself: that's the sole of the right foot; that's the toe; that's the heel and so on till I knew I had enough. They're keeping them at Norwell's till Monday. They fit too, I've tried them on."

Helen laughed, "Is that what you've been muttering about while we've been crawling about in the glaur?"

Then her smile faded and she suddenly burst out, "Oh, Grace, what I'd really love is a new frock for John coming home but I don't like to ask my mother."

"Och, don't be daft, Helen. Your mother wouldn't mind I'm sure. Ask her anyway. After all, you've worked all the holiday."

Still, Helen was undecided about voicing her thoughts when she got home to Bridgend. She said nothing about it while her mother bustled about giving her dry clothes and getting her tea ready.

"Well, pet, you'll be thankful the tatties are in for another year. I'll get these things washed when this rain decides to stop. You and Grace and all the other bairns have done well."

While her mother chattered on, Helen made up her mind. "Mum, here's my tattie money."

She hesitated and then stammered, "Oh, Mum, do you think . . . ?"

Before she could finish, her mother broke in. "Oh, thanks dear. Now – I have a surprise for you!"

Helen stopped, her question only half voiced. Rummaging about in the chest of drawers, Mrs Wilson produced a large parcel wrapped in newspaper.

"Jimmy Dick was here and he brought this. Open it up, pet."

Jimmy Dick, that name and the shape of the parcel meant one thing – dress material! Helen's fingers shook as she struggled with the string but the parcel was undone in seconds. Inside lay folds of checked pink and green vyella. Helen shook out the soft wool and cotton mixture and held it against her.

"Oh, Mum, that's lovely!" Her eyes shone and Mrs Wilson shared her pleasure.

"There's enough there for a frock for you, dear."

"Is it really for me, Mum? How did you know? It's just lovely."

Her mother smiled a quiet smile, "How did I know, when I've watched you pouring over the fashion pictures in the Stirling Observer these last few weeks? And, you've grown like a weed over the summer months. So when Jimmy gave me the chance of the material I jumped at it knowing that your tattie money was coming in. So there we are. You can take it down to Mrs McDonald after school on Monday and she'll fit you for a frock."

"Thanks, Mum!"

Helen threw her arms round her mother's neck. Grace had been right, she thought, but her mother had been one step ahead of them.

It was the night of Hallowe'en when Helen went down Bridgend to collect the finished dress. Mrs McDonald had fashioned the warm fabric into a smart dress with long sleeves and a neat pink peter pan collar. The straight skirt was softened by a couple of pleats. The dressmaker seemed as excited as Helen about it.

"My, you look so grown up, Helen. – It's been a nice wee change for me to be making a frock for you instead of school blouses . . .There was just enough cloth for these two wee pleats."

They were interrupted by children at the cottage door.

"Can we have our Hallowe'en?" they choroused.

"Come away in then and give us your party pieces."

Half a dozen children crowded into the kitchen and led by the biggest one gave a rendering of Vera Lynn's 'We'll meet again.'

Mrs McDonald fished in her bag for small change. "That was lovely, but I've nae sweeties for you, bairns."

"Oh, that disna matter, Mrs McDonald. We're collecting for Mrs Churchill's 'Aid to Russia' fund again. We got a fancy thank you letter for the one pound fifteen shillings we sent after Hallowe'en last year. It said that 'the heroic Russians' were having a 'terrible but victorious struggle against the wicked invaders of their country', and it was signed, 'Your sincere friend, Clementine S Churchill.' " The Hallowe'en witch stopped for breath.

"My, you've got the memory for big words! Here's all my small change."

"Thanks very much," the guisers said as the coins jingled and they left to visit other neighbours.

Mrs McDonald turned back to Helen. "I got the idea of the pleats from an advertisement for Menzies in Stirling. Turn round, dearie, till I check the length. That's fine, your knees are well covered."

The dressmaker turned her attention to the top. "Do you like the row of wee glass buttons? They're from an old dress someone wanted cut down to make a skirt. I think they just finish it off!"

9

Twirling around and peering in the mirror, Helen exclaimed, "Oh, yes, thanks Mrs McDonald. It's really lovely. After my mum sees it I'll hang it up in the wardrobe with a lavender bag."

On the train to school the next day, Helen and Grace exchanged notes on their newly acquired treasures.

"How are the new boots, Grace?"

"Oh, they're smashing – but I'm not allowed to wear them to school, of course. They're to go with my good coat for Sunday or visiting."

"You should see my new frock, Grace. It's gorgeous. I'm keeping it to wear when John comes home."

But as dreary November days came and went, John Wilson did not come home and neither did Donald Carmichael. After the excitement of the summer and the hard work of the harvest it was back to the old routine. For Helen and her friends there was studying after the 'holiday' with lots of homework and difficult exams ahead.

For the war weary mothers still coping with rationing and with growing families to clothe, there was the continued effort to 'make do and mend'. On the kitchen front, housewives struggled with food shortages and wondered how many ways they could disguise the plentiful things like corned beef and cabbage. And all the while they worried quietly about their absent men folk.

Perhaps in the succession of soldiers, English, French-Canadian, Norwegian, Scottish and Polish who were billeted in and around the village, Dunblane women were reminded of their own husbands, sons and brothers. Anyway, they baked for them and made sandwiches from whatever was available and opened canteens in their church halls, providing a little comfort for men who could be facing death at a moment's notice. Sometimes Grace and Helen helped with serving tea. They giggled at the gallantries of the Polish soldiers who always seemed able to produce sweets for the children and charming words in delightful broken English for their mothers.

While allied soldiers fought on pushing the Germans back in Europe, on the home front civilians anticipated peace. With the fear of invasion over, the local Home Guard celebrated the end of their wartime activities with a St Andrews night dinner at Kippenross House, while in the village of Dunblane limited street lighting was re-introduced. Now when Helen and her friends went to Girl Guide meetings, they could see where they were going instead of feeling their way along walls in the blackout.

Yet, as Christmas drew nearer there was still no sign of the victory which months before had seemed to be just round the corner. Doubts over the early return of soldiers, sailors and airmen took the fun out of the preparations for Christmas. Still, Mrs Wilson was determined to make the best of it for her girls.

"Look Helen, I've been saving our food coupons for the Christmas cake and dumpling. Will you go the messages for me, pet? Here's the list. Try the Co-op butcher first for the suet or else go to Bennet's. The Buttercup dairy might have butter, but if not get margarine. Abernethy's should have the dried fruit or try across the road at McEwan's."

Helen laughed, "All right, Mum, I've got the idea. I'll keep my eyes and ears open," and she was off down Bridgend across the river and into the High Street.

It was a bit like a treasure hunt, she thought as she queued with all the other girls and women in the shops, and trotted from dairy to grocer's and butcher's buying all the precious ingredients for the cake and clootie dumpling.

The village was busy with Saturday morning shoppers each determined to have a share of whatever scarce goods were available. Outside Ting-a-Leerie's, the hardware store, an indignant customer was grumbling.

"I asked him to keep me some white cups the next time they came in but he didn't bother!"

"Well, it's first come first served," retorted a successful purchaser, clutching her newspaper wrapped parcel.

"Aye, that's right," said another. "There was a queue even before Ting-a-Leerie opened the day. The cups were lying along the window where the blind stops."

The disappointed customer was not appeased, "Huh! I'm just desperate for everyday cups, and I'm a good customer here. I'll be taking my business elsewhere!"

Helen chuckled when she heard the retort, "Suit yersel, missus!"

Further up the street at the stationer's, the centre table was laid out with Christmas cards and calendars. Helen joined the Wilkie girls inside as they looked through them.

"Hello, Helen. We're looking for a nice calendar for our Grandpa Buchanan," Ann told her.

"I see. Oh, maybe I could get one for our John. But maybe he wouldn't like that."

"There are nice wee diaries for one and eight," suggested Isobel. They were interrupted by the smallest sister, Margaret, hopping up and down.

"I choose this one. I choose this one!"

She was waving a calendar with a cheerful Scottie dog complete with tartan tammy.

"No, Margaret, Grandpa wouldn't like that. He'd prefer a nice view. Put it back."

The small face was defiant. "No, Grandpa likes wee doggies!"

"Put it back before you bend it and I'll tell Mummy!"

Now the small girl was almost crying, so Helen quickly asked her, "How are you getting on at school, Margaret?"

The diversion worked. "I can read some words. The teacher says I'm a clever wee girl." She looked at her sisters and sniffed, "So she does!"

Enjoying Helen's attention, Margaret went on, "We're back in St. Mary's school now. The army men went away and we got our own school back."

Helen laughed and looked at the two older girls, "Oh, yes. I mind the day we all marched from St Mary's, up Braeport to the public school, carrying all our books and things. That was the day the teacher's strap got lost in the flitting. A wee bird told me it landed in the river!"

She winked at Anne who raised a finger to her lips. "Shoosh! You know the saying, 'wee jugs hae lang lugs', and our Margaret's ears are flapping!"

The wee one's hands went to her ears, and she protested, "No, they're not!"

There was more laughter as the Wilkie girls made their purchases and left Helen looking at the diaries. She chose one with an air force blue cover and gave a florin to the assistant. With her change in her hand she was off back home well pleased with her successful morning's shopping.

Mrs Wilson was pleased too and she admired the diary.

"Well, we'll just hope that the war doesn't drag on any longer. There's still a chance that John and the other boys will be home for Christmas. Anyway let's get the fruit picked over for the baking."

So the weeks till Christmas passed with everyone still hoping that their families would be re-united by then. While appeals went out for bedding and small furniture for London's latest war victims, the residents of Stepney bombed out of their homes, Dunblane folk were treated to 'Music, Mirth and Melody', a concert party in aid of the Victory Fund. But victory itself was still elusive.

Christmas came and everyone tried to enjoy it. Mrs Wilson had managed to get a chicken for dinner and Helen wore her new dress. They cut the cake and had a small slice each but the rest went back into the tin in the larder. John's presents lay unopened, Helen's diary with them, and they too were put away safely in the chest of drawers.

New Year came and went, and disappointed hope was replaced by resignation, as the school children returned to their books. Neither Helen nor Grace asked any more when their brothers would be home.

As if they knew that the young people needed cheering up, the Polish forces in the area organised an entertainment in the Victoria Hall for the older school children. Some of the local girls put on a repeat performance of the Christmas play and then a choir of soldiers sang deep-throated melodies that reflected all the melancholy of men far from their homes and loved ones. But then they altered the mood by increasing to a mazurka tempo with a cheerful little folksong that had the audience foot tapping and clapping along.

Afterwards, walking the few hundred yards to Bridgend, Helen and Jean Napier looked eagerly into the gift bags that the soldiers had given each departing child.

Jean spoke first. "Look, Helen, there's an orange! I haven't seen an orange for ages."

"And a lovely red apple – that'll be from Canada," Helen added.

Jean went on excitedly, "Yes, and chocolate and some nuts. It's like Hallowe'en in the good old days!"

"I'm going to share my orange with my mum and my big sisters," said Helen in a fit of generosity.

Jean laughed, "Well, I'm keeping mine to myself. There's eight of us in the house. That would just be a sook each! Cheerio then."

Helen was still laughing as she pushed open the door of number twenty, Bridgend.

"Look, Mum, I've got an orange – where's the knife till I quarter it . . ."

Her voice tailed off. There had been no cheery "There you are pet!" and there was something strange about how her mother was sitting. She hadn't turned round as Helen clattered in and she sat very still in front of the fire, head bowed and shoulders bent.

A cold knot of fear went through Helen. Her voice came out unsteadily. "What's wrong, Mum? Are you not feeling well?"

As she went over to her mother she saw the piece of paper lying on Mrs Wilson's lap. A buff coloured paper, a telegram . . . Fearfully, Helen picked it up, but the words on it were a blur.

"John's dead," Helen thought. "Killed in action, like John McInroy and the Guthrie boys." Then her eyes cleared and she could read the message from Royal Air Force Headquarters.

'. . . . Your son, L.A.C. John Wilson, wireless operator, is missing, believed to be a prisoner of war in Greece . . .'

Relief and confusion mixed together in Helen's mind. Her mother was ashen faced and it was clear that she feared the worst, when she whispered,

"Missing, that's what they say to prepare you . . ."

Friends and neighbours tried to reassure the Wilsons, but no words of consolation could help.

"There's no Germans fighting now in Greece. There's been an armistice," someone told them.

But Mrs Wilson was only more confused by the information. "Then who else would take our John prisoner?" she wondered.

So what had been four years of vague anxiety became a dull ache of fear, fear that did not go away no matter how busy the family kept.

Well meaning but thoughtless friends advised them, "Don't worry. It's no use worrying."

Helen bit her tongue, but she thought, "What a senseless thing to say." Just a look at her mother's grey, suddenly old face showed how useless a piece of advice it was, "Don't worry!"

Still, her older sisters did try to take all their minds off it, when the weekend came.

"Come on, Mum, let's go to the pictures. There's a Bing Crosby and Fred Astaire film on. Oh no, that's at the Queens. We don't want to go to 'the bug-house'."

Number twenty, Bridgend.

13

Helen added, "You know what they say about 'the bughouse'. 'Itchin to get in and scratchin to get out'!"

Her old joke raised a faint smile all round, but Mrs Wilson shook her head.

"No girls, I've never been to a film and I'm not starting now. But you three run along."

Helen's sisters wouldn't hear of it, but they packed Helen off with her friend Grace to the Stirling 'Picture House' where Roy Rogers was starring in 'The Cowboy and the Senorita'. So for a few hours Helen escaped to the 'Wild West' with its handsome singing cowboys, but when the songs faded and the lights went up, the dull ache of anxiety was still there at the pit of her stomach.

Neither Helen nor her sisters talked about it but they could see it on their mother's face all through what remained of that dreadful January. As if to match their mood, gales, wind, rain and frost combined to cause havoc throughout Scotland. Subzero temperatures froze the River Allan till a sudden thaw released tons of ice blocks to float downstream towards the small town of Bridge of Allan. There, a mile of solid ice choked the river and threatened to flood the town till Royal Engineers and Polish paratroopers risked their lives to blast channels through the ice floes.

And in Dunblane, the sad news that a George Street lad, Peter McIntosh, had been killed on the Western Front did nothing to lessen the fears of the Wilson family.

Helen's days were filled with the routine of school but when she came home she was almost afraid to open the door of number twenty, Bridgend, knowing that she would be able to read any bad news on her mother's face. She would not have to read any second telegram.

Then it was Grace's turn to be upset in February when word came that Donald had been wounded again. Helen heard from her friend about her brother's injury – shrapnel in his leg – sustained while attacking the Seigfreid line on the German border. Helen sympathised but secretly thought, 'Poor Donald's hurt but at least he's out of the fighting now - and his family know where he is….'

Now anger mingled with the quiet despair of waiting families. When was it all going to end? Where was the promised victory? Nine o'clock in the evening found households huddled round their wirelesses tuned to the B.B.C. Home service. When the chimes of Big Ben announced the news from London, they listened intently through crackles for the answers to their questions.

According to the war commentary on the third Monday evening in March, British and American troops were now poised to move on Berlin from the west of the River Rhine, while Russia's Red Army was already advancing on the German capital from the east. Helen was only half listening but she saw her mother shake her head and heard her say, "Still it goes on. Still boys being killed." She stopped there but Helen read the words on her mind . . . "and still no word of our John."

The child rose to put on the kettle. "Do you want a cup of tea, Mum?"

Mrs Wilson nodded. "Yes please, pet, and then you'd better be off to bed. You've got school in the morning."

Helen was stretching up for the tea caddy when the knock came to the door.

She fumbled with the caddy while her mother half rose out of her chair, but before Mrs Wilson could reach the door it was pushed open.

A uniformed figure stood framed in half shadow. Below the Air Force cap the thin face was vaguely familiar. Then the man stepped forward and smiled. As if from a distance Helen heard the tea caddy clatter to the floor and she saw her mother sink back into her chair, shock written on her face.

The man held out his arms, "Hello, Mum!"

"John! Son! You're home. Thank God!"

The rest was lost in tears. The pent up emotions of the anxious months of hoping and fearing and endless waiting suddenly spilled over. Tears eventually gave way to smiles and laughter as first mother and son, and then sister and brother embraced. When Betty and Jessie came home the scene was repeated. Only three days later the Allied troops under General Eisenhower succeeded in crossing the Rhine. Then Grace's big brother Donald arrived in Britain for hospital care, and at last six weeks later the lights went on all over Britain as victory in Europe was celebrated.

Dunblane Cathedral was floodlit for the first time in its seven centuries of history. Multicoloured lights and streamers decorated Victoria Hall for the grand victory dance. Among the scores of Dunblane bairns who watched the fireworks display and saw the effigy of Hitler burn on a huge bonfire were the Taits, the Wilkies and the Napiers who were also celebrating the safe return of their brother Ian.

Beside Grace, Helen stood wearing her good pink vyella dress, but even as folk danced and sang in celebration, Helen knew that for her, none of this could be compared to that earlier evening in March – the long awaited night that her big brother John had come home safely to number twenty, Bridgend.

BAIRNS OF BRIDGEND
DUNBLANE

HELEN WILSON 1944-1945

NOTES

Her big brother told Helen very little about his weeks as a prisoner of war in Greece. Along with several hundred other British troops he had been captured by E.L.A.S, a Greek partisan organisation, and force-marched across country from Athens to Trikkola. There, two Americans engineered the group's escape back to Athens. From there they were repatriated via Italy.

At the end of the war, the girls from St Anne's College, Sanderstead, Surrey, returned as quietly as they had arrived. The Hydro was derequisitioned having been in service for most of the war as a military convalescent home. It continues in use today as a luxury hotel.

Helen and her friend Grace still live in Dunblane in houses that have been built since the war in a town that has greatly expanded around its core. After the war both Donald Carmichael and John Wilson resumed work in their fathers' businesses. Donald's family business was situated in what was formerly Upper Bridgend. Following his retirement, the timber buildings of the joinery workshops were demolished in 1989 to make way for modern flats.

Miss Margaret Wilkie provided invaluable background information for this tale. Of the other children in the story, including those who sacrificed the Hallowe'en pennies for the 'heroic Russians', some remained in Dunblane while others scattered. Meanwhile, number twenty Bridgend has been modernised internally and is still occupied.

BAIRNS OF BRIDGEND
DUNBLANE

HELEN WILSON 1944-1945

SOURCES AND BIBLIOGRAPHY

1980s Reminiscences of Dunblane during the 1940s:
Miss Helen Wilson and brother John Wilson formerly of Bridgend;
Mrs Grace Ross *nee* Carmichael;
Farmer Millar, formerly of Hillside.
Mr. A (Sandy) Hunter;
Miss Mary Sharp;
Mrs Isobel Smith *nee* Wilkie;
Miss Margaret Wilkie; Mrs Wilkie.

Stirling Journal and Advertiser   1939-1945
Stirling Observer   1939- 1946
Stirling Sentinel   1939 –1941, 1944

CASE, S L, *The Second World War.* Evans Brothers, 1976
HOARE, Robert, *World War Two.* Macdonald Educational Ltd.
GILMOUR, Ian, *Britain at War* 1939- 1945 Oliver and Boyd, Edinburgh 1982
LONGMATE, Norman *The Home Front- An Anthology 1938- 1945* Chatto and Windus
   1981

BAIRNS OF BRIDGEND
DUNBLANE

LAWRENCE MARSHALL 1918

Dae ye mind lang syne
When the simmer days were fine,
When the sun it shone far brichter
Than it's ever dune sin' syne?
Dae ye mind the ha'brig turn,
Where we guddled in the burn,
And were late for the schule in the mornin'?

Dae ye mind the sunny braes,
Where we gathered hips and haes,
An fell amang the bramble busses,
Tearing a' our claes;
An for fear we might be seen,
We cam' slippin' hame at e'en,
And got licket for our pains in the mornin'?

Rev. George James Laurie

BAIRNS OF BRIDGEND
DUNBLANE

LAWRENCE MARSHALL 1918

The clickety clack of the wheels and the swaying of the railway carriage made Lawrie's head nod as the train travelled northwards towards Dunblane.

As he dozed, he relived his fortnight's holiday in Glasgow. What a lot he had to tell Jake and Jimmy when he saw them. The highlight had been his first trip on the subway train. He could still feel the fearful excitement of leaving sunlit Bridge Street and going down endless steps with his uncle. The warm fusty draught of air had swept up towards them before they reached the dimly lit underground station. Distant rattling grew louder and louder till suddenly their train emerged from the black tunnel, opening its doors to swallow up its passengers.

"It's awful shoogly, Uncle John," Lawrie had shouted out while they stared at the dark walls speeding by.

Rising to get out at St.Enoch Station, Uncle John had said, "You've just been under the River Clyde, Lawrie!"

Wide eyed, the boy had blurted out, "What! Why did the water no come in?"

His uncle laughed, enjoying the lad's bewilderment.

His Aunt Bella, not so keen on underground adventures, had taken Lawrie and his cousin Tib by electric tramcar through the centre of the city to explore the Kelvingrove Museum. Lawrie had stood with his nose pressed against the glass cases, fascinated by the models of elegant sailing ships and modern ocean going steamships. The working models were a 'wonder of wonders' to him.

Then not far from the Eglinton Street tenement above his uncle's fish shop, Lawrie and his cousin had admired the green velvety lawns and brilliant patches of packed flowerbeds in Queens Park. Still, Lawrie reflected, you couldn't run around these well-clipped lawns or the 'Parkie' with his official cap would be out with his whistle giving a blast for all to hear.

No, it couldn't compare with running barefoot with his pals, Jake and Jimmy, around the Laighills of Dunblane.

His thoughts wandered to the ploys they might get up to during the rest of the summer before they had to face Miss Walker and all the hard work at St Mary's school for another year. There was still plenty of time left for whatever fun they could cook up – 'devilment', his parents sometimes called it! The possibilities were endless … Maybe they'd be off to the Kilbryde Burn guddling trout … that was another pleasure unknown to city bairns. Yes, Glasgow was a grand place to visit, thought Lawrie, but all in all he was glad to be going home. Still day dreaming, he suddenly realized he had reached familiar territory as the train drew in at Stirling Station. Soon the castle stood high on the left as the train crossed the River Forth. Lawrie felt growing excitement as they went through Bridge of Allan. Would someone be there to meet him he wondered as he struggled to get his suitcase down from the luggage rack.

'Dun-blane, Dun-blane!" shouted the guard. "This is your stop, son. Here, I'll gie ye a hand wi that muckle case. It's nearly as big as yersel!"

"Thanks, Mister", replied Lawrie as the train halted amidst clouds of steam. He scanned the platform eagerly. Yes, his father was there! Just in time Lawrie remembered the other package that his uncle had given him early that morning.

He jumped down to the platform clutching the brown paper parcel.

"Hello, dad, here's the haddies from Uncle John. He was back frae the fish market right early the morn."

His father laughed and clapped him on the back. "That's fine, son, you can gie them to your mither. She's waitin at hame for you. You haud onto the parcel and I'll manage the case."

Father and son chatted as they left the station and walked the short distance to Caledonian Place. The whitewashed walls of the cottages were bright in the afternoon sun. Smoke drifted above the ripples of the corrugated iron roof of their cottage at the end of the row. Much cosier looking, Lawrie thought, than the four sandstone storeys of the Glasgow tenement.

And there was his mother at their open cottage door beside the joiner's shop and smithy. Kate Marshall hurried forward smiling and giving her boy a welcoming hug.

"So you're back safe and sound, Lawrie! Did you hae a nice time? How are your aunt and uncle and Tib? When will they be comin up here?"

Lawrie's father interrupted the flow of questions.

"Well, I'll get back to my paintin while you two blether. I'll be hame for my tea at six o'clock."

"Right, John. Now, Lawrie, get out of your good Sunday claes while I open the parcel. Oh my, there's bonnie Loch Fyne herrins here too. They must hae been caught last night. Let me see, we'll hae the haddie the day and I'll pickle the herrin for later."

His mother continued, "Your Uncle Willie has been right busy at the smithy. Every wet day, the farmers all want their horses re-shod when they canna work the fields. And every dry day it's been mendin tools. The forge has been goin like a fair frae sun-up till its near enough dark! Oh, I'll need mair vinegar for the herrin. Off you go to Eadie's for some now you're changed. Here's sixpence and

Dunblane Railway Station.

21

mind and no spend the change!"

Lawrie escaped from his mother's chatter into the sunlight again. As he passed the forge his Uncle Willie called out to him. "Hello, Lawrie! So the wanderer's returned! Just in time. We're needin a hand here in the morn, ringing wheels."

"Right, Uncle Willie, but I'm away a message for mam the now."

Running over the railway footbridge, Lawrie looked over the railings and spied his friends below on the riverbank, sitting with rods and string dangling hopefully in Allan Water.

"Jake! Jimmy! Hae you landed anythin yet?" he yelled.

The lads looked up and waved.

"Och, it's yoursel, Lawrie. Na, they just hae a wee nibble and aff they go!"

"You'll hae to change your flies then." Lawrie laughed at his own joke, knowing full well that a bent pin with a worm was all the bait they ever used.

"When are you comin out then, Lawrie?"

"No the night, boys, but maybe the morrow after tea. I've my milk round first thing and then I'll be helpin my grandpa and Uncle Willie at the smithy."

"Lucky dog!" said Jake. "So we'll see you the morrow. We ken a rare place for plunders!"

"Ssh, ssh!" interrupted Jimmy. "Dinna let the hale world ken! We'll come roun for you, Lawrie."

Back at the cottage with the vinegar, Lawrie helped his mother to gut the herring. She rolled them up and placed them neatly with peppercorns in an earthenware dish. In no time at all his mother had them sprinkled with salt, almost covered with vinegar and popped into the oven at the side of the kitchen range.

"Now," she said, "some pancakes for the tea."

Quickly she mixed the batter and greased the girdle as it heated over the coals. Lawrie watched as his mother chose just the right moment, when the blue smoke began to rise, to drop spoonfuls of the soft mixture into sizzling circles on the flat iron disc. As the pancakes rose, the sweet smell made his mouth water, while his mother deftly flipped them over to turn golden brown on the other side.

The hungry lad couldn't resist helping himself as the first delicious pancakes lay cooling. He thought that his mother was too busy with the next batch to notice but he was mistaken.

"That's enough then, Lawrie. You'll no be able for your tea. Here, you can scrub the tatties. They'll be fine wi the haddies. Hurry up now. Your dad will soon be hame lookin for his tea."

Later when the meal was over and Lawrie had told the family all about his stay in Glasgow, he was ready for his bed. His father seeing him yawn remarked, "Well, son you've had a rare holiday, but it's back to 'auld claes and parritch' in the morn. Off to bed now."

It was an early start the next morning to meet the milk cart from Stockbridge Farm at Kilbryde. Lawrie was given his big metal can of milk with its measuring jugs hooked on to the side handle. He lowered it carefully into his homemade cart complete with wheels that he'd salvaged from the smithy, and off he went to deliver to his customers in the cottages of Chuckie Row. Then it was on to the fine big houses in Doune Road where he had to trail round to the back doors. Ladling the milk from the big can, he carefully tipped the full measures into the customers' waiting containers. He didn't take time to admire the pretty matching sets of china milk jugs but he did make sure that he replaced the beaded muslin covers that kept dirt and flies of the top of the milk. Many a scolding he'd had from a cross housemaid who found a speck of dust in the jug or a splash of milk spilled on her scrubbed doorstep!

Then it was along Kilbryde and down to Springbank Mill before crossing to the other side of the river. He paused on the Faery Bridge across the Allan. The early morning light sparkled on the water. Maybe it would still be warm enough after tea for a paddle in the basins where the big flat stones made natural pools. If the sun shone all day, maybe that was where he'd go with Jake and Jimmy in the evening.

Still, standing there wasn't getting the milk delivered thought Lawrie. So manoeuvring the cart he heaved it along and up the sloping path on the other riverbank. At the Haining, a housewife was out sweeping her steps already.

"I'll tak half a pint o cream, son."

"Sorry, Missus, no cream today," he replied, keeping his fingers tightly crossed behind his back. There had been cream on the cart right enough, but he hadn't taken any.

Along Kirk Street and Cathedral Square and at last his final delivery was to the jail at the top of the High Street. The cells must be full, thought Lawrie when he saw four cans outside the big arched doorway. Good, all the less for me to humph back to the dairyman, he said to himself as he completed his circular tour with his can almost empty.

Back in Caledonian Place the porridge was ready for him and then he was off

Bridgend of Dunblane from Caledonian Place.

23

to the forge. Uncle Willie and Grandfather Ferguson were both up and about. All three fires were going so Lawrie knew that it would indeed be a busy day. Sure enough, his grandfather was working on a cartwheel repair and there were others already stacked in a corner.

"What dae you want me to dae, Grandpa?"

"Tak the bellows and gie that fire some air. It looks gey poor. Then gie me a hand wi this wheel."

A few brisk pumps with the bellows pipe poked into the dull ashes brought a red glow to the coals and tiny flames danced on the surface of the fire.

Grandfather was putting the final shaping to a replacement segment of a wheel rim. "Right Lawrie, steady this while I tap this section intae place."

The lad helped his grandfather to manoeuvre the wooden arc on to the spokes of the cartwheel before tapping it into position to close the oak circle.

"Good, I'll get the wedges intae the spoke holes and smooth aff the wheel now. Then we'll gie your Uncle Willie a hand to get all the wheels ringed."

Willie Ferguson already had the first iron hoop on the fire gradually becoming a dull red. The blacksmith kept turning the band in the heat so it would expand evenly. Wiping the sweat from his brow he called his assistants.

"Right," he grunted. "Ready now."

Armed with long metal ring carriers, Lawrie and Grandfather helped to retrieve the metal circles from the fire, their eyes half-closed against the fierce heat. Quickly but carefully they carried the glowing ring to the waiting wooden wheel. While they eased the iron tyre over the wheel, Uncle Willie knocked it into position with his sledgehammer in a frenzy of activity before the metal rim had time to cool and shrink.

Then the wheel was lowered into the stone horse trough. What a steaming and hissing as the hot metal met the cold water and what a cracking and squeaking as the shrinking metal rim gripped the protesting wood. At last, Lawrie rolled the newly ringed wheel out of the way.

As the process was repeated again and again, all the lively action and noise attracted an audience of interested passers-by. Lawrie was only able to wave to Jake and Jimmy but he felt a surge of pride as the watchers followed the activity. They toiled all morning getting black and sweaty as wheel after wheel was repaired. Few words were spoken amidst the clouds of smoke and steam and the smell of molten metal and charred wood. There was no time for chat as the three workers combined their skills in a concentrated team effort.

Lawrie's throat was parched and he realized that he was hungry when his grandmother appeared at the forge with soup and bread for them all.

"Right, we'll hae a breather the now," said Uncle Willie. "Only this ane to dae. Then we'll hae a bite to eat."

The small audience began to drift away, but one small girl remained.

"What dae you want, lass?"

"It's my gird, Mr Ferguson. It's cracked - see? So it winna run smoothly. It keeps goin squinty."

"We canna hae that then. You'll no win any races that way! Here, Lawrie. Here's a customer for you!"

"Hello, Annie. Gie me the gird till I solder it wi a bit of this old iron." He was half embarrassed; half proud to be doing his very own repair even it was only a lassie's hoop. Annie chatted on while Lawrie worked.

"You missed our concert last week, Lawrie. It was great fun!"

"Where was that then?" the boy asked.

"Along at our own bit, in the back-green. We even had a notice, 'Entertainment at Springfield Terrace in Aid of the Red Cross Auxiliary Hospital."

"Oh, aye, and who were the entertainers?"

"All of us, my brother Murray, all the Cairns family and your cousin, Danny. We had singin and dancin and even acrobatics! We collected one pound fourteen pence and we got our names in the papers," she added proudly.

"Very good. Well, here's your gird." Lawrie thrust it at her. "I'm away to get my dinner."

"Thanks, Lawrie," she smiled and skipped off.

His Uncle Willie was grinning at him as he got his bread and soup.

"Funny that Annie McGregor's gird cracked the day you're here, Lawrie."

He winked at grandfather but the older man said, "Och, leave the laddie alane, Willie. He's ower young for that nonsense."

Lawrie was grateful for his grandpa's support and that there was no more time for his uncle to tease him since there was still work to be done.

With the wheel ringing finished, Lawrie helped to stack them in the joiner's shop yard ready for their owners to collect. Now the pace of work slowed down a bit.

"Just one mare to shoe and then there's a binder and some scythe blades for urgent repair. You can heat the shoe while I get the mare ready, Lawrie."

The blacksmith's hammer rang out as he shaped the horseshoe on the anvil, but now there was some time for chat with the waiting customers. It was a mixed bag of information and gossip that was exchanged.

One farm hand had them all laughing about the sight he'd seen in Stirling, when a runaway carthorse had dashed along Port Street dragging its load behind it. "The best part was watchin everybody loup out the road when all the empty barrels on it rolled off and scattered all ower the place."

"Aye, but we shouldna laugh," said another. "I'll bet it was one of thae new fangled motor cycles backfirin that startled the beast. They're just a menace!"

"Och, well, we canna stop progress. As lang as they keep to ten miles an hour in toun they're awright."

Lawrie chuckled to himself, recalling how often he'd waved cheekily to a motorcyclist that he'd overtaken while riding his pushbike around Dunblane.

Inevitably there was war news, this time from France and Flanders and for once it was good news from the European Western Front. All the newspapers were reporting a speech by Field Marshall Foch, Commander in Chief of the Allied armies after the recent battle at the Marne. He had declared that the Black Watch – 'Les Gardes Noir' – had been the fiercest of all the Scottish highlanders, ignoring the shellfire around them in the hand-to-hand fighting that 'threw back the Boches.'

"Maybe the war will be ower soon," said one lad.

"Aye," said Uncle Willie, "but that winna bring back the dozens of Dunblane lads that are killed out there in the trenches."

"Well, it's a glorious thing to die for your country," the lad went on.

"Huh, I just wonder if the McLeans in Well Place feel it's glorious that three of their sons have died, or if the fatherless bairns in Bridgend think they're honoured!"

Lawrie had only hazy memories of the young men who had marched proudly to war four years earlier, but they certainly bore no resemblance to the patients he'd seen this summer from the Dunblane War Hospital at the Hydropathic Hotel. Some of these soldiers were blind, their eyes swathed in bandages. Others were missing limbs and certainly none had the carefree look of youth. All had pain etched on their faces.

"Pair souls," he'd heard his mother say. "Shell shock, they call it."

"Oh, aye," another farm hand added, "and I hear that John McLean leaves for France soon."

There was much shaking of heads and Lawrie was relieved to get away when his uncle said, "Awa with you then, Lawrie. You've earned your keep the day. We'll mak a blacksmith o you yet!"

Out of the smithy he scampered, glad to be into the sunshine and away from the talk of war. After a quick wash to get the soot and ashes out of his hair and face, there would be time for that swim before tea.

In the cottage he was met by the sweet smell of newly made gooseberry jam.

"Can I hae a piece to keep me goin, Mam?" asked the lad hungrily, watching his mother carefully ladling the preserve into jars.

"Here you are, son," Kate Marshall replied and off Lawrie went happily with a big slice of bread, covered in still warm, runny jam. He was licking his fingers clean of the delicious stickiness when Jake and Jimmy joined him for their jaunt.

In no time they were swimming in Allan Water, opposite Springbank Mill. The three lads splashed and ducked each other till they were breathless.

Allan Water and Faery Bridge.

'This is the life, right enough,' thought Lawrie as he clambered out after his swim. "Oh, aye, this beats all the delights of Glesca," he decided as he stretched out quite refreshed in spite of his busy day.

But it wasn't over yet. The long light summer evening was still ahead and lying on the grass of the Laighills, the boys put their heads together.

"What will we dae after tea?"

"I telt you. I ken where there's great plunders!"

"Where?"

"No very far frae your place. Just up the Doune Road at Springbank Cottage. I had a keek ower the wall and the bushes are thick wi grossets."

"Great!" Lawrie could still taste the fruit from his mother's gooseberry jam.

"Right, grossets are my favourite. We'll hae to tak care all the same, the Harrower ladies live in there and they ken me frae deliverin the milk."

"After tea then," said Jake and it was agreed.

That evening when the boys met up, they planned their strategy carefully. Jimmy would be the lookout so that Jake and Lawrie could climb over the wall in Well Place and crawl safely into the gooseberry bushes without being seen from Doune Road. If anyone appeared from Springbank Cottage, they could always say they were looking for their ball and make their escape. If all was safe, they could whistle Jimmy over to join them.

All went perfectly and soon the three lads were crouched in the bushes that hung heavily with ripe fruit. And they were just right, plump and juicy and tinged with pink. The skins burst when bitten and the sweet insides squirted into the boys' eager mouths. 'Ah,' thought Lawrie, "This is heaven. This beats walkin around the paths in Queen's Park in your best claes and shiny shoes."

Silently the conspirators moved quietly from bush to bush plucking and eating the best of the crop. Jimmy was the first to speak. "Oh these are rare but I've had enough."

"Just a couple mair," mumbled Jake with his mouth full.

"Right, what next?" asked Lawrie, "I'm full up too."

"How about hide-an-seek at the stables in Stirling Road?" Jimmy suggested.

"Good idea. Now keep your heids down and we'll get back ower the wall. I'll hae a keek and see if the coast's clear."

Lawrie went forward between the bushes on his hands and knees. Reaching the wall he peered over. No one in sight. He turned to signal to Jake and Jimmy.

His hand froze in mid wave. Miss Harrower stood calmly watching him from the cottage. How long had she been standing there he wondered, as her voice reached him clearly.

"And just what do you think you're up to?"

Jake and Jimmy ducked down out of sight.

"Run for it, Lawrie!"

Lawrie hesitated, weighing up the situation.

"Come here at once, Lawrence Marshall and tell your friends in the bushes that they are not invisible."

"The game's up, lads," he said, "Miss Harrower kens my dad. If we bolt now, she'll tell him and I'll no be able to sit down for a week!"

Reluctantly the three culprits made their way through the garden. They stood, heads hanging in front of Miss Harrower.

"Well, well! What are we going to do with you?" Her toe tapped on the gravel path. Suddenly she made up her mind.

"I know," she said, turning to speak to her sister. "Jean, could you bring three baking bowls from the kitchen please? Large ones."

Jake, Jimmy and Lawrie looked at each other, puzzled.

Miss Harrower continued, "Since you're all so fond of fruit picking, you can each fill a bowl for me."

Back to the gooseberry bushes went the boys and they began to put the berries in the bowls. The berries that were easily reached had all been picked, so now the boys had to stretch right into the middle of the bushes, and soon their hands were scratched and bleeding from the sharp thorns. Still, they kept at it and gradually the bowls filled up. All three of them knew it was a 'fair cop'.

"If Miss Harrower just wants us to fill these for her we've got off quite easy."

"Just as long as our faithers dinna find out," added Jimmy.

At last the bowls were full and the boys knocked on the door of Springbank Cottage. Waiting for Miss Harrower, Lawrie said, "We'll hand these in and then we'd better get hame. No hide and seek the night."

The door opened and Miss Harrower inspected the containers brimful with berries.

"Good, these look fine," she said, "Right, in you come and put the gooseberries on the kitchen table."

Relieved to be finished, the boys filed into the kitchen and carefully set down the bowls. They turned to leave, eager to be off, but Miss Harrower raised a hand to stop them.

"One moment," she said, "Now sit down and eat them!"

The lads gasped in disbelief. With despairing glances at each other, they reluctantly pulled out the chairs and sat at the table. The baking bowls were suddenly massive. Without enthusiasm, Jake, Jimmy and Lawrie began to eat. The gooseberries which had been delicious less than an hour earlier now had to be forced down. Lawrie wondered how many more he could eat without being sick, but Miss Harrower was watching the lads carefully. After the longest two minutes of the boy's lives, she broke the silence.

"That's enough," she said, "Off you go now."

Lawrie couldn't understand why she had a sort of twinkle in her eye, but he took his chance to ask anxiously, "You'll no tell our faithers, Miss?"

"No, but don't let me find you here again!"

No fear, thought all three as they thankfully took their leave of Springbank Cottage. Three very subdued boys walked very slowly down Doune Road.

Nothing was said but each lad was busy with his own thoughts. In Lawrie's mind a longer stay in Glasgow suddenly seemed more attractive and much less hazardous than being back in Dunblane. Maybe he should have stayed there a bit longer!

Bidding his friends goodnight, he slipped quietly into the cottage at Caledonian Place. His mother was by the fire, knitting khaki stockings for the troops. Kate Marshall's hands flew over the needles and she kept working as she turned to Lawrie.

"You're in early the night, son. Are you off tae bed already? You must be weary after your busy day. There's some supper for you on the table, milk and

28

a piece and grosset jam."

Kate Marshall was surprised and puzzled when Lawrie gave her a funny look and a strangled, "No thanks, Mam. Goodnight."

She often wondered why he never – ever – ate gooseberry jam again.

BAIRNS OF BRIDGEND
DUNBLANE

LAWRENCE MARSHALL 1918

NOTES

The cottage and smithy of Lawrie's childhood are now gone marked only by a triangle of grass between Doune Road (once Upper Bridgend) and Caledonian Road. However, his neighbours' cottages have survived and one is now a coffee shop. The stone marker from the blacksmith's forge is kept in Dunblane City and Cathedral Museum at The Cross. The stone has a horseshoe and also bears the initials WF for William Ferguson, Lawrie's grandfather.

The jail, which was the last delivery of Lawrie's milk round, has gone from the corner site, which earlier had been occupied, by Lord Strathallan's house. Now it is a pleasant garden area.

Mr and Mrs Maclean of Well Place lost their fourth son, John, in September 1918 after only two weeks in France. His surviving youngest sister, Margaret, said that her mother bore it all with fortitude based on her Christian faith, summing it up with the remark, "No cross, no crown."

Her daughter's reply was, "Mother, your crown must have diamonds on it."

Springbank Cottage is now called Acredale and the gooseberry patch is now occupied by a bungalow, Glendevon.

Lawrence Marshall's childhood 'adventures' were recollected when he was in his seventies and living in a modern flat within a stone's throw of his childhood home and of the forbidden garden. He was thirteen years old at the end of 1918 old enough to leave the public school.

Throughout his long life he never again ate gooseberries in any form!

BAIRNS OF BRIDGEND
DUNBLANE

LAWRENCE MARSHALL 1918

SOURCES AND BIBLIOGRAPHY

Personal recollections of Mr Lawrence Marshall, Dunblane.

Stirling Journal and Advertiser, 1914 –1918.
Stirling Observer, 1914 -1918.

GLASGOW Museum of Transport, *Glasgow Tramcars*.
McKERRACHER, A C, *Portrait of Dunblane 1875* – 1975 Publ. A C McKerracher, Dunblane.
NORWOOD, J *Craftsmen at Work*, John Baker, 1977.
WYMER, Norman, *English Country Crafts*, Batsford 1946.

BAIRNS OF BRIDGEND DUNBLANE

ANN PETTY 1874

The clinkum-clank o' Sabbath bells
Noo to the hoastin' rookery swells,
Noo faint an' laigh in shady dells,
Sounds far and near.
An o' through the summer kintry tells
Its tale o' cheer.

The steerin' mither strange afit
Noo shoos the bairnies, but a bit
Noo cries them ben, their Sinday shuit
To scart upon them,
Or sweeties in their pouch to pit,
Wi' blessins on them.

From 'A Lowden Sabbath Morn' Robert Louis Stevenson.

A gray old minster on the height
Towers o'er the trees and in the light,
A gray old town along the ridge
Slopes winding downwards to the bridge –
A quaint old gabled place,
With Church stamped on its face.

Begrimed with smoke, a monotone
Of equal streets in brick or stone,
With squalid land, and flaunting Hall
Infrequent spire and chimneys tall,
You know the place wherein
The weary toil and spin.

From 'The Bishop's Walk' O W C Smith

BAIRNS OF BRIDGEND
DUNBLANE

ANN PETTY 1874

The baby slept soundly in his wooden cradle in the corner unaware of the activity around him. His sister, Ann, stood at the fire pouring water from a tin kettle into the large black pot that was bubbling over the flames.

"That's the way, Annie. Dinna let the dumpling dry out. Are you shair the cloot's tied tight enough?"

"Aye, mam, it's daen fine and I've left plenty room for it tae swell."

The rich aroma of butter, fruit and spices from the clootie dumpling made Ann's mouth water. This pudding was a rare treat, made only for very special occasions like this one, the baptism of the latest addition to the Petty family. Mrs Petty had her hands full getting the family ready for church. Seven-year-old Christopher was looking unusually scrubbed but unhappy with his feet encased in polished black boots that pinched. His complaint met unsympathetic ears.

"Stop girning. I ken fine you dinna want tae wear them, but whoever heard tell of goin tae the kirk barefoot? Dae you want us all tae be black affronted?"

His mother didn't expect a reply and while she spoke she wiped the face and hands of John, the toddler. That done she deposited him on his brother's lap.

"There now my wee man, sit at peace with Chris, while I change the wee one."

Turning to the cradle, she lifted and changed the baby with expert hands, and then it was four-year-old Agnes's turn.

"Hold the bairn, Annie, while I brush Agnes's hair. Christopher, mind that John doesna get his hands black on the grate. Sit there on the bed and dinna let him go!"

Mrs Petty brushed the small girl's hair till it shone while Ann crooned at the baby lying like a doll in his long white robe. He was the fifth Petty to wear the fine cotton christening gown so carefully hand stitched.

Ann smiled to herself wondering aloud, "Did I really get intae that wee gownie, Mam?"

"Of course you did. It was bought for you. Nothing but the best, from Menzies in Stirling. Your faither and I were sae pleased when you arrived safely that we didna grudge it. And it's been put tae good use since then with the rest of you bairns. Gracious me! Is that the cathedral bell I'm hearing? We'll hae to be up at the kirk soon. Let me sit doon for a minute."

With a sigh Mrs Petty sat and surveyed her children. She allowed herself a moment's satisfaction at seeing them all so spruce.

"Well, you winna disgrace us if you all mind tae be good in the kirk. But where's your faither? We'll be late!"

"He's out the back, Mam," said Ann, just as Joshua Petty appeared at the door, drying his hands. He filled the frame and had to duck to enter the but and ben.

"Are we all ready then? Come on. Annie, you carry the bairn for your mother. Lads, you stay by me, and Agnes, keep by your mother."

Mrs Petty rose wearily to her feet and put on her straw bonnet. Off went the small family procession along Mill Row. Up they went past the jail at the head of the High Street, and on to Church Street, skirting the cathedral and making their way between the thatched cottages of Kirk Street. Before they reached Leighton Church at the foot of the Braeport, the family could already hear the hearty singing from inside.

They waited for the closing hymn to begin and entered the church to its strains. As they were ushered to the empty row at the front, Ann still held the baby while the singing came to an end.

Nodding towards the family, the minister spoke.

"Our Lord said, 'Suffer the little children to come unto me'."

As he spoke about the sacrament of baptism, Ann rocked her small brother, anxious in case he should waken and cry. At last the minister held out his arms for the tiny baby. Carefully, Ann handed the sleeping bundle to her father who awkwardly passed it to the minister.

"What is this child to be named?"

Joshua Petty spoke quietly to the clergyman who responded, "Ah, a fine name!"

Then holding the baby firmly with one practised hand, the minister dipped his free fingers into the font. Sprinkling the water on the tiny upturned face, he spoke clearly, "David Livingstone, I baptise thee in the name of the Father, and of the Son and of the Holy Ghost. The Lord bless thee and keep thee."

The voices of the congregation rose in chorus to continue in song, the blessing for the newly baptised baby who slumbered on. Many an eye was moist as the worshippers looked at the tiny boy with the hero's name.

Leighton House, formerly Leighton Church.

Back at Millrow, the family were helped to celebrate the event by friends and neighbours who consumed vast amounts of tea and slabs of the delicious clootie dumpling. The day flew by and when the last guest had gone and the last crumb was swallowed, Ann helped to wipe the sticky mouths of her younger brothers and sister.

All were tired out by the excitement, but as Ann cuddled up in bed beside Agnes, she looked forward to telling everyone at school about her wee brother's distinguished name.

Miss Campbell's school for infants and girls was on the other side of the River Allan and the railway line at the foot of the road to Doune. There the next morning, Ann sat on the bench at the back looking over the heads of the other children right down to the youngest at the front. As always, the day began with the catechism. This morning's session was the Ten Commandments. Ann's mind was still on the events of the previous day as she automatically joined in the responses to Miss Campbell's questions. She suddenly came to at the end of them when she heard the teacher asking, "What are the sins forbidden in the tenth commandment?"

Fifty voices responded in ragged unison, " The sins forbidden are, discontentment with our own estate; envying and grieving at the good of our neighbour, together with all inordinate motions and affections to anything that is his."

"Amen."

"Amen," echoed the children.

Now Miss Campbell told the girls in the Bible class at the back to look up the morning's Scripture story.

"Begin please, Mary Drummond. Exodus, chapter two, verse one."

It was Ann's favourite, the story of the baby Moses in the bulrushes. Taking her turn to read with the other girls on the back bench, Ann pictured it all. As the story unfolded she shared the anxiety felt by the young Hebrew maiden sent to watch over the helpless infant in the basket.

Ann could keep her story to herself no longer. Up went her hand as the children closed their Bibles.

Miss Campbell tutted impatiently. "Well, Ann Petty, what is the matter?"

"Please, Miss Campbell, I've got a new wee brother."

"Indeed! I trust that you are not interrupting lessons just to tell us that."

Ann faltered, . . . "No Miss" . . . . She gulped. "He's David Livingstone. . . . I mean that's the name he's got!"

Miss Campbell's lined face softened into a smile. "Ah, I see."

She looked around the class. . . "I'm sure you all remember hearing about Dr Livingstone?"

"Yes, Miss Campbell," came the chorus.

"Where did Dr Livingstone serve God as a missionary to the poor heathens? Christopher Petty?"

"Darkest Africa, Miss Campbell."

The teacher looked towards the world map on the wall.

"Elizabeth Eadie, can you show us Africa on the map?"

"Yes, Miss Campbell." The child pointed to the landmass of the African continent and put her finger on the bright pink patches of British East Africa.

"Good! But we digress. . . . Multiplication tables, children!"

When classes were over at last, the children poured out through the garden gate at the foot of Doune Road eager to be out in the June summer sun. Ann and her friend Mary Drummond ran round the corner past the fine new two-storey tenement and across the railway footbridge. Clattering through Bridgend they were soon over the bridge and back home in Millrow.

Mrs Petty was waiting for Ann with an enamel basin of wet washing.

"Oh, good! You're hame lass. Tak aff your good pinafore and keep it clean for school. Then tak the bairns' washin ower tae the mill lade: It's washed through but it could dae wi a good rinse. Hang it out tae dry at the grass yaird. The washin line's in the basin." As she spoke, Mrs Petty pushed her hair back from her forehead and Ann noticed how tired she looked.

"Will I tak Agnes wi me, Mam?"

"Aye, that would be fine, but mind she doesna fall intae the lade, like that poor old body did last month. Drowned she was, wi her washing beside her and naebody noticed till too late."

" I'll keep an eye on her, Mam. Come on, Agnes, and help Annie wi the washin."

Away went the two sisters on the first of many tasks that Ann carried out for her mother over the summer weeks. There was water to be fetched from the well beside the Gasworks, coal to be carried and errands to be run. Sometimes it was to the fleshers for some dripping to mash in with the potatoes for dinner, or to the grocer's for some tea and sugar, always there were the younger ones to look after. During the school holidays it was easier to get through the never ending round but still Mrs Petty seemed tired out all the time. When Ann mentioned it to her father, Joshua Petty tried to reassure her.

"It's early days yet since wee David was born. Your Mam doesna hae her full strength back yet, but with your help, she'll manage.

In spite of his optimistic words Ann could sense that her father was worried too by her mother's careworn look. "Dae you think she'll be better soon, faither?"

Usually a man of few words, especially with his children, Joshua Petty surprised his daughter by suddenly pouring out his thoughts.

"The cottage here is suddenly awful cramped with five bairns now. And at times I've wondered if the smell of the gasworks there might be upsetting your mother. I've been thinking about a move frae Millrow."

Ann thought about the fine stone tenement that she passed on her way to school, 'The Skye Blocks', but her father poured cold water on her suggestion.

"Oh, aye, these are fine sturdy buildings, lass, and near enough my work at Springbank Mill, but I fear that the rent would be too high."

No more was said about it for the next few weeks till one evening as Ann lay in bed she overheard her parents in conversation.

Joshua Petty spoke first. "I've been findin out about the Skye Blocks, the tenements belonging tae Mr Wilson's company. There's some of the Springbank Mill workers in them already but the rent's high, five pounds a year."

"Well, Joshua, we canna rise tae that. Agnes should be startin school soon at Miss Campbell's and Chris is too big now for the Infant School. He should be movin tae the Public school and that's three pence a week."

"I ken there's naethin to spare but there is a way we could manage. That's for

Annie to come wi me to Wilson's Mill at Springbank as a half-timer."

Ann heard her mother's gasp of surprise. "Oh, I dinna think so, Joshua. Annie's too young to be working in the spinnin mill! Anyway, Mr Hird, the manager wouldna tak her."

Lying rigid with shock, the child heard her father's reply.

"Your wee lass is growin up. She'll be ten soon and she's wise for her years. I'd like to see us all in a new place away frae the gasworks."

"Aye, I'd like that fine. I wadna miss that byre next door wi the muck heap and the flies buzzin round, but we hae tae think about Annie's schoolin."

"She'd still get lessons at the Mill School. I'll speak to Mr Hird and see if there's room for a piecer."

As her father brought the discussion to an end Ann lay with her eyes tightly closed but her mind was in a whirl.

Leave Miss Campbell's nice wee school with its garden. Suddenly her teacher's sharp tongue and leather tawse were forgotten while her occasional words of praise and rarely seen smile were recollected. The monotony of listening to the younger children stumbling over the words of the 'carritch', the catechism, faded in Ann's mind while Miss Campbell's singing lessons were recalled with pleasure. And what about the Mill School? It wouldn't have a nice garden for playing during breaks and wasn't the teacher there a man? He could probably shout louder than Miss Campbell and would lay on the whang o leather with a will!

A restless night tossing and turning left Ann tired and unsettled. In the morning, things didn't look any better and worst of all, there was no one she could discuss it with. If she mentioned it to her parents, they would know that she'd been listening to their adult conversation and they might be angry. Children were supposed to close their ears to grown up talk. There was no point in telling her brother Christopher. He was a boy and wouldn't care.

So Ann was left to worry about it all day, knowing that she just had to wait till her parents spoke about it. As she automatically helped her mother that day, her anxiety made her irritable. Agnes bore the brunt of it when she dropped the loaf they'd just bought in the Millrow bakers.

Instead of picking it up and dusting it off as usual, Ann slapped the astonished Agnes. Her wee sister's tears made Ann feel ashamed but they did not melt away the gnawing fears in her heart.

The day seemed unending and Ann was still on tenterhooks when her father came home after his long day's work. He seemed to take ages over his meal but at last Mrs Petty broached the subject.

"Did you manage tae speak wi Mr Hird, Joshua?"

"Oh, aye. I did that. . . . Annie, are you listenin lass? Mam and I hae been thinkin. . ."

Ann had to pretend ignorance as her father outlined what she'd overheard the night before. He went on to tell what the mill manager had said about it. Thomas Hird had explained it all. Ann would have to show that she'd reached Standard Four in her reading before she'd be allowed to leave full time school and she'd have to take her birth lines to prove that she was ten before she'd be allowed in the mill.

"Oh, well, we'll just hae to wait a while then," said Mrs Petty wistfully and

Ann looked at her mother's weary face.

Mixed feelings swept through her once again. Relief that the prospect of going to work at the mill was not immediate, mingled with her desire to see her mother happier and the family in a better home.

Now, though the idea still dismayed her, she prepared herself for the change. She practised her reading for the test while waiting for her tenth birthday to come around.

At last on a chilly December afternoon Ann found herself with her father at the mill gates awaiting Mr Hird. The child clutched her reading book nervously as she read aloud from the notice board: 'Springbank Mills. Alexander Wilson and Co.'

With that the manager appeared. "Is this your lass getting in some practice, Joshua?"

Thomas Hird smiled as he took Ann to his office.

"Right lass, let's hear your reading. What's your book then?"

"Chambers' Reader, part seven."

Ann read a page aloud, remembering to give it good expression as Miss Campbell had taught her.

"That's fine, but some wee lassies here have learned their books off by heart. Let's see if you can read this."

He took a huge leather backed ledger from the desk and opened it at random. Ann looked at the copper plate handwriting and columns of figures.

"Do you ken what this is, lass?"

"Is it some kind of sums, sir?"

"Aye, you could call it that. See, you just read the words I point to."

Beginning at the top the child read where the man indicated:

Day Book December 1872
Morton and Sons, Kidderminster
C. Harrison, Stourport
31 Bundles
J&J.S. Templeton, Glasgow
77 Bundles.
Quitzoe & Company, Bradford
120 Bundles

Thomas Hird turned over a few pages and continued pointing. Ann read on:

Dunblane, July 1874
D.J. Dillon & Company, Manchester
96 Bundles Black
Palmer & Company, Kidderminster
18 Bundles White

Mr Hird closed the heavy book and turned to Ann, "And dae you ken where Kidderminster is?"

"Somewhere in England, sir?"

"That's right and it's famous for its carpets. These are English firms using the wool spun in our mill. And now you can help to spin it."

"Hae I passed the test then, sir?"

"Indeed, wi flyin colours! Now! Your wages will be two and nine a week, if you're satisfactory. You'll get paid startin the morrow."

Ann couldn't believe her ears. Two shillings and nine pence! What riches!

"Thank you, Mr Hird!"

"All the thanks I need is for you to be a good wee worker. But I'm certain that the daughter of a skilled wool sorter all the way from Yorkshire will be a nimble fingered wee lass. Right, we'll show you where you'll be workin, no time like the present."

With that Thomas Hird called to a young woman.

"Will you tak this lass to Willie Cairns. Tell him he's got a new piecer. She'll start right away."

As she followed the young woman, Ann felt her doubts return. A new 'piecer' Mr Hird called her. She wished she'd asked her father what a piecer did, but it was too late now. She'd just have to keep her eyes and ears open.

The young woman was holding open the door of the Old Mill building. As Ann ducked below her arm and went through the doorway, a wave of noise hit her.

She stood rooted to the spot by all she saw and heard in the large open room chock-a-block with machinery. Men were moving about pulling levers, puppet like among the machines they operated, a confusion of rollers in steady motion. Looking up at the one closest to her, she was dwarfed by the huge cylinders turning in front of her. Around them wide ribbons of soft wool moved steadily with smaller rollers turning against them. When one machine slowed down Ann could see that the cylinders' curved surfaces were covered with fine wire points brushing and cleaning the stream of fibres sandwiched between the rollers.

Her apprehension increased. Was this where a piecer worked she wondered briefly, in the shadow of these huge machines? But now her guide was moving through the ground floor and Ann forced herself to move and follow her. The young woman must have seen the question in the child's eyes as she told her,

Springbank Mill, Dunblane.

40

"That's the carding. You'll be upstairs on the spinning floor."

Again a wall of noise hit them on the first floor. The machinery here was quite different and young women and girls, as well as a few men attended it. Above the noise Ann was handed over to the department supervisor, Willie Cairns.

"Just bide here a while and watch what's happenin," he told her.

She stared around her wide-eyed at the scene. There were three huge machines, stretching across the room. Later Ann learned that they were called mules, but for now all she knew was that they were nothing like the spinning wheels that she'd seen in cottages around Dunblane. These were monsters, upright frames with three long rows of big reels one on top of another. As they revolved, the lengths of soft fibre around these bobbins were drawn out. Following the machine's movements Ann traced the woollen lengths three by three, meeting and entering rollers where they blended into one strand. Then she watched in horrified fascination while the lower part of the machine seemed to come suddenly alive and roll away from the back frame, pulling the length of wool out from its rollers.

A young woman standing between two machines looked as if she were in danger of being crushed! In terror, Ann let out a yell . . . . just as the whole carriage juddered to a stop. . . .

The young woman turned and laughed and Ann blushed crimson, wanting to cry. The supervisor was back and he laughed too.

"Dinna fear, lass. The carriage wheels are on rails. They winna come ony further. Martha here was in nae danger."

As Willie Cairns spoke he beckoned to the young woman. "Martha, here's your new piecer. Show her what tae dae."

"Aye, Mr Cairns." She looked none too kindly at Ann and when the supervisor was out of earshot, added, "Well, I hope you're no as daft as you look! Come on then and watch me."

She turned and made her way back towards the middle of the spinning machine and Ann followed feeling confused and foolish. Now the long carriage was reversing on its rails and she could see the single row of spindles at the front still rotating, winding on the newly spun yarn.

Again the carriage juddered to a halt, close to the rack of bobbins, while the rollers continued to feed through the triple lengths of fibre. This time, as the carriage started again on its outward movement pulling and twisting the fibres into a strong yarn, Ann kept her mouth tightly closed but she did notice that Martha kept well out of its way.

The child's head spun with the rattling of the bobbins, the creaking and grinding of the wheels and agonised shaking of the carriage as it halted. The whirr of the spindles taking up the finished woollen thread brought the process the full circle.

Meanwhile Martha moved up and down keeping a close eye on the yarn as it reached the spindles. Sometimes there was a break in the soft wool and the young woman quickly reached out and rejoined the ends.

"Are you watchin noo?" she asked Ann sharply. "This is the wey it's done. Pick up the broken ends and gie them a good twist thegither till they're firm again . . . .See there's ane broken alang there. You try noo."

Ann's heart was in her mouth as she reached out. Would the machine burn her or knock her down? Her fingers were all thumbs as she tried to follow Martha's example and her twisting of the ends produced an ugly lumpy join.

Martha tutted impatiently, "You'll hae to dae better than that. Try again here!"

She pointed to another break.

This time the carriage was at a halt and the three strands seemed to blend together more easily, but Ann's inexpert join unravelled as soon as it was pulled.

"Here, gie it tae me and watch again!"

So the afternoon wore on with Ann's fumbling efforts being largely unsuccessful. Each failure brought yet another cutting remark from Martha.

"Did Mr Hird look at your haunds afore he sent you up here? I dinna think so!"

Ann grew more miserable with each failure and her fingers seemed to get clumsier the harder she tried. She must have looked as unhappy as she felt because Willie Cairns spoke to Martha in the passing.

"Gie the lassie a chance. Dinna be sae hard on her."

The young woman was unrepentant. "I've enough to dae here wi'oot watchin ower a haundless bairn!"

"Somebody did it for you when you started, Martha."

"I was never as useless as that! Anyhow, up tae last week, me and Maggie Hutchison worked fine thegither on this machine!"

"Well, Maggie went and got married. Married women hae nae place workin in a mill. They hae enough to dae wi a house and a man to look after. And then there will be bairns."

"Huh!"

"Just you keep a civil tongue in your heid, young woman, or you'll be followin Maggie!"

Martha glared at her supervisor's back as he moved on but she did curb her tongue, as Ann renewed her efforts to follow her instructions. By the time the signal came for the end of the afternoon shift, the child had managed to piece the ends together a few times and had been given a grudging word of encouragement from Martha.

"Aye, that's mair like it."

After work, Ann and her father made their way along the riverside path towards Millrow in the winter darkness. Ann said nothing till Joshua Petty broke the silence with a question.

"Who are you workin wi?"

"Martha. I dinna ken her second name."

Her father laughed, "Martha, - that'll be Martha Cameron, but she's called 'Clip-cloots', for her sharp tongue.

It's all very well for him to laugh, thought Ann, but before she could reply her father continued, "Aye, nae doubt you've had the rough edge of it already. Just mind that her bark's worse than her bite, and she's a good worker. Otherwise she'd hae been out the door lang since."

There was small comfort in Joshua Petty's words for the weary child whose eyes closed almost as soon as she had eaten her tea. Her mother smiled at her.

"Awa tae your bed, Annie. I'll see tae the bairns. You hae an early start in the morn."

Ann was already sound asleep before her father added, "And a gey lang day

42

ahead."

It was still dark outside when she felt someone shaking her by the shoulder. It was her father.

"Time to rise. Here's your tea and a piece, bread and treacle."

"But it's the middle o the night!"

"It's well after five o'clock and we hae to be at the mill sharp at six."

Only the glow of a winter moon guided their footsteps as they crossed the bridge and turned through lower Bridgend and along the opposite riverbank. Ann shivered and pulled her shawl closer around her. Other shadowy figures joined them as they went along under the railway bridge. It was a strangely quiet procession that made its way past the mill lade, the only sound their cobbled boots ringing out on the frost-hardened path.

Now the mill was in full view, the shafts of gaslight from its windows piercing the darkness. It looked like a massive lamp, Ann thought, attracting people instead of moths to its warm glow. Certainly everyone's footsteps seemed to quicken, eager as they were to be inside away from the dark chill.

Upstairs on the spinning floor, one of the men was setting up the mule, putting the bobbins full of roving in their triple rows on the vertical frame. If Ann had imagined that Martha might be friendly, she was to be disappointed. The young woman's greeting was unsmiling.

"There you are. Right, mak yourself useful. While the men are settin up we hae tae clean the fluff frae the machines. You're wee, sae you can get in below the carriage. Clear the oose frae the roller in there, all the way alang."

Ann crouched down and reached in through the bars of the carriage. Her hands were quickly covered in grease as she made her way along clearing the fluffy wool from the machine.

"Are you ready then, Martha?" It was a male voice. The wool spinner had completed his setting up and the dozens of fat bobbins were ready to be drawn and spun.

"Right, Tam," came Martha's voice and then she turned to Ann.

"Get oot o there, gowk. Dae you want tae be knocked ower?"

Ann looked up and saw Tam reach out to start the large wheel at the end of the mule. Her heart was hammering as she scrambled out of the way of the carriage.

Martha laughed. "You'll hae tae learn tae move faster. The machines winna wait for you. Noo, watch oot for strands needin pieced and mind how I showed you. Wipe that grease aff your haunds first."

Ann was kept so busy that she didn't notice the sky lightening outside till a bell rang at nine o'clock.

"Breakfast time. We've an hour aff noo. Mind and no be late back."

The child needed no second bidding and she was down the brae to the footbridge and across it ahead of her father this time. In the cottage her mother had a pot of porridge hanging from the swee above the fire and she was just finishing feeding the wee ones. She looked up when Ann entered. "My, is it that time? There's plenty parritch, Annie, but the bairns hae finished the milk. Run up tae the Hainin farm and tak Chris wi you."

The boy protested, "Oh, Mam, I dinna. . . ." but he was cut off in mid sentence.

"Wheest, you'll hae to start goin' the messages now, Chris. Annie winna hae time. You'll be by yoursel the morrow. Tak the big jug."

With her brother in tow, Ann rushed back, through the grass yard below the ruins of the bishop's palace. Christopher was panting as they climbed the steep riverbank and passed the roofless nave of the cathedral on the way to the Haining dairy. There the enamel jug was filled with the day's supply of fresh milk.

Ann carried the jug carefully and reminded her brother, "You'll hae to be earlier for the milk the morrow, so it's ready for the mill workers comin hame, Chris!"

There was just enough time for Ann to sup her porridge before her father warned her,

"Right, Annie, we'll hae to be getting back. You'll lose pay if you're late."

Her mother smiled, "Well, she'd be the first Petty ever to be late. Here you are, Annie, your pieces for dinnertime. You'll no hae time to come hame at midday."

Back at Springbank Mill, the spinning machines went on relentlessly, back and forth, turning, pulling, twisting and winding till the spindles at the front were full and the triple bobbins at the rear were empty. Ann found that if she kept alert she sometimes spied a break in the wool before Martha did. By getting there first and piecing the ends, the child managed to avoid some of the young woman's cutting comments, but as the morning wore on the small girl grew weary.

Martha showed no sympathy when Ann's attention wavered.

"Dinna just staund there. See, you've missed a break ower there. Move yoursel and join it up."

When at last, the half-timers' bell rang at noon Ann was only too pleased to turn away from the machine and join the other girls and boys making their way downstairs. The cold air outside jerked her back to wakefulness as the children lined up outside the mill. She found herself beside an older girl and recognised Liz Eadie from Miss Campbell's school.

"Eat your piece now. We dinna hae a proper break when we're on early shift. We just go right ower tae school."

With that the group of children threaded their way across the busy mill yard. Coming towards them was another group of youngsters finished with their morning's lessons. As they passed there was some jostling and pushing and Ann overheard a boy ask, "Is he in a good mood?"

The question caused loud laughter as Ann's group reached the school building that stood alone in the yard. Its red pantiled roof was bright in the midday sun. A horse was tethered to a hook on the stone wall.

"Is that the teacher's horse?" Ann asked her companion.

Liz laughed. "No," she said, "That's Mr Wilson's. Noo and then he comes intae class to see us, but maistly he's in the office. My faither told me that he used to ride all the wey frae Bannockburn every day. That was a while ago before he was wed. Now he just has to ride frae his big braw hoose, Alford, on the Glen Road."

"What if we meet him?" Ann wanted to know.

"Oh, he doesna bother wi us. We just hae to mind and curtsey and say 'Good morning, sir', if he passes. It's Auld Kingie, the teacher you hae to look out for.

He's got a terrible temper when he's roused. S-sh, there he is – glowerin as usual!"

Certainly the person standing at the school door looked less than welcoming and Ann's heart was heavy as she reluctantly entered her new school. After the warmth of the mill, the schoolroom was chilly and she shivered with cold and fatigue.

"Try and get close tae the stove," Liz advised her as they slipped past the teacher.

When the class settled down the dominie stood in front of them. He rapped his pointer on the floor and glared at his pupils.

"What is the chief end of man?" He barked the question.

"Oh, well," thought Ann, "at least that's familiar," as she joined in the well rehearsed response to the catechism, "To glorify God and enjoy. . ."

Her head drooped and nodded and she would have fallen asleep if Liz had not dug her elbow into the younger girl's ribs.

"Dinna fall asleep. He'll go daft if you dae," she whispered.

Ann shook herself awake just in time to find the teacher standing over her.

"Ah, a new face, I perceive. Name?"

He wrote Ann's details in the register, and then continued to question her.

"And just what did you learn at Miss Campbell's? Singing and outdoor games, I suppose? You'll get no such nonsense here! It's the three Rs we have here. Reading, Writing and Arithmetic! How many yards are in a furlong?"

"Two hundred and twenty, Mr King."

"Good. It seems you've learned something useful. Right class, copy this sum on to your slates."

Ann was relieved when the teacher turned his attention elsewhere.

Somehow, with help from Liz, she stayed awake till the three o'clock bell told them it was time to go home. Wearily, she struggled to her feet while the boys scrambled past her to tumble out the door. In vain the teacher roared at them to be quiet and mind their manners. They just laughed as they hurtled across the yard.

Liz shrugged her shoulders. "They're just showin aff because you're new here. They like to rile Mr King. Dinna let them bother you!"

The days that followed were a haze of fatigue for the small girl, trying to survive in the new routine. As her skill as a piecer improved, Martha's complaints lessened, but the school hours were a constant struggle. Every second week when her shift of half-timers began their day with early school at nine o'clock, the bigger lads seemed more determined than ever to make Auld Kingie lose his temper.

Sometimes, their antics earned them more than sarcastic comments and many a lad found his head gripped under the teacher's arm while being pummelled by the dominie's clenched knuckles. However, such punishment had little effect on the miscreants who compared bruises like war wounds.

Ann found the boys tiresome but at least they diverted the teacher's attention from her while she saved her energy for the long hours at the spinning mule. After morning school, when the two shifts of half-timers passed in the yard, news was always eagerly exchanged, and the rough lads were always delighted if they could boast, "Oh, the dominie's in a right bad mood. Somethin seems to hae riled him the day!"

Back in the mill, the morning pupils worked till they had their dinner break from two o'clock till three and then it was back till the final bell for everyone at six o'clock. Ann didn't know which was worse, the early start before dawn or the late finish after sunset.

Gradually as the days lengthened into spring the child's anxiety lessened, and she looked forward to Thursdays when she lined up with the other mill workers for her pay. How proud she felt when she took her week's wages to her mother who hugged her wordlessly and put the coins away safely in a tea caddy above the fire. Queen Victoria, smiling on the side of the tin seemed to be adding royal approval for the child's contribution to the household.

Some mornings at the mill, while Tam was setting up the spinning mule, Willie Cairns sent Ann with a message to another department. She loved being out even briefly in the fresh air away from the airborne fibres that always floated about the spinning room. She felt quite important crossing the yard going to the new building, dodging the cheeky barrow boys transporting their loads of empty bobbins and avoiding the horses and carts bringing coal for the steam engines. If the drivers called out greetings to her she just hurried on determined to perform her errands without mistakes.

The place she really liked to visit was the packing department up one stair in the new building. She was fascinated by the sight of the railway goods wagons at the doorway being stacked with parcels clearly marked with the names of large carpet firms, the names she'd read in the big ledger for Mr Hird. That seemed so long ago Ann thought as she realised that these parcels were the bundles of yarn that she was helping to spin, going off on their long journeys south by Caledonian Railway.

As the weeks wore on Mrs Petty had to use two hands to lift the tea caddy with its hoard of coins and Ann was sure that Queen Victoria was fairly beaming with delight each time her mother added the child's wage for the week.

At last one evening in early summer Joshua Petty hurried into the cottage at Millrow calling for Mrs Petty and Ann.

"Grand news, my dears. There's a house for us in the last of Mr Wilson's tenements. We can move in whenever we want."

Ann and her mother clapped their hands with delight and asked one question after another.

"Which block is it?"

"Is it upstairs?"

"How much is the rent?"

"When will we flit?"

Joshua Petty laughed. "Haud on a minute! You're like a pair of cluckin hens! It's the newest block, the one at Well Place and we hae an upstairs flat. The rent's twa shillins a week and we'll move on Saturday afternoon. Rob Dick is bringin his coal cairt to dae the flittin."

"But that doesna leave us much time, Joshua!"

"Well, lass, the sooner we're away, the sooner we'll settle in and the sooner you'll be feelin better."

So, on Saturday afternoon Ann and Mrs Petty made their way on foot from Millrow with Davey wrapped firmly inside his mother's shawl and Agnes trotting alongside. Through Bridgend, over the railway bridge, past the thatched cottages of Caledonian Place and then they went round the corner into Well Place. Ann and Agnes ran up the outside stairs on to the balcony and along to the empty house in the middle.

The original 'Skye Block', Springbank Terrace.

"Oh, Mam, look at the size of the rooms, There's plenty space for twa big beds ben the room!"

"Aye, and the kitchen here can tak twa mair. Oh, look Annie by the windae, a jawbox wi a tap!"

Mrs Petty turned on the single tap and after a few gurgles and splutters a jet of water poured into the black iron sink. Her eyes sparkled as she exclaimed, "Just imagine, Annie, nae mair traipsing tae the well for buckets of water!"

From the front window Ann saw the coal cart with Chris and John riding triumphantly with blackened faces amidst their furniture and their father at the front directing the driver. While the men unloaded the furniture, the children dashed up and downstairs with bits and pieces.

From the next flat on the balcony a neighbour called to Mrs Petty.

"Come awa in for a cup of tea, lass. Tak the weight aff your feet while the men shift your things. I'm Mary Boyle."

While Mrs Petty took Agnes and Davey next door, Ann and her father unpacked. Arranging cups and plates on the dresser that was her mother's pride and joy, the child wondered for a moment if the shelving had shrunk in the flitting, but a glance round the room made her realise that all their furniture now looked sparse in the bigger rooms.

From the balcony she overheard their new neighbour pointing out the washing house in the backcourt. Mrs Boyle was talking about the lavatories at each corner of the building.

"You'll share that one wi oursels and the Calders next door and we tak it in turn tae clean it. You'll get the key tae the wash hoose door aince a week and there's plenty room for hingin the washin out tae dry."

Ann joined the women leaning over the balcony. Her mother turned to her, "Nae mair kneelin at the mill lade to rinse things out, Annie. Mrs Boyle tells me that we can light the coal fire under the big boiler in the wash house tae boil the clathes clean."

Ann was more interested in all the children playing below.

"See Mam, there's plenty room in the back court for Agnes and John tae play. Nae horses and cairts and nae river tae fall intae."

"Aye, and plenty ither bairns tae play wi," laughed Mrs Boyle.

"It's like bein' in the country," Mrs Petty exclaimed, "wi naethin but fairms between here and Doune!"

'Except Springbank Mill!' thought Ann, her face clouding a little.

Then she looked at Mrs Petty and it seemed to her that her mother had already got the roses back in her cheeks. A surge of affection went through the young girl and she asked. "Dae you think you'll like it here, Mam?"

"Oh aye, Annie, and it's thanks tae you, love!"

As she spoke, Mrs Petty dabbed her eyes with the corner of her shawl while she pulled from inside it the precious tea caddy. "Here, lass, you put it on the new mantelpiece."

Stretching up to place the tin on the ledge, Ann felt a glow of satisfaction. She knew that ahead of her would be many a long dreich day at the mill, but she would thole it for her mother's sake.

In the evening with the younger children tucked up in bed, she sat watching the dancing flames of the coal fire and pondered over her own future. One thing she knew, she would not stay at the mill forever. Oh, no – when she was old enough she would find different work. Maybe she'd be a maid in a fine house like the Wilsons' at Alford in Glen Road, or better still she might be a cook. Didn't she make a fine clootie dumpling? Aye, that's what she wanted to be, a cook. Her mind settled she kissed her mother goodnight and rose to go through to the other room.

She took the oil lamp from the mantelpiece to light her way to bed. The flame flickered, throwing its light on the tea caddy. Tired though she was, Ann smiled happily at the royal portrait, and she could have sworn that Queen Victoria winked back at her!

BAIRNS OF BRIDGEND
DUNBLANE

ANN PETTY 1874

NOTES

The Petty family's baptism records show that when the family was complete, Ann was the eldest of eight. Her father Joshua Petty later became the manager of Springbank Mill after Thomas Hird left. It was common practice for mill workers to 'speak for' their children to secure employment.

By 1874 a series of Factory Acts had made it illegal to employ a child under the age of ten, while the Education Act of 1872 made at least part time education compulsory for under thirteen year olds.

Unfortunately, no registers have survived for either the Infant and Girls or the Mill School. Pupils' names, like Ann's, are taken from the baptism records of her contemporaries whose family names are known to have a later connection with the mill.

However, both school buildings are still intact. Miss Campbell retired in 1877 after 32 years teaching in the infant school that had been built by the Laird of Keir, Archibald Stirling. The building at the foot of the Old Doune Road is now a private house, Rosebank, while the mill school is preserved as part of a new housing complex. The oldest of the mill buildings dating from 1853, having provided employment for Dunblane folk up till 1980, has now been converted to flats.

The late Mr John Wilson, the last of the family to own and manage Springbank Mill, provided valuable information on the layout and day-to-day work of the mill. The Springbank Wilsons were closely related to the better-known Wilsons of Bannockburn who famously produced regimental tartans for Scots regiments of the British army.

Two of the tenements blocks, including the one in Well Place to which the Petty family moved were replaced by modern flats, but the original 'Skye Block' still stands round the corner from Rosebank facing across to the railway line. The original occupants' names including the Petty family's are registered in the voters' rolls held in Perth Archives.

Strangely, none of the Petty family's boys joined their father at the mill while Ann fulfilled her ambition to be a cook, though not at Alford but at another 'braw big house' in Dunblane. Her niece, Mrs I. Lindsay, supplied the details about the christening gown from Menzies in Stirling, which is still an independent company.

The names Joshua and David continue to be used in the Petty family today.

BAIRNS OF BRIDGEND
DUNBLANE

ANN PETTY 1874

SOURCES AND BIBLIOGRAPHY

1980s Recollections of Dunblane residents of 'Skye Blocks' and Well Place buildings and of families who had formerly occupied them: Mr Duncan Fraser; Mrs Bell; Mr and Mrs James Crockett; Mr Reg McCabe; Mr Lawrence Marshall; Mr and Mrs Walter Lambert; Mrs Margaret Scobie *nee* McLean
Information on Petty Family – Mrs R. Lindsay, Dunblane.

Baptism Register, Dunblane U.F. Church 1836-1890. Stirling District Archives.

Stirling Observer Newspapers, 1865-1880
Stirling Journal and Advertisers. 1865-1880

WILSON & SONS, Springbank Mill. *Day Books and Ledgers* 1853-1888.
Advice on Springbank Mill layout and technical operations, Mr and Mrs Wilson, Dunblane.

BARTLETT, J Neville. *Carpeting the Millions,* John Donald, Edinburgh.
BARTY, Elizabeth. *Old Kirk Street.*
   In Society of Friends of Dunblane Cathedral. Vol XII, part 2 1975
British Parliamentary Papers. 1867 Statistics relevant to Schools in Scotland.
CATLING, H., *The Evolution of Spinning* in J Geraint JENKINS, in
   The Wool Textile Industry in Great Britain. Routledge and Kegan Paul, 1972.
DUNCAN, Robert *Textiles and Toil,* The Factory system and the Industrial Working
   Class in Early nineteenth century Aberdeen, Aberdeen City Library, 1984.
Evaluation Rolls of the County of Perth, 1874- 1878, Perth Archives.
HILLS, Richard L. *Richard Arkwright and Cotton Spinning.* Priory Press Ltd., 1973.
JENKINS, D T and PONTING K G., *The British Wool and Textile Industry,* 1770-1914
   Heineman Educational Books, 1982.
LENMAN, Bruce, LYTHE, Charlotte and GAULDIE, Enid, *Dundee and its Textile
   Industry 1850-1914.* Dundee Abertay Historical Society Publication, No. 14. 1969.
MARSHALL, Jean C., *Half-timers,* Ed B thesis, St Andrews University, 1967.

BAIRNS OF BRIDGEND DUNBLANE

WILLIAM HOGG 1846

Chaunt of the Weaver

Oh, what a world is this!
How toil and want are wed:
Today I dream of bliss –
Tomorrow all is fled.

What though, from day to day,
With busy hands I weave,
And wear myself away,
Ere noon to life's sad eve:
My gains, though war'd with miser care,
Can life sustain no more,
And I breathe a prayer, well nigh despair,
When my children cry for more.

Think not within a school
My children you will see,
In rags much out of rule
Ev'n for the 'Charity'…

Anon, Allou, 1845.

BAIRNS OF BRIDGEND
DUNBLANE

WILLIAM HOGG 1846

Willie balanced on his stomach as he stared over the bridge into the brown depths of Allan Water. He searched the rapid flow for the silver flash of salmon – but the only breaks on the rushing surface were white patches of foam. He wriggled along the wall to relieve the hunger pangs in his belly and lifted his head to listen intently.

In the distance, but coming closer was the sound that the six year old was waiting for, the unmistakeable clip clop of horses' hooves cantering up the road from the south. Willie was down off the wall and along the short distance to Kinross's Inn before the coach from Glasgow came into sight. Swinging round from the Stirling Road, 'The Defiance' crossed the bridge into Dunblane, the hollow ring of sixteen hooves echoing on the cobbles.

By the time the horses had clattered to a halt outside the inn, Willie had squirmed through to the front of the small crowd of curious onlookers and he was ready to wedge the first stone behind the wheel of the stagecoach. Just as he moved forward out of the corner of his eye he spied another lad moving towards the opposite wheel. Outraged, Willie jammed his stone into place and darted round to the other boy. There was a yelp of surprise and pain as Willie dug his sharp elbow into the other's ribs.

"Get awa Rab Cramb," he hissed, "This yin's mine!"

He picked up the stone that Rab had dropped and wedged it in, while his rival slunk off holding his side. No one else challenged his right to wedge the other wheels, while at the front of the coach the stable boys were loosening the girths of the four panting horses. Willie quickly moved round to the side of the coach where the guard was holding open the door for the passengers inside.

The small boy waited expectantly for the travellers to descend. Sometimes a grand lady in a crinoline would step down and charmed by Willie's engaging smile would give the lad a farthing. Today, however, there were only frock coated business gentlemen in tall hats on the long stager and they ignored him.

As the last outside passenger clambered down and disappeared into the Inn without tipping, Willie's well-practised smile faded. From a safe distance at the fringe of the onlookers, Rab Cramb grinned wickedly and Willie could only glower back, failing to mask his disappointment.

Now the tired horses were completely unharnessed and the lads led them to the stables. Willie helped to hold the empty harness to prevent the leather straps and shining buckles from getting tangled. Replacement horses were expertly harnessed and the eager animals together with their splendid coach, made an impressive sight in the crisp autumn morning. The driver pulled out his watchcase from his inside pocket, snapped it open and declared,

"Weel done, lads. That was thirteen minutes. Twa minutes to spare."

Back by the passenger door, Willie hovered hopefully while the straggling passengers resumed their seats. The last two gentlemen were deep in conversation.

"Indeed," said one, "Progress has been satisfactory. The first permanent rails were laid in spring."

Willie heard only fragments of the reply as he circled the coach removing the stones from behind the wheels. "Ah yes, but I doubt if the railway will ever replace the coaches completely. . . . Nothing quite like a brisk gallop on a fine day. . . ."

Now the coachman checked the time, tucked his watch inside the folds of his cape, swung himself up on to his box, and gathered up the reins. From the rear came the guard's warning shout, and Willie stood well back.

With a crack of the whip, the Defiance was off turning through the main street of Dunblane on its northward journey to Perth.

As the small crowd dispersed, Willie gazed forlornly after the disappearing vehicle. That would be the only stagecoach through all day. And the omnibuses that brought summer visitors from Bridge of Allan and Stirling to the mineral springs at the Laighills had stopped for the season. With the departure of the 'Well Folk', Willie's hopes of a steady supply of farthings had faded and this was not the first time that his help with the stagecoach had been unrewarded.

Now his hunger pains returned and there would be no delicious hot buns fresh from baker Malcolm's oven this morning. But his stomach was empty oftener than not, so he shrugged off his disappointment and wondered what to do with the rest of the day.

He could go back to Widow McLaren's at Balhaldie but she'd been glad to see

Stirling Arms and the Bridge, Dunblane

53

the back of him this morning after he'd complained about his meagre helping of porridge. No, he'd be better off keeping out of her way till she calmed down a bit.

He turned and walked slowly back across the bridge and up into Bridgend. The click-clack of shuttles came from the dwellings on both sides of the street and in the shadowy interiors men bent over their looms, intent on their work. Willie could just recall his own father, John, weaving hour upon hour to produce lengths of cotton in their Bridgend cottage, but that had been two years earlier before there were any signs of railway construction. The boy had only hazy memories of his mother who had died giving birth to his sister Bell.

When the Railway Company had routed its line right through the middle of Bridgend, the heart had been ripped out of the local handloom industry. But it was a heart that had been beating feebly for some years. Where hundreds had once thrived, weavers were struggling to feed their families, working longer and longer hours for lower prices for their cloth. There had been little protest when the navvies had moved in and cut a swathe through the old settlement sweeping away the weavers' humble dwellings.

All Willie knew was that on the day that their home had been destroyed, his father had given up his desperate struggle and had disappeared leaving his homeless children to the care of the parish. It was then that Widow McLaren had taken in Willie, his sister Bell and his young brother James.

They had all been delighted when John Hogg had reappeared in Dunblane. They did not know that their father had been arrested for begging in Glasgow and had been returned under escort to his own parish. For a few weeks he had taken an interest in his family but John Hogg found that now there was even less chance of earning a living by weaving. Like so many other weavers he had gone again in the spring, seeking work with Scottish Central Railway somewhere to the north further up the line.

At first the bairns had expected their father to come home and every night they'd waited patiently for him to reappear. The weeks had gone by and summer days had been busy with the visiting 'Well Folk' who had sometimes given Willie quite generous tips. Gradually, the children had stopped looking out for John Hogg, but today as he stared at the railway site where his home had once been, Willie suddenly longed to see his father again. The almost forgotten yearning, for their own family and home for James, Bell and himself, returned in a rush.

But what could he do about it he wondered. Then he came to a decision. . . . He would look for his father himself, 'somewhere up the line'. That wasn't much guidance, but suddenly his mind was made up.

Willie set out across the excavated area, the centre where wooden sleepers lay in readiness for the rails. It was easy going at first, jumping from sleeper to sleeper as he crossed the new railway bridge high above Allan Water. He had a fine view of the cathedral and its yard, bringing back memories of a scene almost a year before. Then, the kirkyard had been choked with hundreds of navvies paying their last respects to one of their fellows, killed by a misfiring charge. That had been a solemn occasion, but by the evening the mourners had become a drunken rabble and Dunblane's disgusted citizens had cowered behind bolted doors. Today the same kirkyard was silent and deserted.

Ahead of Willie at the Laighills scores of men were at work carting away barrow loads of sandy soil from the cutting that formed a gash through the hills. As they trundled back and forth with their barrows, Willie scanned their faces eagerly for a familiar one. There were some he vaguely remembered from Bridgend, Sandy McLean and Duncan Cameron amongst them.

He spoke to Sandy McLean. "Hae ye seen my faither, John Hogg?"

The labourer took the chance to lean on his shovel. "Let me think. Aye, he was wi us for a whilie in spring when we went up the line tae Auchterarder. That was efter the strike there when the wages were cut."

Sandy McLean turned to the other former weaver and continued, "Duncan, dae you mind what happened to John Hogg?"

The other man shook his head. "I dinna ken, but there was word o him stayin on at the Kincardine Viaduct when we were sent back here. I couldna be certain."

"If I was you, son, that's whaur I'd look. Just keep goin up the line but steer awa frae the tunnel that's bein dug. See, up ahead? That runnin sand's a real danger. It could cave in and kill you like yon puir lad, Peter McQeen frae Skye!"

"Thanks, I'll mind that," replied Willie, "but Auchterarder, is that far frae here?"

"Far enough for your wee short legs," Duncan Cameron answered, grinning at the small boy, "but no too far for a day if ye dinna dawdle! It's aboot twelve mile."

"Oh, that's no sae bad then. I should find him quite easy!" said Willie.

Then thinking of the long walk ahead, he blurted out, "But I'm awfu hungert!"

Sandy McLean smiled as he reached into his pocket.

"Oh, I think we can spare ye a bite tae eat, lad. Here, some breid tae keep ye goin'."

"Thanks. I'll tell my faither ye helped me!" With a cheery wave, Willie scampered off, keen to be on his way. Up he clambered between the Laighills tunnel works and the Well House, deserted now by the invalids who took the mineral waters as a cure-all.

Within minutes, he was overlooking the water cut where the railway engineers had diverted the River Allan. In the cutting below him at Barbush, Willie could see a squad of men hard at work, shovelling muck into a row of stationary wagons. They worked rhythmically, in pairs, digging their shovels into the dirt and swinging them over their heads to tip out into the open carts. Willie sat down to eat his bread and watch the men below.

From their sturdy hobnail boots, moleskin trousers and open necked canvas shirts, to the upturned brims of their white felt hats, their clothes marked them as experienced English navvies. These strong men had learned their skills on the first railways south of the border and they wore their bright rainbow waistcoats and gaudy handkerchiefs with the swagger of men who were rightly proud of their prowess.

When all the wagons were full, they were dragged on a short railtrack to a spot about fifty yards from the edge of the bank overlooking Allan Water. Willie could hear the gaffer shout his instructions to his men.

"Right, Joe. Hitch up!"

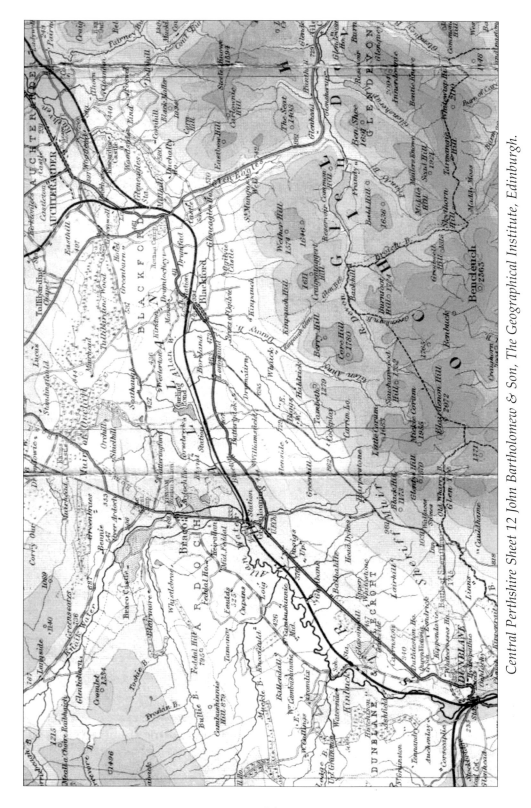

Central Perthshire Sheet 12 John Bartholomew & Son, The Geographical Institute, Edinburgh.

"Ready, Punch," came the response and the first wagon was harnessed to a sturdy carthorse. At the side, the man called Joe held firmly to the reins and he led the horse as it pulled the wagon on its tram rails faster and faster till they were galloping towards the river's edge. Willie held his breath sure that horse, man and wagon must all plunge over into the water!

At the last moment Joe loosened the horse's halter and with a yell of, "Hup, now!" both man and beast leapt aside! The open truck careered ahead till it hit a stout wooden barrier where it tipped forward spewing its contents into Allan Water below. Little islands were appearing in the river where none had been before, as one after another the wagons of spoil were emptied by galloping horses and men. Willie was tempted to stay longer watching the excitement, but he remembered he had a long way to go on the search for his father.

He kept to the east bank of the river while the railway route followed its own course crossing and recrossing the curves of Allan Water. Scores of men were working on the bridges but no one paid any attention to the small boy. At the Mill of Ash Cut he found himself following the first new shining permanent rails as they pointed their way north east. After Kinbuck, the track left the river wending its own twisted watercourse and Willie was able to make good time over a long straight stretch of rail.

Off to the right Sheriffmuir seemed to loom over him and he suddenly felt very small and lonely in the vast empty landscape. Now there were areas quite empty of human life and the track ahead seemed to go on forever. . . .Past Greenloaning, he was somehow comforted to find Allan Water again parallel to the track and he plodded on, encouraged again by the sight of some houses in the distance. The viaduct must be close now.

His legs ached and he was breathing hard now but he kept going till he came up to another group of workers at a bridge just outside the settlement. Again, he searched for a familiar face but saw no one he knew among the labourers busily shifting materials.

Willie stood, unsure of what to do next, when one of the men spoke to him.

"Are you the laddie that takes the tools for repair?"

From his soft accent, Willie guessed he was Irish.

He hesitated before he answered … "No, I'm lookin for my faither, John Hogg. I was tauld he was workin near the toon, on the viaduct."

The labourer looked at the small boy. "Well, you'll no find him hereabouts, son. Kincardine Viaduct's more that four miles up the track near Auchterarder."

Willie couldn't believe it. He was sure he'd come more than a dozen miles. He pointed to the houses only a few hundred yards away. "Is that no Auchterarder then?"

The Irishman shook his head, "No," he said, "This is Blackford."

Willie's heart sank but he tried to put on a brave face.

"I'll be on my wey then."

"Wait a moment, son. Ye'll ne'er reach Auchterarder before nightfall. Ye had best be goin' home."

"I canna dae that either," said Willie, trying to keep the tremble out of his voice. "I live awa back there in Dunblane."

The labourer looked at the small boy and thought for a minute. He called to one of his mates.

"Michael, here's a young fella who's stuck miles from his home with the night drawin in. It'll soon be dark."

"Ah, I'm sure we can find a berth for him at the camp, Sean. God love him! He's no much bigger than my own lad."

Willie sniffed and wiped his nose with his sleeve. He tried to look unworried but his tiredness and disappointment showed through. And he was hungry again.

"Thanks," he whispered.

The Irish encampment was in a quiet spot outside Blackford and the cluster of shacks blended in with the countryside. From a short distance only the smoke rising from low roofs that perched above turf walls betrayed the whereabouts of the settlement.

"We keep oursels to oursels," explained Michael, "but there's always room for a stranger in real need."

Pushing aside the door, Michael called to the woman inside, "Mary, we've one more for supper the night!"

Willie blinked against the smoke as he entered the ramshackle dwelling. Mary Hulligan looked at Willie without surprise and she smiled. She began to ladle food from a big cooking pot into tin bowls. The tired boy sat alongside four small ragged children who gazed at him solemnly. But when he was given his bowl, Willie's tiredness and disappointment melted away as he smelled the rabbit stew with onions and potatoes. A meal fit for a king! The lad tucked in to the best meal he could remember.

Afterwards, when the men sat and smoked and the small children scraped the pot clean, Willie looked around.

The place was cramped and it was filthy. The children huddled together on a makeshift bed, one of two in the tiny square room. Yet he'd been made welcome here with no questions asked. As he pulled off his boots and stretched out to sleep he puzzled over it. He thought about the meagre bowl of porridge that Widow McLaren had given him that morning. . . . There was more warmth in this Irish labourer's hovel than in all Dunblane's cold charity.

In the morning Willie was up with the light to make the rest of his journey. Mary Hulligan gave him some oatcakes to take with him.

"God speed, son," she said, "and I hope you'll find yer daddy soon!"

"Thanks, Missus," he called cheerfully. "I'll be seein him afore lang."

Beyond Blackford, Allan Water was reduced to a burn's width and soon even that disappeared as the railway track swung northward. Somehow the river's disappearance, combined with leaving the warmth of the encampment, left Willie feeling quite alone again, but his excitement at the prospect of finding his father kept him going. On he went, up the incline, through cuttings and embankments thronged with workers. Now the track took him upwards through woodland and he found his view restricted by trees all around. Quite suddenly the way was totally blocked by men, horses and materials.

He had to leave the track and make his way through the undergrowth. Then without warning the ground seemed to disappear just ahead of him. Gingerly, Willie made his way forward and peered over the edge. He gasped when he saw the land fall away steeply and he held tightly to a tree at the top of a slope. Peering over, he had a bird's eye view of the scene a hundred feet below at the bottom of a narrow gorge. There, from the dry riverbed, pillars of stone were rising block upon block, and Willie realised with a start that this was the viaduct at last. This was where he had to look for his father among the hundreds of ant-like figures scurrying about below.

He made his way along carefully till he found a zigzag path down to the dry riverbed. It was when he reached the bottom and found himself among the workers that he felt the enormity of the task he'd set himself. This was no straightforward cutting or embankment where picks and shovels and human muscle were all the tools required. On this vast site there were men mixing batches of mortar, men erecting scaffolding round the piers and men standing looking at plans and discussing them earnestly.

Where was he to begin among the hundreds of men spread over such an area?

Emerging from the wooded slope into the open base, Willie drew in his breath. From this angle the solid stone piers towered above him dwarfing him and the men who swarmed over the site. And now he could see a monstrous piece of apparatus that stood alongside a wagon train loaded with massive lumps of roughly cut stone. Willie had never seen such a machine and he watched in awe while the contraption lifted up one of the huge blocks, swung it across and laid it down on the ground under the direction of one man.

When he got over his amazed fright, Willie returned to his search. He made his way over to three of the serious looking men with the drawings. From their clothes he could tell that they were gentlemen so he shuffled his feet and cleared his throat nervously, waiting his chance to speak to them. His voice came out in a squeak.

Kincardine Viaduct, Auchterarder.

59

"Please sirs, I'm lookin for my faither."

The engineers looked down in surprise and raised their eyebrows. One of them laughed and turned to the youngest of the three.

"We'll leave this non-technical problem to you!" he said rolling up the plans and moving off.

The young gentleman bent down, half amused, half annoyed.

"What is it, boy?"

"I'm lookin for my faither, John Hogg."

"Oh! Is he a mason?"

The young engineer was pointing to the men who were chiselling the stone into shape.

Willie shook his head.

"Is he a carpenter then?"

Now the engineer indicated the men who were erecting the scaffolding.

Again Willie shook his head.

"No sir. He's a weaver. . . . I mean that's what he did afore the railway cam through Brigend."

"Ah, a labourer then. Well, that's like looking for a needle in a haystack! We have thirty-five hundred men on the line between Stirling and Perth!"

Then looking at the small boy's anxious face, the young man said more kindly,

"There are big gangs up at the quarry – where that load of stones comes from – just a mile up the track there."

Then he suddenly changed his mind saying, "No, what am I thinking about? The place to go is to our office – the contractor's office in Auchterarder. The clerks there have the names of all our workers."

With those words of advice, the young man was off with other more important matters on his mind, leaving Willie thinking how lucky he was in his search. It was only another mile to Auchterarder. So the lad left the site of the Kincardine Viaduct with its seven massive pillars and took the track to town, whistling cheerfully.

In the contractor's office in 'The Lang Toon' of Auchterarder, the snooty clerks made him wait, but eventually one of them took down the wages book to scrutinise it.

"Let's see, here in the spring you say? . . . Let's try the month of March, . . .

'Clark, Patterson, Harshley, McKenna, Cheatam, Ritchards, Hogg' – Yes, here it is, J. Hogg."

Willie's heart soared as he burst out, "Whaur is he workin then, Mister?"

The clerk turned over the pages of the wages book and ran a finger down the handwritten page. He tutted impatiently.

"Wait a minute. We must check later in the year. April – Aye, there it is . . . May – Uh-huh. . . .June – Let's see – 'Cheatam, Ritchards, Jamieson, Malloch' . . . .No, he's no there. May's the last entry. . . . What's this in brackets? 'Left site after payday'. Oh aye, I remember now. Quite a few left then, Highlanders mostly though, complaining that they weren't paid the same as experienced railway men!"

But Willie wasn't interested in long explanations and his heart sank as the clerk's meaning became clear.

"Did he no come back then?" he interrupted impatiently.

"It's not likely, and even if he did he'd use a false name so he could be taken on again. The Company does not want unreliable workers," the clerk added with a sniff. "Anyway he's not in the book after May."

The clerk snapped the book closed and with that sharp sound Willie's dream of finding his father evaporated. As suddenly as his search had begun, just as suddenly he knew it had ended. Without a word he left the railway office too choked even to thank the clerk. He stumbled along Auchterarder's main street, his high hopes completely dashed now.

He realised that it was pointless to go further up the line when there were over three thousand men at work. Yesterday's journey through the squads of workers, Highland and Lowland Scots, Irish and English men had given him some idea of what those numbers meant. Sadly, he concluded that he had no choice but to return to Dunblane, but this time he'd take the road.

As he trudged along, Willie could not bring himself to believe that his father could have chosen to desert him and James and Bell. He must have been hurt or even killed somewhere on the line. . . . That was it, and now he and his brother and sister were orphans, left in the charge of the Widow McLaren.

He thought about the reception he'd get from her when he reached Dunblane and he knew that it would include a good smacking for him. Wasn't the Widow McLaren fond of saying, "Spare the rod and spoil the child!" There was little chance of that happening but Willie was too good at dodging her skelps for them to hurt much.

Near Blackford he thought once more of the kindness he'd been shown at the Irish encampment and he decided to stop there again. Mary Hulligan listened to his sad tale and shook her head. Her sympathy weakened Willie's resolve and in his desperate loneliness he blurted out, "Dae you think I could bide here wi your faimily, Missus?"

The Irish woman smiled sadly and touched Willie's upturned face. "I'm right sorry, son, that can never be. Yer Widow McLaren will have the constabulary

Blackford Level Crossing.

lookin for ye if only for the shillings she gets for yer keep. They'd be chargin us with stealing ye away from yer own people. And never forget yer brother and sister at home."

Willie nodded. It was true that with his father gone, he was now the head of the family. That would be something to say to Widow McLaren!

But it was not until the next morning when he was only a couple of miles from Dunblane on the turnpike road that he made up his mind that he was not going to Widow McLaren's after all, at least not right away. He was going to the Scottish Central Railway Contractor's Office in Dunblane to get a job. He squared his shoulders and marched along the rest of the way.

In the railway office the local contractor, Mr Phillips, was amused at his request.

"And what use would a small fellow like you be to us? I doubt if you would last a day on the railway!"

Willie stood looking as tall as he could.

"I've just been these last twa days tae Auchterarder and back lookin for my faither, but he's no there. I'm in sore need of a job. Could I no be a tool carrier?"

Mr Phillips was shaking his head. "We've plenty of boys for that." Then he added slowly, "But we are short of hands for leading out the soil wagons in the Kippenross Tunnel. More than a score of the foolish fellows ended up badly wounded or in jail after Tuesday's riot between the English and the Highlanders! And we've lost three men in accidents. It's been a bad week."

"I'm guid wi horses," replied Willie, eager to please.

"As long as you're good at keeping out the way of wagon wheels in the dark, you should keep your head in one piece. All right, we'll let you try that."

So next day Willie made his way through Dunblane to start work at the Kippenross Tunnel. As he passed the Inn at the bridge he saw Rab Cramb, stones at the ready, waiting for the arrival of the Defiance. Willie gave him a cheeky grin.

"That's aw right, Rab. You can keep the wheel wedgin! I'm aff tae dae a man's work!"

Later that morning in the mouth of Kippenross tunnel his bravado deserted him as he entered the darkness. For a panic stricken moment, he imagined that all Widow McLaren's warnings had come true and that he'd landed in the jaws of Hell. Distant rumblings and explosions together with the acrid fumes of gunpowder brought to mind her vivid descriptions of Satan's tortures. The groaning sounds must be the agonies of the damned souls!

Willie stood transfixed, his heart hammering in his chest. Only gradually as his eyes penetrated the darkness did he realise that the weird distorted shapes on the walls were the shadows of the miners whose pickaxe blows and grunts echoed through the chamber.

"Come on,"urged the lad beside him. "Ye're no feart are ye?"

Willie took a deep breath. There was no going back now. He cleared his throat and when the reply came, it was unnaturally loud.

"Of course I'm no feart! Just show me what to dae!"

He took his first unsteady steps into the candle lit gloom. Then he straightened his shoulders. He'd show them all, that now he really was the man of the family!

BAIRNS OF BRIDGEND
DUNBLANE

WILLIAM HOGG 1846

NOTES

The Hogg family were regular recipients of Poor Relief during the 1840s. Most of the assistance took the form of small amounts of cash from church funds but occasionally entries mention other items such as *'Shoes, stockings and clothes to Hogg's children.'*

At the end of the Kirk Session Accounts of 1845, a mysterious entry appears: *'Expenses in apprehending John Hogg incl. Agency fees.'*

His name is last seen in January 1846: *'blankets to J Hogg'.* Thereafter board wages were paid for the children who continued to receive help till 1852, part of that being Bell's fees at the Parochial School in 1850.

Other orphans are mentioned and one Dunblane girl, Catherine McCrea, had her board paid at the Deaf and Dumb school, Edinburgh. Among the fifty-two names on Dunblane's Poor Roll are the old, the infirm and widowed – 'The deserving poor'.

Transport in Britain was undergoing revolutionary change with the building of the railway network. Thomas Carlyle, writing to a friend in 1846 described railway labourers as 'sunk … in brutality. . . The Yorkshire and Lancashire men . . . are reckoned the worst; and not without glad surprise I find the Irish are the best in the point of behaviour'.

The navvies did indeed take Dunblane and district by storm and in April 1846 their antics resulted in 'the appointment of a number of the respectable inhabitants as special constables to aid in the preservation of public peace'. Upward of fifty eager volunteers were sworn in 'and each of them received his baton of office'. (Perthshire Constitutional)

With the completion of the railway line in 1848, the navvies moved on, but local able-bodied men were thrown once more into unemployment. Since there was no poor relief for the able bodied, a soup kitchen was proposed for Dunblane. The situation was such that the traditional system of Kirk administered Poor Relief was no longer able to cope and the Parochial Board was forced to implement a compulsory poor-rate as proposed in the Poor Law (Amendment) Act 1845.

Although in 1842, children were prohibited from working in coalmines, other industries continued to use very young children until the Factory Act of 1863. * During railway construction children were frequently involved in 'light work'.

* *'Bairns of Bridgend, Dunblane. Ann Petty 1874' is based on conditions after these improvements in conditions for working children.*

BAIRNS OF BRIDGEND
DUNBLANE

WILLIAM HOGG 1846

SOURCES AND BIBLIOGRAPHY

Minutes of Parochial Board of Dunblane, 1845- 1852.
Reminiscences of Dunblane, People's Journal, 1889.
Scottish Central Railway Company Reports, 1845-1848.
Accident Reports. Stirling Journal and Advertiser, 1845- 1848.
Dunblane Sheriff Court Reports. Stirling Journal and Advertiser, 1845- 1848.
Stirling Observer, 1845.

CAGE, R A., *The Scottish Poor Law,* Scottish Academic Press, Edinburgh. 1981.
CLARKSON, W W., *Postal History of Stirling,* Mini Print, Edinburgh, 1981.
COLEMAN, Terry, *The Railway Navvies,* Pelican, 1968
FERGUSON, Thomas, *The Dawn of Social Welfare,* T Nelson, 1948.
FERNEYHAUGH, Frank, *The History of Railways in Britain.* Osprey Publishing Ltd.,
    1975.
HALDANE, A R B., *Three Centuries of Scottish Posts* Edinburgh University Press,
    1971.
LOXTON, Howard, *Railways,* Hamlyn, 1968.
MURRAY, Norman, *The Scottish Handloom Weaver,* 1790-1850.
    John Donald, Edinburgh, 1978.
NOCK, O S., *The Caledonian Railway,* Ian Allan Ltd., London, 1961.
ROBERTSON, C J A., *The Origins of the Scottish Railway System,* 1822- 1844,
    John Donald, Edinburgh 1983.
SIMMONDS, J., *Scottish Railways,* J. Pike, 1975.

BAIRNS OF BRIDGEND
DUNBLANE

SCHULE BAIRNS 1782

The Schules o' Dunblane

In yon days the maisters keepit the Schule
At the back o the Kirk, in the wee chapter hoosie:
Twas a dungeon o learning, sae dark and sae dool,
In dim Gothic vault, like the nest o a moosie.

But though the auld Schule has seen transformation,
An' aince mair is a Kirk, fu' trig and fu' braw,
The names o' auld scholars shine thro' restoration
In the dumpy nick't pillars that haud up the wa'.

Amang oor great Dominies o every description,
The great name o Coldstream stands foremost o a',
His virtues are tauld in the learned inscription,
In the auld tongue o Rome upon the kirk wa'.

Anon.

The Cock-pit

The carpet's laid – pit money drawn –
    All's high with expectation,
With birds bereft of Nature's garb,
    The handlers take their station.

What roaring, betting – bawling, swearing
    Loudly assail the ear.

But hark! – What cry! – 'He's run! - he's run!'
    And loud huzzas take place –
Now mark what deep dejection sits
    On every loser's face.

R Tannahill (Extract)

BAIRNS OF BRIDGEND
DUNBLANE

SCHULE BAIRNS 1782

The two lads sat on the bench with their heads together. The smaller, Colin Lennox, looked anxiously at the Latin text in front of him. 'Alexander et Julius Caesar sum praestantissimus dux, qui ill domo Asia, at hic subigo Gallus.' The older lad looked at the youngster's translation, 'Alexander and Julius Caesar were great commanders, the former of which dwelt in Asia and the latter subdued the Gauls'.

Robert Haldane smiled and dug his elbow into the smaller boy's side.

"Domo is not 'dwelt', but conquered. Alexander conquered Asia. Otherwise it is correct. Now translate this into Latin: 'I and my Brother read Terence; Thou and thy brother are elder than we are, and read Cordery'. You can come and show it to me when you're finished, before you give it to Maister Coldstream. Now I must continue with my Greek."

'Greek!' thought the small boy, 'Wi all that strange writin! This Latin is enough o a struggle. Hoo can Rob cope wi Greek?!' Colin sighed heavily and looked up at the arched ceiling of the chapter house of the parish church. His eye caught a break in the crumbling plasterwork. He followed the cleft as it wandered down the wall, meeting other cracks and widening as it reached the flagstone floor. It was like a wee river, he mused, running between banks of green mould.

The Chapter House, Dunblane Cathedral.

CRACK! The Master's stick slammed on the desk in front of him and just missed Colin's fingers.

"Ede nasturtium, Rouse up dullard!" William Coldstream did not need to say another word.

Jerked out of his daydream, Colin dipped his quill into the ink. 'I and my brother. . . .' His pen scratched the paper, 'Ego et meus frater. . . .'

At the other end of the chapter house a group of boys and girls sat huddled together chanting the measures of length: '3 barley corns make 1 inch; 12 inches make 1 foot; 3 foot make 1 yard; 3.3/4 foot make 1 ell; 6 foot make 1 fadome. . .'

The assistant Master Malcolm Coldstream tapped out the rhythm of the chant while keeping a vigilant eye open for slackers.

When at last the handbell was rung to signal the end of morning lessons seventy pupils of assorted ages poured out into the kirkyard of Dunblane Cathedral. Delighted shouts went up from the boys when they found the gravedigger at work in a corner.

"Hae ye found anythin interestin the day? Any buried treasure?" The gravedigger grunted at them. "Awa wi ye! There's nae treasure hereaboots!"

But one lad had already spied something white peeping from the heap of newly dug earth. Eager hands grubbed at the soil to pull the object out, and shook the dirt from it.

"Braw! See here, lads, a braw skull!" Its finder held it up with pride.

"Pass it ower then, Tam," came the shout, and the boys were all over the yard throwing and catching their 'ball'. If they heard the gravedigger's protests they ignored them anyway. Round the church went the players throwing and kicking the skull. Inside the ruined cathedral nave, they dodged round the pillars, pushing and jostling each other to get possession.

Hunger and breathlessness made them pause to eat their mid-day pieces before returning reluctantly to the church and into the adjoining chapter house to start the afternoon's classes.

As the day wore on more candles were lit to throw some light on the dim interior while reading and writing lessons were in session. At one bench girls and boys were laboriously copying the cursive alphabet. The old schoolmaster moved along behind the row lifting each paper to peer at it. He tutted and shook his head as he looked at one splotchy paper.

"Joseph Smith! Read aloud this line, sir!"

The lad scrambled to his feet.

"Keep free from Blot your Piece and Writing-book," he stammered.

"And hast thou, sir?"

"No, Maister Coldstream."

"Indeed not. Thy mother pens me worried letters from England enquiring of thy progress. What shall I write in reply? That under the tuition of the dancing maister thou hast perfected an elegant minuet, yet thou cannot hold a pen?" Joseph hung his head unsure of whether to reply, but William Coldstream went on. . . . "Indeed no, my lad. Your mother, my niece, learned from me the art of penmanship and by Jove I will not accept this from her son. Thy writing is a disgrace but thou canst mend it. Observe the following lines."

"Learn the command of hand by frequent Use.

Much Practice doth to Penmanship conduce."

"Good, then pen it, Joseph, twenty times, without a blot!"

The dominie moved slowly down the bench scrutinising each child's effort and commenting briefly. Each pupil breathed a sigh of relief as the master made his remarks and moved on. He stopped again at the last lad in the row. "And thou, sir, is this thy best endeavour?"

William Campbell stood up looking defiant.

"Yes, Maister Coldstream. My fingers are numb with cold."

"Ah, but thy tongue is quick, sirrah! What is the month, lad?"

"February, Maister Coldstream."

"And what season do we endure in February?"

"Winter, Maister Coldstream."

"Exactly, then we cannot expect to be warm. We all must thole the cold. Make the best of it, young man. Breathe on thy fingers, improve thy penmanship and perhaps thy elder brother will require thy presence in Jamaica when thou hast learned to write a fairer hand than this!"

The schoolmaster smiled as he moved from the still scowling William Campbell to check the work of his most advanced pupil. Robert Haldane was quite oblivious of the spelling being chanted by the younger pupils and the scoldings being given to the writing class. Open in front of him lay the Greek text of Aesop's Fables that he was translating into Latin.

William Coldstream nodded approvingly as he checked it.

"Let me see, Lupus et Pastores. Ah yes, a tale of misplaced confidence. When you have completed the translation give it to class four to render in English."

Returning to his desk, the dominie faced the whole school. He shook a hand-bell and held up his hand for silence. The general hubbub died down and seventy faces looked up expectantly. The schoolmaster spoke.

"Let me remind everyone that next week will be Shrove tide and that Tuesday will be Fastern's E'en. We are all aware of what that signifies - the annual cock-fight. . . ."

A ripple of excitement went through the audience and William Coldstream had to stop for a moment. When all was quiet again, he continued, "All who intend to enter fighting birds shall give their names to Maister Malcolm and pay the fee of a shilling. Those who will not enter a cock shall pay twa shillings as forfeit. The ballot for battle order will tak place on Saturday. That will be all. Stand for the closing prayer."

Out in the cathedral yard after dismissal, excited knots of pupils discussed the forthcoming event. During the next few days the competitors would have to find fowls to pit against each other, and they would be given some time off school to do so. The farmers' sons from around the parish were confident. "Och, we hae plenty guid cocks at Whitiestone. I can bring a couple!"

"Stop yer braggin, John Dawson! Yer dunghill birds winna stand lang against real fightin cocks frae Wester Kinbuck!"

The challenge was no sooner out of Tam Millar's mouth than the two lads were rolling about the grass in mock battle while the other boys cheered them on. But the fight came to an abrupt halt when Malcolm Coldstream's cane swished down on the breeches of the uppermost lad. John leapt to his feet with a yelp, holding his rump. Swish went the cane again, this time on Tam's rear as he struggled to his feet. The spectators roared with laughter at the rough justice.

"Enough, lads. Hasten hamewards, for it will be dark afore lang."

The assistant master's words reminded his pupils that many of them had two or three miles to walk to outlying farms, and so they scattered going their various ways.

John and Tam were still grimacing and rubbing the seats of their breeches as their group turned north up Braeport in the direction of their farms. In the midst of the lads who started off in the opposite direction, Colin Lennox was wondering how he would get hold of a fighting cock. In the yard behind the Lennox family's vintner's shop in Bridgend there were a few scrawny hens,

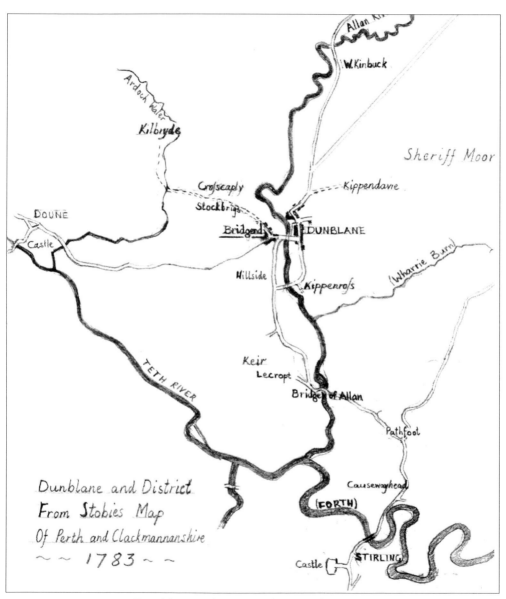

Dunblane and District from Stobie's Map
c. 1783

but the one male was not much more than a cockerel.

Some of the lads paused at the Leighton Library and William Campbell ran up a few of the outside steps to speak to them.

"We must mak certain that nane of these scoundrels frae Kinbuck direction can win the championship. I propose that we each bring twa bonnie fighters."

"That's fine and easy for ye, Will!"

It was Andrew Gentle, the dyer's son from Bridgend, who continued, "But it's no sae easy for us to get decent birds."

The young Campbell dismissed the lad's remarks with a wave of his hand. "Och, dinna worry! If there are nane in Brigend, come wi me on Friday, when I go hame to Kilbryde. We can beg, borrow or steal some fighting cocks frae our farms."

Colin jumped at the chance. "Can I come wi ye? We've nae really braw birds."

"Of course. All the farms on the estate supply my faither with poultry as part of their rent."

"Are ye sure yer faither, - I mean Sir James – winna mind?"

William Campbell laughed. "Oh, we winna even see my faither. He's in London helpin my brother Thomas's preparations to voyage across the sea to Jamaica."

"Lucky fellow! I wad love to sail in a trader across the Atlantic Ocean!" said Joseph Smith. "Will ye follow him to the Indies like Maister Coldstream said?"

The young Campbell's face clouded at the reminder of the altercation with the schoolmaster.

"I have nae intention of travellin' to foreign lands. And Maister Coldstream is too familiar wi his remarks – just because he taught my brother Alexander! He forgets wha I am, and wha he is – just a parish school dominie!"

It was Joseph Smith's turn to bristle.

"Never forget, William Campbell – that my great uncle is a respected scholar. As for ye – bein' the fourth son of a baronet is nae great distinction. Ye'll hae to make yer ain way in the world like the rest o us!"

For a moment it looked as though there would be another fight but the young Campbell just clenched his fists and said disdainfully, "You'll not be comin to Kilbryde for fightin cocks then, Smith?"

Joseph's reply was unrepentant. "Nae. Indeed I winna be enterin the tournament at all. Cock fightin is uncivilised and unchristian!"

And then as a parting shot he added, "And so is usin black men as slaves for sugar plantations in Jamaica!"

"That is enough, Joseph. You're bein' unfair!" It was Robert Haldane who pulled at Joseph's sleeve and led him down Millrow to their lodgings near the schoolhouse.

William Campbell could only glare at their backs and try to recover his composure. He addressed the remainder of the group.

"So my invitation is open. Wha will accompany me to Kilbryde Castle on Friday?"

The two lads from Bridgend had lost none of their enthusiasm and Colin jumped in with another request.

"My sister Isabel would fairly love to visit a castle. Can she come wi us?"

The young gentleman smiled indulgently at the vintner's son.

"As lang as she does not delay us, that will be fine."

Isabel Lennox was indeed delighted and she begged to include two of her friends, Janet Faichney and Jean Moir, from the Spinning School.

So it was a mixed band of half a dozen youngsters who met up at the bridge over Allan Water on Friday, small boys from the parish school and older girls from the spinning school and proudly leading them all was the nine-year-old William Campbell. The girls wore their best clothes for the outing. All three had on their Sunday dresses of linsey-woolsey over warm red flannel petticoats. Bright coloured ribbons held their bonnie hair and let it hang loose over the back of their wide cloaks. They looked like ladies apart from one small detail, - their bare feet!

The young Campbell nudged Colin to whisper, "Where are yer sister's shoes?"

Colin laughed as Isabel overheard.

"Oh dinna worry," she said. "Our shoes and stockins are here, see, tucked aneath our cloaks. We'll cairry them. There's nae sense in spoilin them in the glaur, but we'll put them on afore we reach the castle."

True enough there was mud where horses' hooves had churned up the rough unpaved track from Bridgend, but they were used to picking their way through streets that were often covered with filth. As they went along the three girls questioned the young Campbell.

"Will Lady Campbell be at the Castle?" asked Jean.

"Dae ye hae any sisters at hame?" Janet wanted to know.

The boy pretended impatience. "So many questions! Wait and see when we get there!"

The boys were more interested in keeping their eyes open for likely looking fighting cocks, and Andrew was the first to spy one.

"Look ower yonder! There's a grand bird. What dae ye say, William?"

The young Campbell laughed. "I say we canna hae that one. That's Easter Crosscaply Farm, and it isnae part of Kilbryde Estate!"

"Oh, aye," Isabel smiled as she spoke. "That's the Finlayson's place. Janet Finlayson was tellin me the other day all about her grannie, how she lost her best stockins that were out to dry when highland sodgers stole them!"

Colin was astonished. "I didna ken there was sodgers hereaboots! I havena seen any."

"Not the now, daftie," his sister answered. "It was durin the troubles years and years since!"

"See ower there", added William pointing, "that cairn is where a highland sodger is buried, Duncan Aubraugh's grave."

Colin was not impressed. "Och, I'm no interested in ancient history! When dae we get to Kilbryde Estate then, William?"

"Just past Bowton Farm there. See there's the remains of Kilbryde Chapel."

"No another history lesson for us I hope!" was Colin's cheeky reply as he dodged the slap that the young Campbell aimed at him.

Past the chapel, the youngsters found that the track swung north between rows of trees, still leafless in the grip of winter. Their leader stopped and pointed across fields to a point in the distance.

"Look ower yon rise beyond the cottages, ye can see the castle roof."

The young folks' excitement rose as their path swung round and the castle was lost to view. Snowflakes started to fall and made them quicken their pace while the girls pulled up their hoods. They plodded on uphill now skirting the steep sides of a glen till William Campbell stopped the party again.

"There, see now through the trees!"

The party gasped in genuine admiration.

Jean was first to find her voice. "Oh my, that's wonderfu! Five storeys high!"

"It looks like Sleepin Beauty's castle," added Janet. "Is there a bonnie princess locked up in ane o thae high turrets, keekin out the wee windae at us, William?"

As they discussed the castle, the girls were putting on their footwear. William laughed, delighted with the impression his home was making.

"Well, when she was a wee lass, Mary Queen of Scots stayed in ane o the rooms. It's still called Queen Mary's bedroom and some of her things are still there."

Colin tried not to look interested in this history, but he asked, "What about ghaists, William? All castles hae a bogle."

"Oh aye. We hae 'The White Lady of Kilbryde' but I'll tell ye about her another day. Are all you lassies ready then, Isabel?"

The young Campbell led the group through the gateway in the high wall that surrounded the castle. He jangled the bell at the arched doorway and the heavy wooden door was swung open by the family butler.

"Guid mornin, Daniel. I hae brought some friends frae schule."

'Old' Kilbryde Castle.

The manservant surveyed the group and its leader.

"Aye, so I see! Guid mornin to ye, Maister William. Now just ye tak yer freens through the back. You lads arenae traipsin upstairs to my scrubbed hall wi yer clarty boots on! I'll tell Lady Campbell that ye're here. On you go ben the kitchen."

A warmer welcome awaited the group in the kitchen where the cook soon had the damp cloaks off the girls. As she bustled about finding places for the young folk to warm up around the wide fireplace, she bombarded young

Campbell with questions.

"Let me look at ye, Maister William. Hae ye grown any? Are they feedin ye right at yer lodgins?"

"No as well as ye feed me, Sarah. I was just tellin my friends here what a splendid cook ye are."

Colin, Andrew and the girls exchanged surprised smiles. The young Campbell had never even mentioned the cook to them but Sarah was pleased anyway.

"Och, yer just tryin to butter me up, Maister William! I ken yer tricks fine."

"Aye, and so dae I!" It was Daniel the butler entering the kitchen. "Now what brings ye here the day, Maister William, wi all yer freens? It's nae a holiday, is it?"

He listened as William told him about the cockfight and their quest for fighting birds.

"Och aye. That shouldna be difficult. We'll see what we can dae. Ye can see Lady Campbell now. But tak aff yer clarty boots like I telt ye!"

With that the butler went off outside muttering to himself.

"Ne'er mind him grumpin at ye, Maister William. He'll get ye the best birds he can. On ye go and see yer mither in the sittin room upstairs. She'll be right pleased to see ye."

Now Sarah turned to the others. "And what about the rest of ye? Ye're nae all at the parish schule are ye?"

"Nae," said Isabel, "My wee brother Colin here and Andrew are, but Jean and Janet and me, we're all at Mistress Gillespie's spinning school."

"Aye, well there's mair sense in that for a lass. There's nae need to fill lassies' heids wi Latin and siclike nonsense. It's against nature!"

"What dae ye think is against nature, Sarah?"

It was Lady Campbell entering the kitchen with her son William and his small toddler brother, Frederick.

"Introduce your friends to me, William, before goin out after Daniel."

The girls remembered to drop a curtsey as they met William's mother, while Colin and Andrew gave awkward little bows and hurried off outside with the Campbell brothers.

Sarah continued where she had left off.

"I was just sayin, yer Ladyship, that it's against nature for lassies to be fillin their head wi a lot o book learnin."

"Girls should be able to read and write and dae their household accounts, Sarah."

"Oh, aye, but they can learn that at hame like you learned Miss Jane, and look at her now, - Mistress Pearson of Kippenross! And Miss Colina is learnin her letters fine in the nursery."

Lady Campbell smiled. "Yes, lasses can learn at hame but there are accomplishments that many governesses cannot offer, tambouring, dancing and French for instance."

"I'm sure Miss Colina winna need thae for a lang time."

"No, we'll keep yer wee pet lamb here for a while, Sarah. But what about you girls? Are ye at school wi William?"

"Nae," interrupted Sarah. "That's just what we were talkin about, the lassies are at the spinnin school in Dunblane."

Her mistress spoke again, "Right, Sarah. Now, our young guests must be hungered. See about a bite of dinner for them, will ye?"

And turning to the girls she continued, "Lasses, tell me all about the spinnin then."

Isabel began, "Well, Mistress Gillespie gies us the flax ready for spinnin and shows us how to dae it."

Jean went on, "We've been goin all this winter

18th Century Spinning Wheels, Dunblane Museum.

and if we dae weel and keep at it till Easter, we'll get to keep our spinnin wheels to tak hame."

"I see, and then ye can work in yer ain cottages?"

"Aye," Jean explained, "The weavers canna get enough spun thread to keep them goin."

"And are you all experts now?" Lady Campbell wanted to know.

Janet joined in. "Oh, at first it's awful hard. The wheel keeps runnin backwards if ye dinna keep the treadle goin nice and steady wi yer foot. Then the flyer wi the spun threid stops turnin or goes backwards and the flax gets in an awful fankle! But efter a while ye dinna think aboot the treadle and the wheel just goes whirr, whirr, whirr. The real tricky pairt is drawin the flax out nice and even so ye dinna get thin or lumpy bits."

Isabel added, "And ye hae to mind to keep the fibre damp or it just snaps."

"Oh dear", said Lady Campbell, "It does sound difficult. How many pupils does Mistress Gillespie hae?"

Isabel thought for a minute – "Oh, there's been mair than thirty this year but some learn real quick."

"Aye." Jean added, "Mind Janet Coldstream cam for a while an it was nae bother to her?"

"But she's a grown woman. It's no sae easy for a wee lass, but Mistress Gillespie winna tak anyone under eight year auld," Janet explained.

"Well, William's wee sister Colina is ower young to learn just now. Perhaps when she is older, ane of you lasses can come and teach her here at Kilbryde. Flax spinning is a maist useful accomplishment. All households hae need of linen for table and bed."

As Lady Campbell spoke the lads burst into the kitchen each with two bundles of feathers flapping about.

Sarah was enraged. "Get thae fowls' legs tied and get them out o my kitchen. I dinna want their feathers and their fleas all ower the place. The only birds I want in here are plucked anes wi their necks drawn!"

Lady Campbell laughed as she took her small son from the butler.

"Come awa now, Frederick, back to the nursery wi ye. Yer brother William and his friends will hae their dinner and then they maun be back on the road to Dunblane afore it gets dark. I'll bid ye fareweel, bairns."

So it was a very satisfied group of youngsters who made their way back to Dunblane, their stomachs well lined with a good bowl of Sarah's broth and a plateful of potatoes mashed with cheese and butter.

The boys compared notes on the virtues of the birds they now held tucked securely under their arms, each lad convinced that he held the champion fighter.

The girls argued jokingly about who should take on the teaching of William's small sister when she was big enough. Even when it started to snow it did not dampen their high spirits and the way back to Bridgend seemed even shorter than the morning's journey.

Back at school, the Saturday draw for the battle order, 'Ordo Gallorum Pugnacium', was the scene of animated debate. The would-be competitors argued about the best position for their fighting cocks to draw. If the bird was too early in the contest, it might be taken by surprise by an experienced enemy – while later in the day the sight of others battling might bring out its natural fighting instincts.

While all those with birds, or hopes of acquiring some before Tuesday, drew lots a few pupils joined Joseph Smith and Robert Haldane in declining to take part and paid the subsequent fine. The lads with the Kilbryde fighting cocks discovered that their first fight was about halfway through the contest and the other two towards the end of the day.

Shrove Tuesday, Fastern's E'en dawned snowy and cold. As soon as it was light the competitors made their way to the cathedral where another part of the chapter house had been opened up for the occasion. This morning there was no sleepy reluctance to reach school. Instead, there was an excited buzz of anticipation.

Overlooking the battleground at one end of the chapter house, a stage had been set up for parents and distinguished visitors who were always ready to advise the judge, Master Coldstream. His was the final word on the outcome of each bout while Master Malcolm held the battle order and signalled the beginning of each round.

Andrew was the first of the Bridgend lads to enter the contest just before noon. His hopes were high when he brought forward one of his bonnie fighters, to face up to one of the Kinbuck farm birds. For a moment or two the birds blinked at each other jerking their heads and pecking the air.

The crowd shouted, "Come on! Get on wi it!" and Andrew's bird lunged at the other.

"On ye go!" yelled his supporters. His opponent struck back and the first Kilbryde fighter turned and flapped out of the arena.

"Fugie, fugie, fugie!" the mocking label for runaway cocks was chanted.

"Ill luck, Andra. That's ane for the dominie's cooking pot!"

"Andrew Gentle, thy second fighting cock into the arena," Master Malcolm reminded him.

This time it was even worse. The bird pecked at the ground totally ignoring the shrieks from the children round about. In vain Andrew, Colin and the young Campbell egged it on. Its opponent looked equally uninterested, scratching at the ground. The schoolmaster looked at his watch. "Four minutes," he said. "Lift them out, baith defeated."

After a few more rounds it was the turn of William Campbell's first fighter. Opposed to him was a fighting cock with two victories already won. The Kilbryde bird faced his fierce enemy as it clawed at him but a feeble peck was all it managed before making off in the direction of the door.

From the onlookers came shouts of derision. "Thae fightin cocks frae Kilbryde Castle. They're too weel bred to strike a blow!"

The roar of laughter that went up made the young Campbell red with suppressed fury. His next bird was ready. Into the arena went the fighting cock. Some of its owner's anger must have infected it. It flew at its opposite number and slashed out with it claws. There was an agonised squawk and its victim fluttered off.

"Fugie, fugie, fugie!" Again the cry rose.

"One victory for William Campbell."

The next fight was over even faster when a bedraggled specimen flapped around the fighting area and up on the stage among the dignitaries. Again amidst squeals from the ladies came the cry.

"Fugie, fugie, fugie," followed by the dominie's verdict, "Twa victories for William Campbell."

Now Tam Miller came forward with a challenger. For the first time the Kilbryde bird had an equal match and they went at it jabbing, pecking and slashing till blood ran from both birds and the onlookers' shrieking could be heard from Bridgend. Sheer exhaustion got the better of the young Campbell's bird and it lost on points.

"One victory to Thomas Miller."

The young gentleman from Kilbryde Castle sank back on the bench in disappointment, tired out by yelling.

Andrew tried to console him. "Dinna fret, William, we still hae Colin's birds."

"Aye, true enough. Oh weel, my second bird put up a brave fight. We'll hae somethin to eat and sup now. It's a lang wait till your first fight, Colin."

The three lads pushed their way through the crowd to the schoolroom where refreshments were being served. The ladies, glad to escape from the noise and heat were sipping negus and the smell of the hot spiced port and lemon wafted across the room. For the boys there was ruby red claret mixed with water, while the gentlemen enjoyed whisky.

The contest went on while the three friends relaxed and they were taken by surprise when Colin's name was called. He hurried through to put his first bird into the battle area where John Dawson's best fighter faced up to it. The lads from the Kinbuck farms yelled their support and the fight was on. Colin hardly had time to get back to the side when the cry "Fugie, fugie, fugie!" went up and John Dawson's supporters were cheering their champion.

Colin, Andrew and the young Campbell were stunned by this instant defeat while their rivals were jubilant.

"John Dawson, fower victories. Colin Lennox, thy second competitor, please."

Andrew nudged his friend. "On ye go, Colin! It's our last hope!"

So in went the last of the Kilbryde fighting cocks and, to its owner's astonishment, it flew at the Whitiestone farmyard fowl. Beaks stabbed, feathers flew, and blood spattered the floor and John Dawson's champion lay dead!

Colin and his friends leapt to their feet while the Kinbuck farmers' sons groaned with disappointment.

"Colin Lennox, one win. Thy next bird, John Dawson."

The onlookers held their breath this time while the fighting birds glared at each other. Peck, slash and claw and the Kinbuck lads moaned their disappointment, as their last bird was defeated. Still, John Dawson's fighting cock was in the lead with four victories, the largest number chalked up all day. "Colin Lennox, twa wins."

The next challenger fluttered into the arena, looked around frantically and took off without taking a stand.

"Fugie, fugie, fugie," the cry went up again.

"Colin Lennox, three wins."

Above the noise, William grabbed Colin's arm. "I believe we hae a chance efter all!"

"Oh, dinna count yer chickens till they're hatched!" replied Colin, but his cautious words belied the hammering of his heart.

Another fresh bird entered the arena but it was a poor bedraggled thing from a midden. It made a desperate attempt to defend itself but it was no match for the speed and power of this Kilbryde fighter. In three minutes it was laid out. "Colin Lennox, fower wins!"

Now Andrew could not contain his frenzied excitement.

He jumped up and down shouting, "Just ane mair victory, Colin and ye're the King!"

His voice was lost as the crowd roared with anticipation. The fresh challenger was no midden top bird. It was sleek and well fed looking with a grand cluster of trailing tail feathers. Round the arena the onlookers craned forward to get a better view. Colin's bird was tired now but its blood was up and it rushed at the newcomer.

Slash, the bonnie feathers were spotted with blood and the Kilbryde fighting cock had darted out of reach. Its handsome opponent turned but its lovely plumage slowed it down and Colin's bird was back pecking at it before it could strike a blow itself. And so it went on – dart, peck, turn, and slash – till the mangled newcomer lay lifeless on the floor.

"Colin Lennox, five wins!"

The three friends could hardly believe it. No one else could match that score now. Victory had been snatched from the jaws of defeat!

So at the end of the afternoon, Colin Lennox was crowned King of the Cockfighters. He thought his heart would burst when a lady placed the 'chapeau plume' on his head and he was hoisted on the shoulders of his fellow pupils. In the triumphal procession through Dunblane, William Campbell and Andrew Gentle were at his side joining in the Latin victory song.

His crown slipped and the tail feathers from the defeated birds tickled him, making him sneeze, much to the amusement of Isabel and her friends joining the procession along Millrow. He was glowing with pride as he was carried across the bridge towards the cottage in Bridgend.

Colin's home was not a grand castle like Kilbryde, but he was King for the day!

BAIRNS OF BRIDGEND
DUNBLANE

SCHULE BAIRNS 1782

NOTES

William Coldstream's forty-three years as schoolmaster of Dunblane ended when his son Malcolm took over from him. His memorial on the wall of the Cathedral is, not surprisingly, in Latin. The chapter house continued to be used as the school till about 1811 when a new parish school was built in the northeast corner of the kirkyard.

Mistress Gillespie's school, which had been founded by the Forfeited Estates Commission, continued under the auspices of the Scottish Society for the Propagation of Christian Knowledge when Jacobite estate owners had their lands restored to them in 1784. Spinning schools were part of the considerable effort being made to encourage the linen industry in eighteenth century Scotland. All the girls mentioned were Mrs Gillespie's pupils in the year 1782.

Farms like Crosscaplie, Whitiestone and Kinbuck grew flax among other crops. Good yields of flax were awarded handsome prizes by the Board of Trustees for Manufacturers.

The twenty-one small farms on the estate of Kilbryde were obliged to supply the laird with 295 hens, butter, cheese and 300 wads of peats according to the Rental of 1798.

Cockfighting was traditional, and took place in Dunblane Parish School on Shrove Tuesday as described. In other areas, it was on Hansel Monday, the first Monday of the New Year and was often accompanied by adults gambling on the results. By the nineteenth century it was considered to be 'a most degrading and brutal pastime' that 'should not be permitted by the authorities.' (1848 West Lothian) By then it had practically vanished from schools.

Of the parish school pupils, the studious Robert Haldane from Lecropt went on to become a minister, a professor of mathematics and Principal of St Mary's College at St Andrews University, teaching theology.

William Campbell of Kilbryde studied law and became a Writer to the Signet. In 1812, his half-brother who owned slaves in Jamaica returned to Kilbryde to become Sir Alexander Campbell of Aberuchill.

In 1777 a landmark decision concerning slavery had been made at the Court of Session in Edinburgh when Lord Kames of Blairdrummond and fellow judges set free a Jamaican slave whose master had brought him to Scotland. Joseph Knight had sought his freedom and his case was upheld on the principle that, 'No man is by nature the property of another'.

BAIRNS OF BRIDGEND
DUNBLANE

SCHULE BAIRNS 1782

SOURCES AND BIBLIOGRAPHY

The Statistical Account of Scotland, 1790s Ed. Sir John Sinclair, New Edition.
  Vol. XII N W Perthshire, E P Publishing Ltd., 1977.
Coldstream Letters GD1/392/ H M General Register House, Edinburgh.
Forfeited Estates Papers E777/ H M General Register House, Edinburgh.
Society in Scotland for Propagating Christian Knowledge, Records, GD/
  H M General Register House, Edinburgh.
An Aytone Schoolmaster's Notebook, 1687, CH2/101/39 Stirling District Archives.

BAIN, Andrew, *Education in Stirlingshire, Reformation to Act of 1872*,
  University of London Press, 1965.
BAINES, Patricia, *Spinning Wheels,* B T Batsford Ltd., 1977.
Burke Peerage and Baronetage, 1953 edition.
CLARKE, John, *An Introduction to the Making of Latin*. B T Batsford Ltd 1977.
DEANS, I F M, *Scottish Spinning Schools* SCRE 1930
DYCHE, Thomas, *A Guide to the English Tongue* 1707. Facsimile reprint The Scholar
  Press 1968.
FYFE, J G, *Scottish Diaries and Memoirs*, Eneas Mackay, Stirling, 1942.
GRAHAM, H G, *Social Life of Scotland in the Eighteenth Century*. A&C Black, 1901.
GRANT, James, *History of the Burgh and Parish Schools of Scotland*. Wm. Collins,
  1876.
HARDING, Albert W., *Education in Perthshire to the Act of 1872*. Ph. D. Thesis
University of Dundee, 1975.
HERMAN, Arthur *How the Scots Invented the Modern World* Three Rivers Press,
  New York. 2001.
MACLEAN, Ella, *Lecropt Church*. Journal of the Society of Friends of Dunblane
  Cathedral. Vol.IX, PtII. 1963.
MASON, John, *Scottish Experiments in Rural Education,* University of London, 1935.
MERCER, John, *The Spinners Workshop*, Prism Press 1978.
MILLER, Hugh, M*y Schools and Schoolmasters* Nimmo, Edinburgh, 1891.

BAIRNS OF BRIDGEND
DUNBLANE

PEGGY LUCAS 1745

Twas on a Monday morning,
Right early in the year,
When Charlie cam to our town,
The young chevalier.

As he came marching up the street,
The pipes play'd loud and clear,
And a' the folk came running out
To meet the Chevalier.

Carolina Oliphant, Lady Nairne.

BAIRNS OF BRIDGEND
DUNBLANE

PEGGY LUCAS 1745

Peggy and Helen squealed with delight at the warm water splashing their legs when they climbed into the washing tub. They hitched their skirts up above the knee high water and face-to-face balanced with their arms over each other's shoulders. Still laughing they began to trample the linen at the bottom of the tub and within moments their skirts were soaked anyway. Half an hour's trampling brought the scum from the cloth to the surface while the squealing and laughter changed to puffing and panting. Helen was thankful when her older sister gasped, "That's enough, out we get," and the two young girls clambered out again.

Sinking down on the grassy riverbank, the girls took a few minutes rest while they looked around the washing green. Other bairns and women were about and their voices rang out in the bright morning air as they all went about their laundry. When they had their breath back, Peggy and Helen heaved the full tub over on its side and skipped out of the way as the dirty water streamed down the bank into Allan Water. Taking an end each of the length of cloth, the girls stretched and twisted it in opposite directions wringing out as much water as possible. Then Peggy paddled into the shallows of the river to give the linen a thorough rinse before the two girls shook out the cloth and pegged it out to dry in the sun.

Now their task was to shoo away any birds that might land on the cloth and to look out too for stray dogs whose dirty paws could ruin their morning's work in a moment's romp across the linen. While they safeguarded the cloth, the girls enjoyed the gossip of all the other washers whose linen now covered the riverbank like a huge haphazard patchwork bedspread. The opposite bank was in shadow but above it in sunshine the sisters could just see the gable end of their own line of cottages in Chuckie Row, Bridgend of Dunblane. The sun's rays had already dried out their skirts and when Peggy felt the linen on the ground she found it just barely damp, ready for the next step in the bleaching.

Carefully detaching the latchets around the cloth from the pegs, the girls returned it to the river to be thoroughly dunked, wrung out and shaken again. A brisk breeze made the beige linen flap like a ship's sail as they struggled to hold it and Peggy anxiously warned her young sister, "Haud ticht to the edge o the claith, Helen. If ye haud the latches, it'll tear and we'll hae to answer to grandfaither for that!"

With the cloth safely anchored to the ground again, the girls relaxed, playing with the pebbles they'd collected to throw at any stray dogs. Tiring of this, Helen wandered off to paddle while Peggy was left to guard the linen. While she sat, now and again clapping her hands to frighten the birds, Peggy almost dozed off in the afternoon warmth only to be startled when she heard someone speak to her. Shading her eyes against the glare of the sun's rays she was surprised to see a sprucely dressed woman who spoke again.

"I see yer hard work has made ye tired but I hae been watchin ye for a while.

You look like a sensible lass. Just the sort I want for my kitchen. What is yer name?"

After a moment's hesitation, the girl answered, "I'm Margaret Lucas, but my family call me Peggy."

"Lucas?" repeated the woman. "Are ye kin to James Lucas o Brigend?"

"Aye, he's my grandfaither. I bide wi him and my wee sister, Helen," she added.

"Ah yes. I ken James Lucas, a maister weaver."

"Yes," replied Peggy, "that's his best linen shirtin that we're bleachin."

"I can see that, a fine web of linen. I'll hae a word wi yer grandfaither."

As suddenly as she'd appeared, the woman turned and was gone across the Bishop's yard towards the meal mill.

Peggy stared after her, bewildered. Who was she and what was she talking about, 'a lass for her kitchen?' Her heart was fluttering as she called Helen. Together they folded the linen and set off past the mill towards the bridge and home. That evening Peggy kept quiet about the woman and her strange remarks, keeping her confused thoughts to herself.

Early next morning, Peggy and Helen were back with their grandfather at the riverbank for a repeat performance of the previous whole operation. In the big cauldron full of hot water their grandfather stirred up the lye that he'd made from wood ashes. Then back in went the linen shirting for another thorough soaking. It was after the caustic solution had cooled down a bit that James Lucas left his granddaughters to do the part they enjoyed most, the trampling. And trample they did, stamping and kicking till they were breathless and their hitched-up skirts, damp around their legs. The rest was a repeat of the rinsing,

Chuckie Row, Dunblane.

the wringing and the drying of the cloth. Only the weather was different. At midday a summer thunderstorm sent the girls scurrying to the shelter of the mill wall and then rushing back again to weight down the linen that looked likely to soar skywards. As suddenly as it had come, the storm departed leaving blue skies and sunshine to dry the linen again.

Home again at the Bridgend cottage, their grandfather inspected the cloth.

"That's grand, bairns. We'll hae to let it lie the morn, it bein' the Sabbath, but come Monday we'll get it intae the buttermilk again and let it steep for a day or twa. Come now, tak yer supper. It'll soon be time to get aff to bed, my hinnies."

Peggy sighed, thinking about the Sabbath day to come. She and Helen would not be allowed to caper about but would have to endure a long church service in the parish church in Dunblane cathedral, listening to Mr Simson preaching. Still, she and Helen usually managed to avoid boredom by examining the attire of the matrons of the congregation. Indeed, sometimes the girls struggled to contain their mirth underneath a show of suitably subdued behaviour.

This Sunday brought its fair share of amusement for Helen and Peggy who nudged each other as they watched some of the women tottering slightly, their feet pinched in the silver buckles shoes which they wore only for such public occasions. Then there were the mutches of the married women, transformed for the Sabbath from plain linen caps to a display of showy ribbons. The men were no less amusing for the sisters, especially those few 'Gentlemen' who sported wigs with rows of curls poking out below their three cornered beaver hats.

Occasionally, Peggy shot a cautious look in her grandfather's direction to make sure that he was unaware of their activity. Those glances confirmed Peggy's opinion that James Lucas, with his own white hair flowing to the shoulders of his Dunblane blue Sabbath coat, cut a more handsome figure than the local gentry.

It was when they were outside in the kirkyard, in the shadow of the great roofless nave of the cathedral, that Peggy suddenly recognised one of the high-heeled matrons. She was the woman who had spoken to her at the bleaching green. The child's light-hearted mood turned to apprehension when she saw the woman bearing down on her grandfather and engaging him in conversation. From their looks and gestures it was obvious that they were discussing Peggy who strained her ears from a respectful distance to catch a few words. From the woman, Peggy could make out, 'kitchen lass' and 'respectable faimily', while her grandfather's shaking head and 'the bleachin' and 'my only help', brought the conversation to a close.

Bursting with curiosity, Peggy rushed up to James Lucas as he gave a slight bow and the woman moved off.

"What's the matter, grandfaither? Wha's that woman? What does she want?"

"Wheest, Peggy, wheesht now and I'll tell ye. That's Mistress Russell, Bailie Russell's wife. She's lookin for a new kitchen lass to tak the place o her lass that's to be wed soon. Is seems she saw ye workin the ither day, and liked the look o ye."

"But, grandfaither, what did ye tell her? What did she say?"

James Lucas laid a comforting arm round his granddaughter and looked at her fondly. "I tauld her the truth, Peggy, that wi yer mither dead since Helen was born and yer faither gone too, we hae only the three o us. I canna be weavin and bleachin at the same time and I need ye baith for that."

Relief swept through Peggy as she asked, "And what did Mistress Russell say to that?"

"Oh, just if I changed my mind to let her ken."

"But ye winna change yer mind, will ye grandfaither? I dinna want to leave you and Helen and I dinna want to be a kitchen lass."

"I ken that, lass. Nane o us want that. Now we'll gae back to Brigend. I believe that Mistress Wright may hae some mutton in the pot for us the day."

As the weaver and his granddaughters made their way down Millrow and turned towards the bridge, they were in time to see Mistress Russell and Bailie Russell entering their fine house at Allanbank. Peggy clutched her grandfather's hand tightly but said no more about the matter.

The next few weeks were as busy as ever with the bleaching continuing till the linen shirting was snow white, for this was an order for a gentleman's household. There was plenty to gossip about at the Bishop's Yard bleaching ground; the price of cattle at the Grosset Fair just past, the weather for the harvest and all the usual subjects, but towards the end of August a new topic came under discussion. Now Peggy and Helen listened eagerly to tales about 'The Bonnie Prince' who was rumoured to be somewhere in the highlands with his followers, the 'Jacobites'.

At home in Bridgend, the girls couldn't wait to tell their grandfather all that they had heard but the old man just shook his head as he listened to them.

"Weel, I hope that he and his men stay awa frae Dunblane. It seems it was just yesterday that yer grandmither and I, wi yer faither, a wee bairn, stood on Hillside watchin them battle it out. It was a Sabbath day bright and frosty and sae clear that we could see the Redcoats runnin pell mell frae Sheriffmuir wi Mar's highlanders screechin like demons ahint them, and cuttin them down as they ran."

"And did the highlanders win then, grandfaither?" asked Helen.

"Nay, nay lass. Naebody won. All the while thae government foot sodgers were runnin backwards towards Stirlin, their horsemen wi the Duke o Argyle further up the moor were drivin the Jacobites awa down to Allan Water at Kinbuck.

"And what happened next?" asked Peggy.

"Well, we heard that Mar took maist o his highlanders north to Perth, but some of them that were taken prisoner were taken to Stirling Castle by Argyle's army. Our own Lord Strathallan was ane o the Jacobites imprisoned and he ended up exiled in France. For a while all was quiet and then efter New Year some government troops came from Stirling and camped nearby. We kept our distance and then the sodgers marched through Dunblane wi the Duke himsel' wi a grand company o horsemen ridin north. They were a braw sight clatterin ower the brig but we were glad to see the back o them."

"Oh, I wish I could hae seen them!" said Helen, but her grandfather's face clouded over.

"Weel, we were lucky here in Dunblane, but the folks of Auchterarder and Blackford were nae sae fortunate. Their hames were burned to the ground and their stores wi them, that is what the highlanders hadnae plundered already. They were left wi neither food nor shelter in the middle o winter. Decent hardworkin folk left like beggars, cold and starvin."

James Lucas shook his head slowly, but then smiled at his girls as he continued, "But all that was lang since. . . . let me think. . . . Aye, it's nigh on thirty years and it finished as quick as it began. We hae to hope that this Bonnie Prince will vanish as quick as his faither!"

'But no before we hae a chance to see him,' thought Peggy as she and Helen exchanged glances in secret disagreement with their grandfather.

The Lucas household was not the only one divided in their views about the Bonnie Prince and his Jacobites. While the girls helped their grandfather harvest the crop of oats at summer's end the arguments went on and excitement grew as rumours flew around the town. When at last one afternoon there was definite news that the prince and his followers were on their way from Perth, Peggy and Helen chattered together about the thrilling news.

"I heard tell that he is vera handsome in his tartan trews," whispered Peggy.

"Aye, all the ladies are supposed to be fallin in love wi him!" added Helen.

Their giggles stopped abruptly when their grandfather cut in, "That's enough, baith o ye! There's plenty needin done here and nae time for blethers. Here, tak the buckets and get some water frae the well!"

Off scampered the girls, glad to be away from James Lucas's unusually sharp tongue.

"What's the maitter wi grandfather?" asked Helen.

"Och, I dinna ken. Maybe his back is hurtin wi the harvestin." But at the back of her mind, Helen was remembering what James Lucas had said about the highland army's activities around Auchterarder all these long years ago.

Well, behind the Cross.

But Helen had no such doubts. "We can plank our buckets here and go and see if the Prince is in Dunblane yet!" Seeing the older girl hesitate she pleaded, "Come on, Peggy, we hae time for a wee look afore it gets dark. Grandfaither winna bother as lang as we get the water."

"Oh, all right then," said Peggy, glad to be persuaded and with that the girls were off down the slope, across the bridge and along Mill Row where other excited folk were gathering and exchanging news. Passing the Russells' grand house they wondered aloud if the Prince might be inside, but a person in the throng redirected them.

"Ye needna look for the Stewart Prince at Allanbank. The Bailie is a staunch supporter of King George in London. It's at Balhaldie House up the road that the Prince will bide the night."

With a glance at each other, the girls nodded their agreement and pushed their way from Mill Row, past the manse and round by the cathedral kirkyard towards Balhaldie House. But their footsteps faltered when they heard shouting from further uphill at Braeport. They could not make out what was being said, but there were angry local voices, protesting, followed by mocking words in Gaelic coming from wild looking highland men who swaggered down the narrow street. The kilted clansmen with their bare thighs and unkempt beards below their blue bonnets made an awesome sight as they came on down the brae.

Even as Peggy and Helen stopped in their tracks, a voice spoke urgently to them.

"Margaret Lucas! What are you and yer sister daen here wi all thae troops about? Get back hame this minute to Brigend!"

It was none other than Mistress Russell who had recognised the girls. They needed no second bidding. Clutching each other's hands they turned and fled back down to Mill Row and across the bridge, stopping only to retrieve their buckets of water. Before they reached home they saw James Lucas out looking for them.

"Whaur hae ye been? There are highland sodgers all ower the place. I should never hae let ye out o my sight!"

As he hurried the girls inside he did not give them time to reply and Peggy squeezed Helen's hand in an agreed silence. It was unusually quiet that night in the cottage where the two very subdued girls took their supper and cooried down under the blankets in bed.

Outside however it was a different story. All night there was little sleep for the girls as the sounds of singing and loud laughter drifted over the river from the alehouses of Dunblane. Their grandfather did not go to his bed but sat by the fire in silence with his eye on the door. As the sky lightened, Peggy felt herself jerk fully awake by sound of voices right outside the cottage. The sound of a musket hammering on the door woke Helen too and the sisters clung to each other. James Lucas was on his feet and he signalled the girls to keep quiet.

Then a voice from further off called to the man at the door and he grunted some sort of reply. From the yard there was a clucking of startled poultry, the frantic flapping of wings and agonised squawks as the hens were carried off.

As these noises grew fainter, they were replaced by the low murmur of many men on the march westward towards Doune. Only when all the sounds had faded completely did James Lucas open the door cautiously and look out in the early morning light.

Throughout the whole town the stories were the same, and from surrounding farms came similar tales. There was hardly a house in the area that had not had unwelcome visitors who had helped themselves to whatever they could beg, borrow or steal. Oatmeal girnals had been emptied, larder shelves were bare of cheeses and in many yards like the Lucas's there was not a hen to be seen. Even the alehouse keepers, normally pleased to have thirsty customers were bitterly bemoaning their empty casks, while indignant farmers' wives told of clothing being stolen from their washing lines.

Of course there were others who had thoroughly enjoyed all the excitement and more than one Dunblane lass fancied herself to be in love with a handsome highland lad who had promised to return to her. And as for the Prince, those who had seen him at Balhaldie House, where Lady McGregor had welcomed him, swore that he was every bit as dashing and handsome as they had heard tell. Local lairds who had come to pledge their support for the Jacobite cause had found his manner courtly as befitted a royal prince, and it was whispered that he had bowed low and kissed the hand of Mistress Russell when she had given him a purse of gold.

Peggy and Helen found the conflicting tales intriguing and confusing but it was not until the evening that the full meaning of it all became clear. James Lucas had said little all day but now Peggy suddenly noticed that her grandfather was sitting by the fire with his shoulders bowed and his face buried in his hands.

"What's wrang, grandfaither?" the child asked.

As the old man slowly raised his head to look at her, the sadness on his face sent a chill through Peggy. He shook his head and struggled to find words.

"It's like this, lass. We hae nae poultry left to give us eggs, there's little enough food of any sort in the town and winter's comin on. The siller for sellin my shirtin winna last lang in the months ahead. I dinna ken how we'll get through the winter wi three mouths to feed."

Peggy rose and put her arms round her grandfather, dismayed to see how he had aged overnight. Nothing more was said, but the old man patted the small hands that tried to comfort him. Another restless night lay ahead of Peggy as she tossed and turned, wondering what was to be done.

Then in a flash it came to her. She must take the responsibility. She must approach Mistress Russell about the position at Allanbank. Perhaps being a kitchen lass would not be so bad after all.

Even as she came to this decision she was having second thoughts. She dreaded the idea of leaving Helen. Through her sadness Peggy had to smile to herself in the dark as she recalled the mischief that the pair of them had got up to in the summer days not long past. And grandfaither, how could she leave him? But lying there thinking of the sudden droop of his shoulders and the hopeless expression on his face, she knew that there was only one sensible choice. Her pillow was wet with tears but at last she slept.

In the morning Peggy was awake before anyone else. With beating heart, she eased herself out of bed taking care not to disturb Helen who slept like a baby. She wanted to be at Allanbank before her grandfather woke and before she had time to change her mind.

Part of Peggy was hoping that Mistress Russell would not want her now as she knocked at the door, but there was to be no escape that way. Mistress Russell agreed straight away that Peggy could start at the end of the week, so there was no going back.

The next few days went by in a whirl of mixed feelings for the small family in Chuckie Row. Peggy saw her grandfather's shock at her news turn to pride as he looked at her. Helen's bewilderment turned to heart broken tears when she realised that for the first time in her life she would be without her constant companion. It was a painful parting when it came and Peggy felt very small and alone as she approached Allanbank, such a grand house, two storeys high with

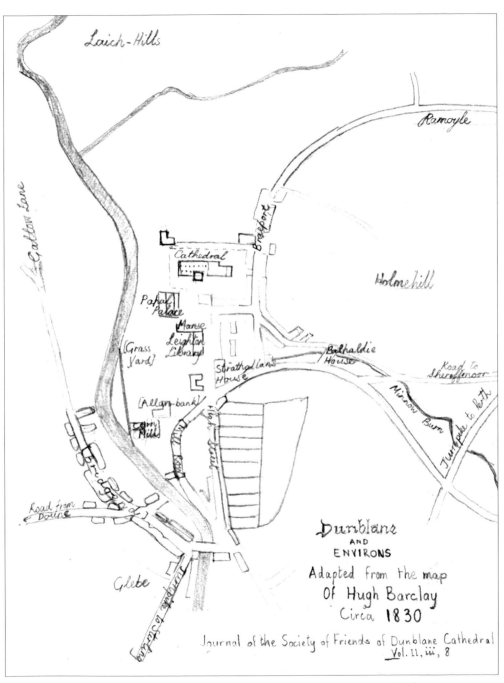

Dunblane and Environs from Hugh Barclay's Map c. 1830.

fancy 'pepper pot' turrets.

However, she didn't have time to feel lonely as she was shown around and given her instructions. Allanbank was the best house in town and Mistress Russell was determined to keep it that way. Peggy soon learned that her duties began at the crack of dawn when she had to be out of her bed in the kitchen corner, coaxing the embers of the fire back to life. Keeping it supplied with peat was a constant task, as was keeping the big black kettle hanging above the fire filled with water. Maggie, the cook, showed Peggy where to get the water in the Minnie Burn that surfaced beside the house before disappearing into the pipe that carried it under Mill Row. It was more convenient than trailing off to the well, but even so on laundry days Peggy thought that her arms might drop off with lugging heavy buckets. Rinsing the soap out of bed linen in the cold water of the burn made her think wistfully of her young sister and long past summer days.

It was a different world from the one she had shared with Helen and her grandfather. Washing the flagstone floors of the kitchen made her think of the cold earth floors in the cottage at Chuckie Row, kept damp even in summer to prevent her grandfather's linen threads from drying out and snapping. 'At least it didna need scrubbin,' thought Peggy as she nursed her raw knuckles grazed on the stone floor.

Whenever she got the chance, she peeped into the main rooms that were Mistress Russel's pride and joy. Here there were carved wooden panels, the like of which the child had never seen before, and fine white plasterwork so very different from the smoke blackened walls of the weaver's cottage. Then Peggy would wonder anxiously if Helen was keeping that fire going, but a voice from the kitchen would bring her back to her new surroundings, "Peggy, whaur are ye, lass? Mair water and the fire needs feedin!"

So there was little time for dreaming as autumn days wore on to winter. In the shorter, colder days Peggy spent less time on outdoor tasks but now she and the other serving lasses were expected to use the lengthening evening hours usefully. There were candles to be made for the long hours of darkness ahead. That was a smelly business, using tallow from cattle that had been killed at Martinmas. Peggy soon learned how to stretch the wicks on a frame, dip it into a trough of warm tallow and let it cool, repeating the process till the candles were thick enough to be stored.

Soap making, using the remaining tallow, was a longer, complicated process. The fatty substance was mixed with salt and lye, made from wood ashes combined with lime and water. After several hours of boiling this mixture a scum of soap rose to the surface to be skimmed off. As she helped to transfer the thick, greasy soap into boxes to cool and harden, Peggy felt her eyes smarting and the acrid smell catching the back of her throat. She was thankful when that task was over, but the sickening smell hung about the kitchen for days.

With these stores replenished, Mistress Russell now set the servants spinning in their spare moments. In the long evenings Peggy and the others would keep both hands and tongues busy as they sat in the warm kitchen. Local gossip was still full of stories about the Bonnie Prince's stay at Balhaldie and about how Mistress Russell and Bailie Russell were in disagreement about the Jacobite cause.

In the weeks after the Prince's departure, stories had come back about his sojourn in Holyrood Palace, Edinburgh, after a surprise victory at Prestonpans. News had become scrappy as the Jacobites moved south, well out of the range of the government's cannons at Edinburgh Castle, but word reached them that they were still marching south.

As the old year passed, Peggy and the other servants looked forward to the first Monday of the year, Handsel Monday when they would have a holiday, the only whole day off since Peggy had come to Allanbank. Like the others she was out of her bed in the corner of the kitchen at early light. She could hear from Mill Row and the High Causeway the sounds of young people already celebrating their free day. The streets were full of lads going from door to door collecting their handsel half pennies from their employers and customers. And woe betide anyone too mean to contribute to the festivities, for they risked having their signboards torn down for a grand bonfire later in the day.

Peggy was relieved to find herself through the uproar and across in Bridgend with her own Handsel money from the Russells' still safe in her pocket. Along with it was the gift of carls, the triangular oatcakes specially made with treacle for the New Year celebrations at Allanbank. At Chuckie Row, Helen ran out to meet her and dragged her by the hand into the cottage where James Lucas greeted her with a hug.

"My but ye've grown, lass! Mistress Russell is feedin ye too weel!"

Peggy laughed in agreement. It was true that she had become taller with the good feeding.

"Aye, the mistress gies us boiled beef on Sundays and Thursdays wi our broth and there's aye plenty o parritch and cream. Oh, and eggs aince a week."

Suddenly remembering their own shortage, she felt guilty and hastily added, "Here, Grandfaither, some carls still fresh and some cheese from Allanbank. Their stores werena touched by the soldiers."

The day passed all too quickly as they exchanged news and this time all three of them were in agreement that they hoped that they had seen the last of soldiers, either government or Jacobite. Peggy was pleased, yet sad in a strange way, to see how well her young sister and her grandfather were managing without her. Helen seemed so independent now, not needing her sister's instructions any more, but there were fond hugs as the girls parted at the bridge in the late afternoon.

Back at Allanbank, the early January days went by quietly enough in an endless routine of kindling and feeding the fire, carrying water, scrubbing, sweeping and spinning.

It was while Peggy was out drawing water from the burn one afternoon that she saw a horseman come over the bridge and approach Allanbank. The rider looked exhausted and his horse's flanks were mud spattered. As Peggy watched, Mistress Russell hurried the man into the house and later in the kitchen the whisper was that he was a messenger from Prince Charlie's army.

He had brought news of a Jacobite victory against government troops at Falkirk but the Prince and his followers were retreating northward, where they would wait till spring for long promised French reinforcements.

The cook was able to report that the Prince's man had dined well, but hurriedly, and had left within the hour.

That evening as they all sat spinuing in the kitchen, there were raised voices from their master and mistress. Straining their ears, Peggy and the others could make out the angry tones of their master. The words were unclear but they could catch some of them.

"Naethin but trouble. . . . a lost cause."

Then in the lighter tones of Mistress Russell came the indignant reply . . . . "the rightful king . . . . German usurpers . . . ." indicating that she was unrepentant.

The last words were from the Bailie and were clear for all to hear. "Leave the plottin and schemin' to Balhaldie and Keir and the likes, but you just leave well alane!"

With that the outside door slammed and the listeners scuttled back to their spinning lest their mistress might catch them eavesdropping.

For the next few days it was a very subdued household where the servants went about their tasks treading carefully, fearful of giving their master or mistress any cause for complaint. But worse was yet to come to the household at Allanbank.

The townsfolk held their breath as the Jacobite army made its way north through Dunblane and few were sorry that 'the rebels' as the Bailie called them, did not stop.

But close behind them at the beginning of February

Minnie Burn, behind High Street, now covered.

came the advance guard of the pursuing government army.

Just what this meant for the household at Allanbank was soon made clear to Peggy in yet another argument between her master and her mistress. This time there were no closed doors between the startled servants and their employers. Mistress Russell was checking the stores when the Bailie hurried into the kitchen.

"Mak ready, Mistress. We'll hae a guest soon. The Duke of Cumberland will bide here the night."

Peggy heard her mistress gasp in disbelief.

"Oh, no. I winna lift a finger to entertain the like o him! Let him camp wi his sodgers!"

The Bailie turned on his wife, his face red with anger.

"Woman, you will dae as I bid! Hae ye forgotten how the folk o this town hae suffered already in the cause o yer Bonnie Prince? We winna mak maitters worse by angering the King's son! As Commissary Clerk of Dunblane, I am offering him our hospitality. It is your duty as my wife to provide it! I will gae wi the minister, Mr Simson, to meet him!"

With that the Bailie was gone, leaving Mistress Russell white faced and open mouthed. But after a few moments of stunned silence in the kitchen she recovered and turned to the cook.

"Ye heard the maister, Maggie. We'll mak a meal fit for a king! Let's see now. What can we prepare in sae short a time?"

The cook rose to the challenge and together she and Mistress Russell planned the dinner. They'd start with broth with barley and onions, followed by roast fowls with egg sauce.

Hasty instructions were given to all the kitchen servants and Peggy began the first of many trips to the Minnie Burn. Then she had the task of plucking one of the hens, still warm after having its neck wrung. With the main courses simmering and roasting, Mistress Russell turned her mind to desserts, while Peggy kept an eye on the hens slowly turning on the spit above the fire. Now and then she dipped a bunch of their tail feathers into melted butter and brushed the fowls with it. She shielded her eyes as drips of fat sizzled and smoked.

"Now Peggy, leave that a wee while. Come and beat thae egg yolks for the flummery."

The cook thrust the bowl and beater at the child. She was happy to sit and rest her feet, letting her arm do the work of beating the yolks with the sugar, nutmeg and rosewater.

"That's fine. Now coup it intae thon bowl wi a mutchkin each o sugar and cream. Let it heat gently ower that pan o water. Dinna stir it and dinna let it boil."

As she issued her instructions all around, the cook was busy herself, using the whites of the eggs to make lemon cream, and slicing preserved apples in syrup. The kitchen lass was quite proud of herself as she removed the thickened flum mery from the heat and watched Maggie add wine soaked currants to the yellow mixture.

Then it was, "Mind the fowls, Peggy, dinna let them dry out. Keep bastin them."

Mistress Russell bustled in and out fetching things for the dining table.

"Here, Peggy, tak these beeswax candles. They smell sweeter than the others. Put them in their holders."

And later, "Peggy, polish up this pewter. I'll no hae it said that our table is no as fine as any in London. Tak it to the dinin room."

There Peggy paused to admire the snow-white linen cloth and napkins. The housemaid had polished the glasses and cutlery till they shone and the china punch bowl was out of its cupboard on the sideboard with the best cups and saucers. The maid's voice broke into Peggy's thoughts.

"Dinna stand there gawpin. If ye hae naethin else to dae bring mair peat for this fire. We canna hae the Duke freezin!"

And so the day flew by with no rest for anyone at Allanbank. But by the time Mistress Russell had changed into her best brocade gown everything was ready, and even Peggy had the chance to wash her hands and face and put on a clean linen skirt and apron.

When the royal party approached Allanbank with Bailie Russell and Mr Simson, fires burned brightly in the main rooms making shadows dance on the mellow wooden panels. Honey scented candles sent a soft glow playing on the dishes, while from the kitchen appetising smells of the carefully prepared dinner wafted through the house.

Mistress Russell allowed herself a moment's pride as she surveyed the arrangements for the royal reception. Minutes later as the Duke entered Allanbank, she dropped a curtsey to welcome the royal visitor.

In the kitchen Peggy and the others awaited their orders to serve the meal while Maggie the cook kept checking everything nervously. It was some time later that the Baillie himself, looking none too pleased, entered the kitchen with two of the Duke's personal staff behind him. In front of the astonished cook the Duke's men produced their own cooking pots and provisions. Just as Maggie opened her mouth to protest the Bailie laid a restraining hand on her arm. He was tight lipped as he spoke.

"His Highness has made his own arrangements and will not be enjoying your fine dinner, Maggie. It will be his loss, I fear!"

He gave his cook a warning look, silencing her objections before she could voice them, and turning on his heel strode out of the kitchen.

Peggy and the others stood dumbfounded. All their work and all that lovely food rejected but, like her mistress earlier that day, cook was quick to recover.

"Right, lasses, get this food intae the larder. Lock everythin awa. These gentlemen hae nae need o it."

That done, the servants cleared out of the kitchen only to be met in the corridor by more strangers, armed sentries from the government army brought in to guard the Duke. Now it was Mistress Russell's turn to calm the alarmed servants.

Turning to the housemaid she said, "Gang upstairs and tak the warmin pans frae the best bed that ye made ready for our guest. The Duke has seen fit to bring his ain bedstead and beddin, but it is to be hoped that he may at least trust our warmin pans between his sheets. Tak the others back intae the kitchen, Maggie. Ye'll be safe there. Help yoursels to a bowl o broth. Just let the Duke's men carry out their orders but offer them some broth too. They must be weary efter their journey."

Still bewildered by it all, Peggy took her bowl to her corner of the kitchen. Her bones ached with fatigue as she supped the tasty broth. Then the wooden bowl slipped from her grasp and rolled across the stone floor. Before it spiralled to a stop, the kitchen lass was sound asleep.

She slept peacefully hearing nothing of this second night of army occupation with its raids on what was left of the town's provender. When she awoke, it was to the sound of jingling harness and marching feet as the government army moved north out of Dunblane. As she helped with clearing up from the previous evening she was still tired but interested enough to listen to the kitchen gossip. The whole household was still indignant about the insults they had suffered at the hands of the Duke.

"Just imagine turnin down good food!" said one, but Mistress Russell, entering the kitchen, silenced them all.

"Haud yer tongues all of you. The Duke's sentinels are still in the hoose and he is close by lookin intae thievin last night frae his army supplies. It will be the worse for all o us to rile him further!"

Later, while she was scouring the splattered fat on the fireplace, Peggy heard the whispers . . .

"The Duke has condemned all three to the gallows . . .", but their mistress's footsteps outside the kitchen stopped further talk.

There were so many pots still to be cleaned that Peggy's hands were never out of water in the kitchen and then it was off to the burn again to refill the big kettle over the fire. It was bitterly cold as the child hauled the full bucket out of the burn and turned to go back into the house. Suddenly her eye caught a movement in the shadows where the burn came out of the culvert a little further up Mill Row, and she gasped in surprise as a young girl's head and shoulders appeared above the flowing water at the mouth of the pipe. Startled, Peggy ran into the house and bumped into her mistress.

"Mistress, there's a lassie like to drown in the Minnie Burn. She's stuck in yon pipe!"

The woman and child ran back to the edge of the burn just in time to see the lass with soaked skirts flapping round her bare legs, clambering out of the burn and making off as fast as she could, through the garden and across the bleaching green.

"Weel, she wasnae stuck, Peggy. I wonder just what she's been daein. No a word to anybody about this! Look, yer bucket's spilt. Fill it up again and get back inside."

As she tipped the water into the kettle Peggy was still puzzling out the whole incident in her mind. She could not make sense of it as she stoked the fire. The mistress was still in the kitchen wondering what to do with the uneaten feast.

"Peggy, when we hae tidied up here ye can tak a roastit fowl hame to yer grandfaither. We hae sae much meat left ower that . . . ." her voice trailed off as she heard her husband's footsteps in the passageway.

The door swung open and there stood the Bailie looking ten years older overnight. He slumped down in a chair at the kitchen table.

Mistress Russell was at his side immediately.

"What is the maitter, my dear?" she asked anxiously.

"You will nae believe this, but some fool has tried to kill the Duke just outside Lord Strathallan's hoose! A pail o boilin water was flung out o the attic windae as he passed by! Lucky for us it missed him but it went all ower the haunches o his bonnie grey charger. The horse lowped forwart and Cumberland landed in the mud. It could hae been funny it had been anybody but King George's son rollin about in the glaur. He certainly didna laugh and I hae just spent the past hour pleadin wi him no to fetch back his troops to tak revenge!"

"And will he pay heed to ye, dae ye think?"

"Weel, we maun hope sae. He did mutter somethin about a promise he's made to 'spare Dunblane' to someone in London but I didna press him further. He was still furious as he rode aff wi his braw coat spoiled and his dignity gone!"

"And hae they found the attacker?"

"Nay, ane o the sodgers lookin up swore it was a young lass that flung the water. They searched My Lord's Hoose frae top to bottom but there's nae sign o her. She's disappeared intae thin air!"

More likely 'thin water' thought Peggy, remembering that the Minnie Burn was open behind Lord Strathallan's house too, before it was channelled into the culvert underneath. Mistress Russell must have read Peggy's thought as she quickly changed the subject.

"Come awa, Peggy. Tak this to Brigend. It will be the last roastit fowl we'll see for a while."

As she hurried Peggy out of the kitchen, she spoke urgently, so low that the child could only just catch her words.

"And no a word to anybody o what we saw earlier! If the Bailie catches her he'll hae her whipped for puttin us all intae danger!"

Then in normal tones she continued. "Be back in an hour mind. There's still plenty needin done here."

Still confused by all that had happened, Peggy felt weary as she made her way along Mill Row with the precious food. At the other side of the bridge the flattened grass of the Crofts was the only sign that the royal army's heavy baggage and artillery had spent the night there.

But the completely empty hen coops, there and in Bridgend, were another reminder of the army's occupation. On her way between the houses Peggy was piecing together all the events of the past twenty-four hours. As she approached Chuckie Row, clear in her mind's eye was that other lass not much older than herself, her clothes dripping, running across the grass.

What a tale to tell Helen!

Then she remembered Mistress Russell's words, 'not a word to anybody'. Peggy paused – but she and Helen had always shared their secrets. Helen was not just anyone; she was Peggy's only sister. That was it . . . . She would tell only Helen, not another soul. No one else would ever find out … would they?

BAIRNS OF BRIDGEND
DUNBLANE

PEGGY LUCAS 1745

NOTES

In 1724, James Lucas of Bridgend was one of four quartermasters appointed for the year to assist the Bailie of Dunblane in the maintenance of order and administration of justice (Barty p127) He may have been the grandfather of the Margaret Lucas whose Testament was registered in 1768.

In later years, Bailie Russell distributed the lint and collected the finely woven linen shirting for which Dunblane's hand weavers became famous in the later eighteenth century. (Clough)

The Russells' fine home, Allanbank, dating from 1633 faced down Millrow beside the river. It was allowed to fall into disrepair and was demolished in 1962. All that remains of it are some wooden panels now housed in Dunblane Museum at the Cross. Its site is now a children's playground. The Museum also houses some of the doors from Braeport houses, damaged by the Jacobites.

The Minnie Burn through which local legend says the serving girl escaped can be seen very briefly between the former co-operative building (now Age Concern) and the block next to the Sheriff Court Building. It remains hidden under the flowerbeds that bloom on the site of Lord Strathallan's house and continues unseen under Millrow until it joins the Allan from a culvert behind Allanside House.

The domestic servant, who attacked the Duke of Cumberland, worked for the Drummonds of Balhaldie but her name is unknown. It is believed that she was never punished for her attack and that she later married a local farmer.

Balhaldie House, though altered internally, still stands between Sinclair's Wynd and the north end of the High Street. If the stonework is closely examined it reveals just a hint of the pink wash with which the houses of Jacobite sympathisers were covered for easy identification by government troops after the defeat of the rebellion.

In June 1746 Dunblane Kirk Session offered a day of public thanksgiving for *'gracious deliverance from that wicked and unnatural rebellion by the success ... to His Majesties armies at Culloden . . . under the conduct of . . . the Duke of Cumberland.'*

BAIRNS OF BRIDGEND
DUNBLANE

PEGGY LUCAS 1745

SOURCES AND BIBLIOGRAPHY

CLOUGH, Monica, *Pink Wash or White Wash?*
  Journal of the Society of Friends of Dunblane Cathedral, Vol. XII. iv, 1977.

DURIE, Alistair, *The Scottish Linen Industry in the Eighteenth Century* John Donald, 1979.
HUTCHISON, R E., *The Jacobite Rising* of 1715, HMSO, 1965.
McPHAIL, I M M, A History of Scotland Book I Edward Arnold. 1954
PENNY, George, *Traditions of Perth*, 1836

BAIRNS OF BRIDGEND
DUNBLANE

JOHN WRIGHT 1724

An it werena for the weavers what wad we do?
We wadna get claith made oot of our woo'
We wadna get a coat, either black or blue,
An it werena for the honourable weavers.

There's fouk independent o' ither tradesmen's wark,
For women need nae barber – Dykers need nae clerk;
But there's no ane o' them a' but needs a coat or sark,
Which maun be the wark o' some weaver.

Anon, Forfar.

The Tryst-time set us plaitin' whips,
And trimming sticks sae trig,
To drive the cattle in our glee,
Across the Bainsford brig.
Where drovers' gutteral Gaelic rang
Aboon the babel rout,
O hawkers, scowmen, cadger folk
And roarin Hieland cattle.

From 'The Bairnies O', Anon.

BAIRNS OF BRIDGEND
DUNBLANE

JOHN WRIGHT 1724

His father's angry words were still ringing in his ears as John stumbled, only half seeing, across the bridge over Allan Water. His stick smacked the rump of the cow that he drove none too gently. He didn't even hear friends greet him as he hurried along Millrow urging the cow forward. All he wanted was to escape his father's harsh tongue but even as he made his way through Sinclair's Wynd and left the houses behind in the climb up to Sheriffmuir, the words kept repeating in his head.

"Ye've broken the threid again, John! This web will be nae use to anybody by the time ye're finished. Naebody will want to buy it!"

John had looked miserably at the shuttle in his hand, not understanding himself how he had managed to make yet another mistake. It was perfectly true that he did not seem to have the knack of weaving in spite of long hours spent with his father at the loom. Not for the first time he wished himself small enough to go with his mother and sisters to scour the wool in the burn, cold work but pleasant enough on a summer's day. But that was women's work and John was

Bishop Dermoch's Bridge (1409).

expected to follow in his father's footsteps, and not just his father's footsteps either as he was harshly reminded by the voice that broke into his thoughts.

"Good Heavens, lad, yer grandfaither maun be turnin ower in his grave to see ye, no to mention yer great grandfaither. The Wrights hae been weavers in Brigend for nigh on a hundred year. It's in yer blood but no in yer fingers by the look o it!"

Things had gone from bad to worse. The harder John tried, the more awkward he became. His fingers were all thumbs as he passed the shuttle across between the double rows of warp threads. At last when the shuttle again slipped from his grasp, landing on the damp earth floor, his father had lost patience completely.

"Wad ye look at that! Ye hae pulled it out o shape again! Will ye get out o my sight! Tak the coo frae the back up to the muir to graze. Dae ye think ye might manage that?"

Now tired, as well as upset, John was glad to fling himself down to rest on the moor above Dunblane while his cow chewed contentedly at the patches of grass. Without meaning to, he slipped into a deep sleep.

It was some hours later that the evening chill of autumn made John shiver and rouse himself. He sat up with a start wondering for a moment where he was. The day's events came flooding back and with them his unhappiness. Then all at once he remembered why he was up there on the edge of the moor – the cow. Where was she? Scrambling to his feet, he looked round frantically but there was no sign of the beast. Hither and thither he ran calling and searching but beyond the patches of grass the broom was tall and made perfect cover for man or beast to hide. Before long the fading light of late afternoon made it impossible to detect movement in the bushy branches and he gave up the fruitless search.

Disbelief turned to despair as the full realisation of his situation dawned on John. He sank to the ground with his head in his hands forcing himself to think out his next step. In his misery he knew that he dared not return home without the cow. He could not face his father's renewed wrath but neither did he relish the thought of a night alone on Sheriffmuir.

It was while he was apprehensively looking around for a place to settle that he heard the faint sound of voices coming across the moor from the north. Listening intently and preparing to hide as the sounds came closer, John was able to make out the lowing of cattle and barking of dogs. As the approaching herd came to a gradual halt in the distance, the lad could hear the strange words of the men with them. Relief flooded over the boy when he recognised them as drovers coming south from the highlands. Rough these strangers might be but at least they were company. Anyhow he'd try his luck with them before he found himself alone in darkness.

The men paid no attention to the young lad who shyly joined the outside edge of the group while they busied themselves settling their several scores of black cattle. The tired animals did not wander far, finding good grazing at the stance where they had stopped. Dogs and men took water from a nearby burn and as John watched one of the drovers turned and noticed him. When the man called out in Gaelic to his friends John wondered if he should run, but while the highlander's words were unintelligible to the lad, his gestures were friendly enough and he beckoned to the frightened boy to join them.

Watching the men stir oatmeal into the clear water from the burn, John realised how hungry he was and he was grateful for the offer of a share in the cold oatmeal mixture. Men, boy and dogs all ate the same supper but the drovers finished off with a mouthful of liquid from the ram's-horn that they each carried at their sides. Winking at his fellows one of the men offered a drink to John. One sip was enough and the boy spluttered and choked as the rough whisky burned his throat. While they chuckled at the lad's discomfort, the men began to settle down to sleep wrapping their plaids around them. One of them, seeing John shiver, tossed a spare plaid at the lad. As he snuggled down thankfully in its warm folds John noticed that two men were staying alert checking the beasts in their care. With this reminder of his own neglect earlier that day, the lad drifted into a troubled sleep.

Next morning he lay awake before most of the drovers and black cattle were stirring. He thought about his next move, and he knew that he had to find his stray cow. Without a word to the drovers on watch, John slipped away from slumbering men and beasts and began his search anew.

He worked in a wide circle around the place where he'd last seen the animal. All morning he searched stopping only to eat the blaeberries that grew in patches among the grass and heather. As time wore on, John's heart grew heavier and as his hopes of finding the cow faded, he rejoined the track close to the stance. To his surprise he found his companions of the night before only a short distance from where he'd left them in the morning. They smiled and greeted him kindly enough and he wearily rejoined the group. There was no question of his going home now. Slowly an idea formed in the lad's mind. If he could stay with the drovers, he could work for his keep. He took a good look at the men he'd seen only in the half-light of dusk the evening before. What a strange lot they

Sheriffmuir Inn.

seemed compared to Dunblane's soberly dressed men. Instead of dark breeches worn by men like John's father, the drovers wore their woollen plaids hung in folds around them and secured by a wide belt round their middles.

The checked and striped materials looked like very short women's petticoats and the men's knees and lower legs were bare. The remainder of the plaid was draped loosely over the men's chests and hung over their shoulders, while their heads were bare. Only one who seemed to be the leader wore a blue bonnet and John noticed that in his belt he had a pistol as well as the broadsword and dirk that all the men carried. The lad must have been staring at the six men and he was startled when his gaze met the alert eyes below the blue bonnet. To John's relief the bonnet wearer gave him an amused smile and beckoned him across to sit beside him.

Another surprise was in store when the drover spoke in a language he could understand. In reply to his questions John gave deliberately vague answers allowing the man to think he was one of the many orphan lads who wandered the countryside. In turn the drover leader let John know that he was Angus Macleod from the island of Skye and the English-speaking spokesman for his fellow islanders. To John's hesitant request to stay with the highlanders he nodded slowly but went on to outline the next few days ahead.

"On the morrow we leave this stance for the Tryst at Falkirk. We rested the beasts today after the long journey south. This is the last chance for them to graze freely until we reach the market two days' journey from here."

As man and boy sat together sharing a meagre supper, the lad was fascinated to hear the drover recall details of the trek from Skye. Place names like Kyle Rhea and Glenelg meant nothing to John but when Angus described the swimming of the cattle across the hazardous strait between island and mainland he could visualise it all – the strings of eight cows each roped to the tail of the one in front, and Angus himself in the stern of the rowing boat holding the rope from the lead animal's jaw while the rowers plied their oars, fighting the current and urging on the swimming beasts. With the sea crossing safely behind them other dangers met them on the mainland. There were rivers to ford and chill autumn nights to endure in wild glens and mountain passes. Glen Shiel, Glen Morriston, Pass of Corrieyairack, Drumochter Pass, Dalnacardoch and Tummel Bridge and so Angus traced their route south through the Sma' Glen to Crieff –meaningless but fascinating names to John and the boy's eyes sparkled at the tales of plundering Macgregor clansmen who tried, sometimes successfully, to 'lift' some cattle from passing drovers.

As he spoke his slow but perfect English, the highlander's fingers strayed to the weapons at his side in recollection of past skirmishes. "So you understand, lad, it is small wonder that drovers alone among us highlanders are permitted to carry arms after the troubles of some years ago. But that's enough of talk. Now we need to save our breath for the road tomorrow."

As darkness fell, John was proud to take the first watch with Angus, and watch he did, never taking his eyes off the herd till the leader roused the next two sentries. For a brief, troubled moment, as he wrapped himself in the plaid John's thoughts strayed to the Wrights' single lost cow before he drifted off into a deep sleep.

There was little time for looking back the next day as the drove began the last

NLS County of Stirlingshire.
Edgar 1745-1777.

leg of their journey. The distant jagged outlines of highland peaks piercing the clear blue sky were gradually lost to sight behind them as the herd moved steadily over the moor. They skirted the battleground where blood had been spilled when John had been very small. The lad's task was at the rear of the stream of cattle where he had to encourage stragglers. Still at an easy pace, the drovers led their charges down the southwest slopes of the Ochils, round the shoulder of Dum-y-at. Below lay the panorama of the carse of the River Forth, a twisting ribbon of silver on its way eastward to the sea. But straight ahead, thrusting upward out of the surrounding flatness, the Castle of Stirling rose from its base of solid rock to dominate the surrounding countryside. The drove wound its way downwards, passing the tiny village of Pathfoot, before taking the causeway across the carse towards the town that spread itself down the slope of the castle rock.

Their easy pace became even slower as they approached Stirling Bridge where an eager toll collector calculated the fee for the drovers and their beasts. As they crossed the cobbled surface the men spoke softly in Gaelic to the cattle, alarmed by the hollow sound of their hooves on the stone bridge. John shivered when they passed the Heading Hill with its stark stone chopping block but soon they were climbing up the shoulder of St Mary's Wynd into the bustling town of Stirling. The lad was sent to buy some more oatmeal and a few onions to add flavour to the men's next few meals. Rejoining the herd resting outside the town walls, John found his companions attending to some cows that looked lame as they trod the hard paved streets. Patches of leather were attached to the feet of these animals and they were on their way again.

Now the droves from the north were joined by others from the west and the stream of cattle became a river. It looked as if all the cattle in the world were surging towards Falkirk and John wondered how they could possibly keep the herds separate. Sure enough, the Macleod drovers kept circling their charges making sure that none strayed into other herds. By late afternoon when they stopped near Torwood they were all tired with the effort of keeping the beasts together.

The evening routine of seeing cattle and dogs fed, watered and settled down was now familiar to John and he was proud when Angus clapped him on the back and said,

"You've earned your keep this day, lad. Tomorrow or the next day the beasts will be sold. I trust that the prices here at Falkirk are better than what was on offer at Crieff last week. Let's hope the extra distance we've walked the beasts was not a waste of time!"

John was asleep as soon as he lay down and he had to be roused for the last spell of watching the cattle in the hours before dawn. When the sun rose it shed its light over wave upon wave of black cattle broken here and there by the silent figure of a drover moving quietly among the animals. As if on a signal, the mass of men and beasts began to stir and they were on their way again. The river of cattle meandered along past open country slowing down to make its way through Falkirk to the moor of Reddingridge a mile to the south.

John could hardly believe his eyes when he saw the scene. Now with all the droves converging on the market area, the river of cattle spilled out into an ocean. Drovers, usually quietly spoken, now raised their voices as they secured a stance for their animals. And what a merging of people and accents as drovers met dealers from the south of Scotland and beyond. Gaelic mixed with Doric from Aberdeenshire and John couldn't understand either! He could follow the speech of dealers from the Scottish Border country but had difficulty with the dialects of the Yorkshire men who looked over the Macleod herd as a possible buy. All day the arguing and discussion went on, drovers and dealers each intent on getting the best bargain. Even the beasts were excited, bellowing and tossing their heads, impatient at being restricted and immobile, while the dogs barked among their legs. Angus Macleod, alone in the melee, kept calm ignoring the sea of activity all around him.

Indeed to John he seemed not to care if he sold his cattle or not as he discussed them with a Yorkshire man. Only when the deal was struck did Angus allow himself to look pleased. John was trusted to help keep watch at the stance while Angus and the buyer sealed their bargain over a dram of whisky at one of the refreshment tents. When the men returned Angus slipped the boy a coin.

"Off you go now, take yourself yonder to the fire. You'll get a heat and this will more than pay for a bowl of broth. Mind your change though, for there are thieves around who would part you from your money if you are not alert."

John stammered his thanks as he clutched the coin. The drover smiled, "You are welcome, lad. We got a good price for the cattle. You see the secret is to keep them in good condition on the journey and then not to look too anxious to sell. Oh, and to keep the scrawny beasts in the middle and the best ones at the outside of the herd!"

John laughed and delighted with his newfound wealth he threaded his way through the throng. He paid attention to Angus's warning and kept a wary eye on the motley crowd who hung around the outskirts of the tryst grounds. As well as pick-pockets there were card sharpers, beggars, ballad singers and fiddlers all trying in their own ways to part drover and dealer alike from their money, but John reached the inviting fire with his coin still safe. The smell of the broth rose to his nostrils and the warmth spread through him as he stood before the flames.

He had just begun his bowl of soup when a voice behind him said, "Here now, dae I no ken that face? Are you no Webster Wright's lad frae Brigend o Dunblane?"

John spun round to find himself face to face with someone he knew instantly. Donald McLaren, chapman traveller from Dunblane, complete with pack stood in front of him. There was no way that John could deny his identity.

"It is you!" went on the pedlar. "So this is whaur ye've got to! Dae ye ken that yer mither is heart broken lookin for ye? She thinks ye're drowned in the Wharrie Burn!"

Shock and then guilt flooded through John. He had hardly given his mother a thought since he had fled from his father's harsh words, but she was worrying constantly about his whereabouts.

He knew now where his path lay. He must go back and face his father if only to put his mother's mind at rest. Anyway, his adventure was over. Though some of the drovers would take the cattle south for their new owner, Angus had done his business in Falkirk and would soon be returning to Skye. Slowly, John finished his soup and spoke to the pedlar.

"Aye," he said thoughtfully, "I'll gang back to Brigend in the morn."

And so, the next day John bade farewell to his drover companions with hearty handshakes and backslapping and he set out at first light from Reddingridge Moor. As he strode away from Falkirk he met other droves still coming to the Tryst, but John's mind was on how he would be received at home.

The Auld Brig, Stirling.

Without the cattle to slow him down and by keeping up a steady pace, John reached Stirling by the afternoon, pausing only to spend the last of his money on some food. As he took the causeway north of the town his stomach began to flutter, but he kept going, through the hamlet of Pathfoot. He took the shortest route to Dunblane, passing the mill at Bridge of Allan and continuing on the track that skirted the slopes of Sheriffmuir where his adventure had begun. When he found himself going through Bridgend, John felt a strange mixture of reluctance and anticipation.

At last, as he cautiously pushed open the cottage door, his mother cried out. His father, startled too, looked up from the loom, rose and gave John a resounding clout on the ear. Yet even as the boy held his stinging ear, there was relief in that wallop.

Then his father pointed out the back. Puzzled, John looked and stared in disbelief. There in the yard was the very cow that he'd taken to Sheriffmuir!

Suddenly remembering something that Angus had said about the strong homing instinct of both cattle and men, John turned and hugged his mother.

He was back home where he belonged, in Bridgend of Dunblane!

BAIRNS OF BRIDGEND
DUNBLANE

JOHN WRIGHT 1724

NOTES

The names in this story are taken from a real family that lived in Dunblane.

The Register of Testaments for Dunblane lists two centuries of the Wright family from one Malcolm Wright who died in 1598 to an Andrew who died in 1796. Three Wrights are specified as being weavers or wobsters at Bridgend while the John Wright who died in 1756 was a merchant in Dunblane. The initials IW 1754 HW are above the door of a cottage in Calderwood Place or Chuckie Row, which marked the western limit of Bridgend for many decades. Donald McLaren, chapman (pedlar) is recorded as living in Dunblane around 1705.

The cattle trade between Scotland and England was legalised following the Union of the Crowns in 1603 and what had begun as a Borders activity was gradually extended to the Highlands. By the end of the seventeenth century Crieff had become famous for its great trysts or cattle markets, for the trade from the northern highlands and islands. In 1723, Macky reported that 30,000 cattle had been sold at the autumn Tryst in Crieff. (Haldane P136) The Tryst at Falkirk dates from 1717, and it gradually assumed dominance over the Crieff Tryst.

Dunblane was just by-passed by the great droves which either came over Sheriffmuir from the north as in John Wright's story, or went directly to Stirling from Doune only three miles west of Dunblane. The battle mentioned is that of 1715 at Sheriffmuir, an indecisive encounter between Jacobite supporters of the deposed Stewart dynasty and British government troops of the Hanoverian King George. It was after the later 1745-46 uprising that wearing tartan was proscribed.

The village of Pathfoot on the way to Stirling lay within what is now Stirling University campus and it was itself the scene of a small local tryst.

Torwood, like Larbert was used as a last stance before the Falkirk Tryst.

BAIRNS OF BRIDGEND
DUNBLANE

JOHN WRIGHT 1724

SOURCES AND BIBLIOGRAPHY

GILLESPIE, Robert, *Round About Falkirk*, James McLehose, 1868.
HALDANE, A R B, *The Drove Roads of Scotland*, T Nelson and Sons, 1952.
POCOCKE, Richard, *Pococke's Tours in Scotland*, Scottish History Society, 1887.
SCOTT, Sir Walter, *The Two Drovers* 1827.

BAIRNS OF BRIDGEND
DUNBLANE

MARIAN CORSAR 1656

A spindle o bourtree,   (elder tree)
 A whorl o caumstane, (limestone)
Put them on the house-tap,
 And it will spin alane.

Traditional.

Fareweel, ye lowland plaids o grey'
Nae kindly charms for me ye hae,
The tartan shall be mine for aye,
For O' the colour's dear to me!

For mine was silky saft and warm,
It wrapped me round frae arm to arm,
And like himself it bore a charm,
And O' the plaid is dear to me!

V. Halley.

If there's a waddin' in a town,
I'll airt me to be there
And pour my kindest benisons,
Upon the winsome pair.

And some will gie me beef and bread,
And some will gie me cheese,
Syne I'll slip out amang the folk,
And gather the bawbees.

And I will wallop out a dance,
Or tell a merry tale;
Till some gude fellow in my dish,
Will pour a sowp o' ale.

From 'A-begging we will go' Alexander Ross

111

BAIRNS OF BRIDGEND
DUNBLANE

MARIAN CORSAR 1656

In the sheltered hollow beside the Bonny Burn, the only sounds were the murmuring of water and droning of the bees on the bell heather. Sitting by the stream, Marian Corsar and Isobel Graham were silently intent on their spinning.

Then Marian sneezed as some wool fibres went up her nose. Her hand jerked and the thread broke letting the spindle fall into a clump of reeds. She was close to tears as she retrieved the pointed stick with its ring of stone.

"I'll ne'er finish this the day! That's it spoiled again!"

Beside her, Isobel smiled and shook her head as she spoke, "Dinna be sae impatient. Lift up the spindle. Pick the wee bits out o the wool. See? There's nae harm done."

But Marian was not so easily consoled. "I'll ne'er be able to dae it like you, Isobel! Your wool's sae even. Mine's all lumpy!"

The older girl laughed. "I hae been spinnin for ages, daftie! Now watch again. Haud the distaff under yer oxter, firm but no sae tight. Now mak ready to play the wool out when I join it up again."

While she spoke, Isobel unwound a soft strand of wool from the long pole sticking up from under Marian's arm. She twisted and joined the soft wool to the broken end of fibre on the spindle in the child's hand. "There! Now drap the spindle and give it a birl."

Trying again, Marian fed a ribbon of soft fibre from around the distaff above her right shoulder and twisted the wool above the spindle hanging from her left

Site of Shielings, Cambushinnie.

hand. Twisting changed the fleecy fibres into a strong woollen yarn. After a few minutes concentrated effort she heard Isobel comment, "See ye're spinnin a fine yarn now, Marian. Just dinna sneeze again!"

So with the older girl's encouragement, the ball of spun yarn around Marian's spindle grew, while the fluffy bundle on the distaff gradually disappeared.

"Finished, Isobel!"

"Aye, sae ye are. I said ye could dae it. Rob will be proud o his wee sister when he sees that."

The small spinner looked proudly at the ball of wool and confided in her friend, "Dae ye ken, Isobel, this work is no sae bad. It's fine here up at Cambushinnie, mindin the kye and sheep, especially when it's no rainin! The air's sae fresh awa frae the town."

"Weel, ye had best mak the maist o it now. Next week ye'll no be sittin, ye'll be harvestin! But I love it mysel' up here on the moor. Through the dreich days o winter I canna wait, first for the spring and then for word frae the laird that we can come back here wi the beasts. Then we ken that simmer's really beginnin."

Then Isobel glanced at the late afternoon sky and continued, "It's time the lads were back wi the beasts. They'll be in need o milkin. Marian, fill the water bucket and bring it wi ye."

Climbing up the slope beside the burn, the girls looked round at the common pasture that was dotted with herdsmen and animals belonging to all the tenants of the Laird of Cromlix. Among them, the lads from Bridgend of Dunblane were returning to the summer huts. James and John Hutcheson, neighbour lads from

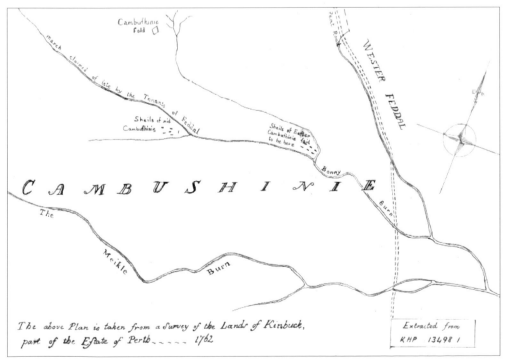

Plan of Shielings, Cambushinnie.

Bridgend were herding their own animals along with the Corsars' and Grahams' cows and sheep.

While Isobel milked the cows and sheep, the Hutcheson brothers told the girls about their wanderings that day, of how they'd chased the cattle from the neighbouring estate off Cambushinnie hillside. "If we see their kye on our pasture the morn, we'll hae them gaithered up as strays. Then they'll hae to pay a fine to get them back!"

Isobel interrupted, "Did ye mind to bring us mair cut heather for the beddin, John?"

"Nay, but there's plenty round here. You and Marian could cut it!"

"Indeed and we couldnae! We hae plenty to dae when ye're awa wi the beasts. We hae butter to mak frae the kye's milk and cheese to mak wi the yowes milk . . ."

It was John's turn to interrupt, "Aye, aye, Isobel! We'll cut ye mair heather but are ye no feedin us the night?"

Isobel laughed, "Marian will cook the oatcakes, while you lads cut the heather! There will be fresh milk ready for ye then!"

"Ye're a hard task-mistress! I feel pity for the man that mairries wi you!"

The girls were still laughing as the lads went off for the heather.

"Ye can save yer pity for yersel, John Hutcheson!" Marian called after them.

And so the days at the summer pasture passed pleasantly. After she helped with the butter and cheese making, Marian practised her spinning and gradually found it easier. And always when the herds returned from the grazing there was a lot of good-natured banter and gossip over supper. The herd lads regaled the lasses with exaggerated tales of how they chased stray animals from the next estate back where they belonged, while the girls passed on rumours of whose cows were not giving milk. It was whispered that a local woman could use water from the nearby Well of the Fairies to charm the cattle.

"Aye, they hae sent for Katherine McGregor to cure the dry beasts."

"But what if the Kirk Session hears tell of it?" asked John.

Isobel shrugged her shoulders. "Och, they'll no hear what's happenin awa up here on the moor!"

All too soon word came from Dunblane that all who could be spared were needed immediately for the harvest. For James Hutcheson and for Marian, summer at the shielings was over.

"Ne'er mind," Isobel consoled her, "Rob will be pleased to see yer spinnin. And dinna forget that when the hairvist's in, we'll all be back at Brigend in time for the Grosset Fair. Now, ye'll cairry the morn's milk back wi ye to Brigend. It will give strength to the hairvisters!"

So next morning when milking was finished, Marian made her way down over the pasture of Cambushinnie, wending her way carefully along the narrow sheep tracks through bracken and heather. On her head, she carefully balanced a wooden bucket full of milk. Ahead of her, James strode on impatient to be back in Dunblane. In the gully below the shieling the Meikle Burn was running high but the lad waded over without a backward glance.

"James, will ye give me a hand ower?" Marian called. "I'm feart I'll coup this stowp o milk!"

"Och! You lasses are helpless!" came the reply, but the lad splashed back over

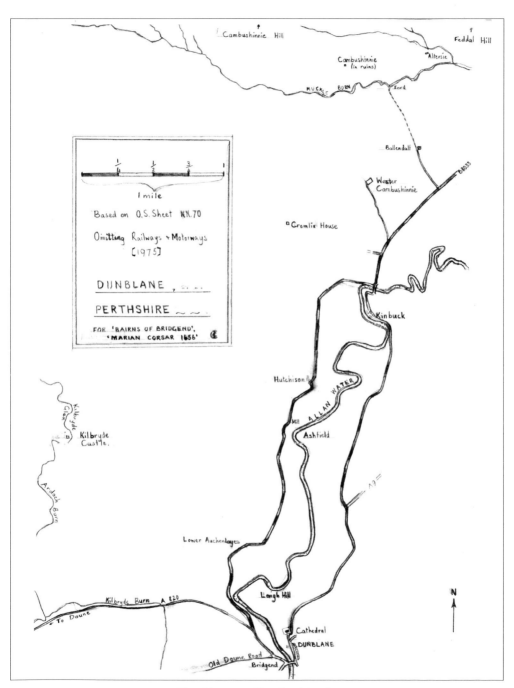

Dunblane to Cambushinnie.

the ford to Marian's side.

"Here," he said, "Gie me yer free hand."

Marian ventured into the cold stream, one hand steadying the precious stowp of milk and the other clutching James's hand. Together they made their way across safely. As soon as they reached dry land, James pulled his hand free and was off ahead of Marian again, up and over the brae on to the well-trodden track that would take them the four miles south to Dunblane.

From the other shielings came more boys and girls whose help would be needed for harvesting and they all made their way across the bridge over the River Allan, past the mill and cottages of Kinbuck and over the gentle slopes of the Laighills. By the time they reached the Braeport of Dunblane, Marian's arm ached with the effort of keeping the milk container level on her head, but as she made her way through the quiet streets of Dunblane she looked forward to seeing her brother in Bridgend.

When he returned from the fields, Robert Corsar gave Marian a brotherly hug and he listened to her tales from Cambushinnie.

"And wha's been learnin ye to spin?" he asked as he admired her handiwork.

"Isobel Graham. Oh Rob, we had a grand time thegither. Ye ken Isobel!"

"Oh, aye," said Robert, "A handy kind o a lass. Weel, she's showin ye the things our mither would hae learned ye if she'd been spared."

Marian could barely remember their mother and father who had died some years earlier when the plague had swept through many of Scotland's towns.

There was no sorrow in her voice when she replied, "Aye, Isobel's like a big sister to me. Oh, I very near forgot, she sent this milk for the hairvisters. I cairried it all that lang road!"

"Weel, we had better sup and hae a guid night's rest. We'll be hard at work frae first light. Just pray that the weather stays fine and we get the corn in safely. I hae seen guid crops ruined by rain at hairvist time."

And so the next morning Marian joined their Bridgend neighbours to start cutting the oats. Every able-bodied person from the youngest had a part to play. The women were grouped in threes across the rigs with the most experienced reaper in the middle. Marian found herself at the outer edge of a rig alongside Margaret Duthie. In her hand she held a sickle with its curved blade ready for her first day's harvesting.

The long strip seemed to stretch ahead forever, wave upon wave of the heavy heads of oats swaying in the summer breezes. She stood mesmerised by the rippling grain till Margaret Duthie's voice broke through her daydream.

"Come on, Marian, follow what the other lass and I dae. Mind and lay the cut corn down on the straw bands that I'm makin."

Marian shook herself and gripped the sickle, bending down low to her task. Copying the others, she grasped a handful of stalks near the ground, hooked the curved blade round them and sawed through, plucking out and laying the bunches of cut grain on the straw band. Across her section of the rig she went to and fro, turning when she reached Margaret's section. All morning the work went on; grasp, saw, pluck out and lay down, grasp, saw, pluck out and lay down, to and fro, to and fro till Marian's eyes stung with the sweat that ran down her forehead.

Behind her came Robert working across two rigs, tying each of the bundles that the shearers left behind them. Glancing round at her brother, Marian saw him stooking three or four sheaves together, leaning inwards, their heads touching and nodding gently, - like so many old wives gossiping, thought the child as she wiped the sweat from her brow.

By noon more than half the rig was cleared and Robert said that they could stop. Thankfully, they sank down into the dip between the rigs where they could shelter from the midday sun. Marian fell fast asleep while the others enjoyed their oatcake bannocks and ale.

"Marian, waken up, lass. I hae kept yer noon-meat. Eat it afore we begin work again."

It was Robert, shaking Marian by the shoulder. She sat up stiffly, and drank some of the milk that she'd carried from the shieling at Cambushinnie. The creamy goodness of it reminded her of the summer moorland, 'Was it only yesterday?' she thought to herself, but Margaret Duthie's voice brought her back to the present.

"Come awa, Marian. Tak yer place." Then looking at the child's weary face, she added, "Aye, we ken! Hard work's no easy! But if ye want to eat, ye maun work for it!"

Marian needed no reminding of that. Only Robert's careful rationing of their precious grain had kept them going over the winter so she knew that a poor harvest could mean real hunger. With that thought in mind, she stuffed her bannock into her mouth and took her place with the women. She carried on mechanically, crouching at the stalks of oats that were like a forest to be felled, small clump by small clump. Grasp, saw, pluck out and lay down, grasp, saw, pluck out and lay down. So it went on through the afternoon. Then quite suddenly the reapers were at the end of the rig and the last stalks were cut.

Slowly, painfully, Marian straightened her back and turned to look over the ground that she and the others had just covered. Where golden grain had rippled, now the rig was bare except for the rough stubble of the remaining straw. And here and there, the bound stooks of corn stood ready for the summer air to dry them out. Robert straightened up from placing the last sheaf and surveyed the scene with satisfaction. He glanced at the sky and read in it the promise of another fine day before he spoke;

"The ither rigs can wait till the morn."

And so Marian was back at the rigs again the next morning, back still aching, and fingers sore from gripping the sickle. Somehow she got through another long day until at last the task was done. Robert was binding the last sheaf of oats and handing it to Marian. The harvest was safely cut and there in her hand was the kirn, the sheaf that would be hung up and kept through the winter.

Back in the cottage, even as she watched Robert tie the kirn sheaf to the smoky branches of the roof frame, Marian felt her head nodding. Her thoughts turned to the return of Isobel and the other lasses and herd lads from the shielings.

'And efter that there's the Grosset Fair,' she murmured to herself as she closed her heavy eyelids and drifted off into a deep slumber.

The tenth of August came round at last and Marian found herself clinging to her brother's arm as he shouldered his way through the throng in the High Causeway of Dunblane. Under his arm Robert kept a firm hold of the shoes that he'd crafted in quiet days and evenings earlier in the year ready to sell at the summer fair. Over one arm, Marian carried a basket of eggs collected from the poultry in the yard at Bridgend.

How very different this was from the day she'd returned from the shielings balancing the stowp of fresh milk on her head: then the streets had been almost deserted with the townsfolk busy in the fields; today all she could see were the backs of the crowd around her as she was swept along past the market cross and into the Cathedral yard.

Suddenly the crowd parted in the path of a runaway ram. Losing her grip of Robert's arm, Marian felt herself being pushed against the wall of the cathedral. While the ram charged on with its furious owner after it, the lass lost sight of her brother. For a moment she panicked, searching the crowd but he had disappeared in the throng of folk who'd been arriving for days for the Grosset Fair, the old Lawrence Day Fair.

The kirkyard was packed with men haggling over the price of their beasts. In August the cattle were at their best, plump and healthy after their days on the summer pastures. If the price was right their owners would sell, if not, then they could wait as long as the Hallowday Fair on November first, before winter set in and with it the shortage of fresh grass.

Today though, the animals were of no interest to Marian. What had caught her eye were the booths crammed side by side around the market cross. Now that her heart had stopped thumping as she got her breath back, it occurred to her that without Robert she could explore the booths on her own instead of following him all day. Once he had found a buyer for his shoes, he would probably be off to the hammersmiths' looking at daggers or maybe a new coulter for the plough, things that were of no interest to her. Still, before she could explore she first had to sell her eggs.

In no time, she had a buyer for her fresh eggs, an empty basket and a few small coins in her hand. Now that she was free she hardly knew where to begin. Maybe she would find Isobel in the crowd and they could explore together. So Marian pushed her way from one stall to another. There were tailors sitting cross-legged, their nimble fingers never stopping as they stitched at trousers and doublets. Nearby, saddlers cut and shaped thick leather into hand-tooled saddles for horsemen whose orders would be ready for their mounts before the fair ended.

At the weavers' booths, Marian fingered the webs of woollen cloth from the Highlands. The material was woven in stripes of purple, brown and blue so lovely in comparison to the plain linen of her skirt and the drab grey wool around her shoulders, and the lass suddenly longed for a plaid like all the grown women wore, with enough material to drape round her head, fold across her chest and reach down to her knees.

The sound of laughter and applause drew her towards a group in a corner of the kirkyard. Squeezing her way through to the front, Marian was delighted to find a group of acrobats whose rapid leaping and tumbling made everyone gasp with admiration. The dark-skinned performers spoke a foreign language but there was no mistaking their meaning when at the end of their act, they indicated that they hoped for payment. The more prosperous onlookers tossed small coins into outstretched bonnets. Smiling broadly, one acrobat bowed deeply in front of Marian and she dropped a curtsey in return.

Laughing and blushing she was just turning away when she caught a glimpse of Isobel in the crowd. She was about to call out her friend's name when she noticed that Isobel was looking up at someone with a very silly kind of smile on her face. Marian frowned and then stopped in her tracks as the taller person turned his head towards her. It was none other than her brother, Robert.

"Rob! Rob!" she called as she started to make her way towards her brother and Isobel.

Pushing through the crowd, Marian suddenly found her way blocked by a trio of burly young men in the uniform of English Commonwealth soldiers. They nudged one another and grinned at her but somehow their smiles were not friendly like the foreign acrobat's.

"Rawb! Rawb!" one of them mimicked her.

"Who's Rawb then darling? Is 'e yer sweetheart?" asked another winking at the others who guffawed loudly in return.

Their unfamiliar English accents made this very different from the teasing of the Bridgend lads that Marian knew well, and she suddenly felt alarmed. Her heart was pounding for the second time that day and there was a tremble in her voice.

"Rob's my brither," she managed to say, shrinking back.

"Oh! I'll be your sweetheart then, a pretty maid like you!" said the third, reaching out towards her.

Dunblane Cross from Cathedral Yard.

The trio guffawed loudly again enjoying their own idea of fun.

Marian stood rooted to the spot but she managed to call out again, "Rob! Isobel!"

Again her tormentors grinned and began to imitate her.

"Rawb! …"

But this time the mocking echo was suddenly cut off as the speaker staggered sideways, reeling from a sudden blow. It was from Robert, and behind him was another familiar figure, John Hutcheson, who shouldered another soldier aside while Isobel reached Marian and put her arms around the younger girl.

It looked as if a fight would break out between the English soldiers and the local lads who were always ready for a scuffle. In the middle of the pushing and shoving, Marian burst into tears.

"We were only in jest, man!" one of the soldiers called to Robert, as the trio retreated into the thick of the crowd.

There was no friendship in Robert's reply, "Dinna show yer faces here again. Gang back to Stirlin and bide there!"

Safe again, Marian wiped her face with the corner of her plaid and took her brother's arm. "I think I'll bide wi ye, efter all," she said, managing a watery smile.

Isobel smiled too. "They didna really mean ye harm, pet. That's just the foolish way sodgers talk. They're far frae their ain hames and folks."

Safe between Rob and Isobel, Marian turned her attention to the bustle around them. Passing ballad singers with tales of battles long ago and pedlars trying to sell their ribbons and trinkets, they made their way to the trestle tables of the ale sellers and found space at the rough benches. While they were relaxing with the ale-wife's brew in front of them Marian glanced at Isobel and saw the silly smile again on her face. Then looking at her brother, she was astonished to note the same foolish expression on his. She turned from one to another as they gazed at each other and then blurted out, "What's the matter wi you twa?"

Isobel nudged Rob. "Tell Marian, then!"

Trying to sound casual but turning a strange shade of pink, Rob nodded.

"Isobel has agreed to be my wife."

'So that's it!' thought Marian and a beaming smile spread over her face. While she hugged her friend and brother in turn, she asked, "And when will ye be wed then?"

"At Martinmas, when the last of the year's work is past," answered Isobel.

"Oh, that will be grand. Will we hae a weddin feast then?"

Rob laughed, "Weel, I canna mind a weddin in Brigend that didna hae a bit o a celebration!"

Then a thought flashed into Marian's head. The lovely Highland plaids! She must have one to wear at Rob and Isobel's wedding! She turned to her brother.

"Rob, come wi me to the highland weavers' stall. I want the plaid there. I'm in need of somethin bonnie to wear at yer weddin!"

The smile faded from Robert's face. "Marian, ye ken we canna lay hands on that much silver. When Will Wright weaves our ain wool, he taks some corn or eggs or the like for his fee."

"But Rob, please come wi me. Isobel, ye must see them. We can speir how much they cost!"

The young couple allowed themselves to be pulled along to the weavers' stalls. As Marian danced along with excitement, Rob was shaking his head and Isobel was trying to calm her down, but she was not listening. At the weavers' booths, Marian darted from one bale to another, feeling the warmth of the wool and pointing out the soft colours of the material.

"I canna think what to pick, the browns or the purples. Ye ken I'm in sore need of a proper plaid, Rob. Ye said so yersel no lang since!" She stopped, looking up at her brother.

Rob was still shaking his head. "I'm sorry, Marian, but think o the cost. We canna afford that."

"But I still hae my egg money." Marian looked at the coins in her hand.

The stall keeper looked at her outstretched hand, shrugged and shook his head while Robert put his arm round his sister's shoulders. "Nae, Marian. That's no nearly anouch, and I canna pay for it either. Sorry, lass."

Choking back tears of disappointment, Marian took her brother's arm again and all three made their way through the crowds. Isobel tried to draw her attention to some jugglers showing their skills, but Marian was no longer interested.

As they made their way down the High Causeway towards the bridge, she heard Robert saying, "Come on now, Marian, it's been a grand day. Think about all we hae seen at the fair!"

Suddenly her disappointment turned to anger, and she exclaimed, "What's the use o the fair if we canna buy anythin?" And then as the tears spilled, she stammered, "Oh, Rob, I did want that plaid. This ane is short and thin and grey and I wanted to hae a bonnie new ane to wear at yer weddin!"

"Weel, lass, if ye work hard at yer spinnin, ye can tak the yarn to Will Wright and he'll weave ye a fine warm plaid in time for Martinmas."

Marian brightened a little at her brother's suggestion, but she went on, "It's the colours, Rob. Our wool is dull, that auld grey. The highland plaids hae the colours o the rainbow in them! I canna spin wool into thae colours."

Then Isobel spoke. "Wait a minute, Marian. I ken wha has the knowledge o dyein' wool .... The auld grass-woman frae out Kilbryde way ... auld Widow Janet, that was mairrit to Angus McDonald, the dyster frae Doune. I mind she used to dae it and she was passin on the skill to her lasses when the pestilence took all her family. I tell ye what, Marian, ye should gang and talk wi Auld Janet. Maybe she wad help ye wi yer wool."

Marian looked up at Isobel and Rob. "I dinna ken. She's a funny auld wife livin alane in her wee cottage. Whiles I see her mutterin to the kye she taks to the moor. The Hutcheson lads said they sometimes hear her sayin some kind o charm."

But even as she spoke, Marian felt a glimmer of hope. Perhaps she would go and see the old woman.

So a few days later, the young girl plucked up the courage to visit Auld Janet. To her surprise, the old woman was pleased to see her. When Marian told her about the lovely highland plaids and about how she longed for one for the wedding, the old woman's eyes grew misty. She seemed to be lost in thought as Marian tried to explain what she wanted.

"And I was wonderin if you could help me, if ye could tell me some o the secrets o colourin the wool."

Auld Janet was silent for a while, still lost in her own thoughts and when she replied at last, her voice was soft and slow. "It's many a lang year since I learned the art frae my guidman, Angus McDonald, and I lost the heart for it when he and my dochters died. But if ye hae patience and can work hard, I'll gie ye a hand to dye the wool for a bonnie plaid."

And so during the remaining days of summer and the weeks of early autumn, whenever Marian could escape from her tasks in and around Bridgend, she and the old woman were busy together. Sometimes Marian would join the grass-woman as she tended the cattle on the moor. Under Auld Janet's directions, she collected the plants that would yield their secret colours.

The child's hands were stained blue picking the blaeberries that grew almost hidden among the moorland plants. Her fingers were grazed scraping at the white crotal, the lichen that encrusted the moorland boulders, and the tough stems of the ling heather hurt when she pulled at them and her feet were soaked in the patches of bog when she uprooted long faded, yellow irises.

Collecting the plants was only the beginning. Under Auld Janet's skilled direction the dyeing was done in the open air by Kilbryde Burn. A big black cauldron filled with fresh, burn water was set to heat over a peat fire. The blae-berries went in to be infused as the water came to the boil. Once all the juices had been leached out of the plant, the dye was strained and some of Marian's precious hanks of spun wool were added. Then she busied herself stirring the pot, stoking the fire and examining the depth of colour of the wet wool. Marian watched as Auld Janet judged the right moment to crumble in some rust from a discarded ploughshare to fix the dye. When the bundles of wool were removed to be washed in the cold burn, Marian's fingers were stiff with cold. But she forgot that in her delight when she saw the blue of the rinsed wool that she hung on bushes to dry. When the fresh breezes had done their work, Auld Janet rewound the dried wool into skeins ready for the weaver.

It was a long process, repeated from start to finish for each colour. The old woman recalled the Gaelic names for each plant as they yielded their dyes: blue from the blaeberry, lus nan dearc*; black from the roots of the iris, seilisdear #; dark green from the heather, fraoch+; and red from the crotal.

And as they worked the old lady began to talk about the days when she had wed her highlandman, Angus, and learned the secrets of the plants. Sometimes she grew sad as she recalled the times and people that were gone, but then the work in hand would bring her back to the present.

"Oh, hark at me havering while that pot's goin aff the boil! Mair peat, Marian, or the colour winna infuse," she would say.

As the days passed, their talk became less of the past and more of the present and Auld Janet enjoyed Marian's chat about the preparations for the wedding. By the time Marian had taken all the yarn to Will Wright for weaving, the young girl and the old woman had become firm friends, each replacing a loss in the other's life. As the wedding drew closer, Marian included Auld Janet in the plans.

Blaeberry, lus nan dearc say loos-nan-jerk; # Iris, seilisdear # say shillister
+ Heather, fraoch+; say froo-ach (ch as in loch). crotal, say crottle

"Ye hae to come to Rob's bridal feast. He and Isobel baith want ye to be there."

"But I heard tell that the Kirk Session has banned weddin pairties wi mair than six folk."

"Oh, aye, but Rob says we'll no tell the Elders and we'll keep the pairty quiet."

"Och my lass, ye hae muckle to learn. Kirk Elders hae eyes and ears everywhere. But I wad love to come to the bridal. I had ne'er thought to be at a bridal again. What will I bring wi me?"

"Ye hae nae need to bring anythin, Mistress. The laird himself has promised to send a fowl, and the folk o Brigend are givin us meal, butter and cheese. Rob is getting ale in plenty frae the brewster so we winna be short."

"Weel, I canna come to a weddin empty handed. I'll just bring a penny like we did when I was young," Auld Janet replied.

During the last few days before the wedding Marian was so busy baking bannocks for all the expected guests that she was taken by surprise when Will Wright came to the cottage with her woven cloth. But when she felt it, her pleasure turned to disappointment.

"Oh, the checks are bonnie, Will, but it's short and sae rough! It doesna feel at all like the highland plaids at the fair."

The weaver laughed. "That's because it still has to gae to the waulk mill, lass. If ye like I'll tak it mysel to Auchenlay wi anither web of claith I hae ready."

It was November tenth; the eve of the old feast of Saint Martin, when Will Wright returned and this time Marian was delighted. The finished article was transformed into lovely soft closely woven cloth. Thanking Will, Marian folded the plaid carefully to keep it safe for the wedding in the morning. Tonight, there would be the fun of the visit with the older girls to Isobel's house for the traditional foot-washing of the bride. And there would no doubt be a great deal of splashing when all the girls scrambled for the wedding ring in a bucket of water. The triumphant winner would be declared the next bride-to-be amidst all the laughter.

At last the wedding day dawned. With her new plaid around her shoulders, Marian skipped across the river with Rob and Isobel. Up the High Causeway they went to Dunblane Cathedral. There in the parish church, with just six people in the congregation, the marriage ceremony was performed by the minister and carefully recorded by the clerk in his big book.

Then it was back to Bridgend where their friends and neighbours were gathered for the celebration. At the cottage door, Will Wright stood with a large two-handled wooden bowl full of strong ale ready to drink the bridal couple's health. While the toast was being drunk, Marion stood on tiptoe to break an oatcake over Isobel's head and everyone scrambled for the lucky crumbs. Then the feast began with everyone eating and drinking more than they had in months, yet there was plenty to spare even for the beggars who always found their way to celebrations.

By the time the fiddlers began to play for dancing, some folk were not fit for it, but many were and Marian found herself whirling around with partners aplenty. Her short plaid floated like a rainbow around her while James Hutcheson almost danced her off her feet.

In the midst of the activity Marian was delighted to see Rob dancing more gently with Auld Janet whose wrinkled face was lit up with pleasure. John Hutcheson spun Isobel round in a reel forgetting all their arguments of the summer days at the shieling. Neighbours, who usually got together to work the land, made the most of the wedding as a rare chance to put aside their daily toil.

Afternoon wore into evening and the heat of the dancing at last made Marian discard the warm wool round her shoulders. And so all through the night the feasting, drinking and dancing continued, until finally the young lass fell into her bed exhausted. Her last conscious thoughts were of the money that Rob and Isobel would now surely have to pay when the Kirk Session imposed a fine for the forbidden music and dancing at the wedding party. She hoped that they would not have to stand in front of the whole congregation in the church….Even so, she thought as she drifted off to sleep, it was worth it…

And so was all the work for this… Marian stroked the soft folds of her precious plaid. With her head nestling in the cosy softness of the cloth she dreamed happily, reliving these past few months: the long summer days at the shieling where she'd learned to spin with Isobel's help; the back-breaking days of harvest with all the other women and girls; the Grosset Fair and all its excitement; and then the late summer days on the moor and by the Burn of Kilbryde.

She stirred in her sleep and smiled quietly at the warm memories of these busy days when she and Auld Janet together had captured all the colours of the moor for her very own bonnie woollen plaid.

BAIRNS OF BRIDGEND
DUNBLANE

MARIAN CORSAR 1656

NOTES

The family name, Corsar, has come down to the present time in Dunblane.
The Register of Testaments (Wills) for Dunblane records a Marian Corsar at the beginning of the seventeenth century who could possibly have been related to Robert Corsar,
cordiner (shoemaker) in Dunblane who died in 1682

Later a dyster, Angus McDonald, is recorded in Doune while the Hutcheson and
Graham families were living in or around Bridgend at the time of the story.
Many Scottish families were affected by the pestilence of 1644-1648. Spread throughout
the country by the armies of the Covenanters and of the Royalist Montrose, it may have
been typhus fever. It is not known how many people it killed in Dunblane, but mortali-
ty rates recorded in towns show that between a fifth and half of their populations died.

Just north of Dunblane, in the estate of Kinbuck, the shiels which tenants used for
summer pastures are marked on an eighteenth century map of the area. (Scottish Record
Office, RHP 13498). This is the southern limit of the areas where the highland practice of
the migration of livestock to summer grazing grounds continued until the end of the
eighteenth century. Quarrels between tenants of neighbouring estates over use of pasture were not uncommon. In 1769 there was a complaint that, *'the tenants of Cambushinnie
have begun to mollest'* Wester Feddals tenants *'in their possession of the said moor and to hunt
their cattle and sheep from the pasture'*. (E777/186/1)

At the time of the story, Cromwell's defeat of the Scots in 1650 at Dunbar had led to
Stirling Castle being garrisoned by the English soldiers of General Monck. Though occupied, and with her King Charles 11 in exile, Scotland was enjoying a few years of peace.
Indeed, Stirling's magistrates had sworn obedience *'to the Commonwealth of England ….
without a king or House of Lords'*.

In 1656 Dunblane Cathedral yard was used for the three annual fairs at Whitsunday,
Lawrence Day and Halloway (All Saints' Day) because it provided a walled enclosure
for animals. Coinage was scarce and most trading was still being done by barter. Later
the Kirk Session banned the use of the yard for trading.

Church discipline extended across the whole community and Dunblane's Session
Records are a catalogue of investigation and punishment of moral lapses: Sabbath breaking; drunkenness and so on. In 1659 a Katherine McGregor was summoned by the
Session to appear because *'she lives and charmes by carrying water out of ye superstitious
well'* in Cromlix district.

In spite of the efforts of the church elders, moral lapses continued to be enjoyed and
'pennie brydals' were still celebrated with song and dance. The bridal couple duly paid
the monetary fine for any such 'unbeseeming conduct' after the event.

BAIRNS OF BRIDGEND
DUNBLANE

MARIAN CORSAR 1656

SOURCES AND BIBLIOGRAPHY

Advice on 17th Century wool dyeing from Peter Macdonald, handloom weaver formerly of Crieff.

Dunblane Kirk Session Records, 1652-1704.
Charters relating to the Royal Burgh of Stirling.

BIL, Albert, *The Shieling, 1600-1840. The Case of the Scottish Highlands,* John Donald, Edinburgh 1990.
FENTON, Alexander, *Scottish Country Life.* John Donald, Edinburgh. 1976.
MAXWELL, Stuart, and HUTCHESON, Robin, *Scottish Costume, 1550-1850.* A&C Black, 1958.
ROSS, Provost Alexander. *Scottish Home Industries, 1895.* Reprinted Molendinar Press, 1974.
THOMSON, Francis. *Harris Tweed – The Story of a Hebridean Industry.* David and Charles Ltd., 1969

BAIRNS OF BRIDGEND
DUNBLANE

ANDREW KERR 1615

There was a jolly miller, who lived by himself,
As the wheels went round he made his wealth;
One hand in the hopper and the other in the bag,
As the wheel went round he made his grab.

Traditional.

The Pyper Knowes are green wi' broom,
Or yellow when they're a' in bloom,
Whence fairy pipings sweetly flow,
While owre the Myre, the gloamin mist
Is like a snowy mantle cast.
And reeds and soughs are hid below …
For there, and several other places,
About mill dams and green brae faces,
Both elrich Elfs and Brownies stayed,
And green-gowned Fairies danced and played.

Cleland.

In langsyne days, in ancient times,
When ruled in Britain's Isle King James,
Then witches wrought their awfu' crimes
in many a house and hame,
'Mang thae was foremost, says auld rhymes,
The warlock o' Dunblane.

Traditional, Adapted.

127

BAIRNS OF BRIDGEND
DUNBLANE

ANDREW KERR 1615

Andrew was wakened by the sound of raindrops plopping on the fire beside him. He opened his eyes reluctantly and looked up at the hole in the cottage roof. The sky was still dark so the lad pulled his woollen blanket closely round him and snuggled down into the crinkly straw of his bedding.

It seemed that he had just closed his eyes again when he heard his mother moving around the fire, blowing on the embers, coaxing the smouldering peat back to life. Now when he looked up, the new flames lit up the soot blackened, timber arches and turf of the roof. Beyond, through the hole in the middle of the thatch, he could see the grey light of dawn. He could hear morning sounds, the low mooing of the cattle in the byre beyond the partition at the other end of the low building, and at the opposite side of the fire his father, John Kerr, yawning and stretching as he rose to begin his day. When his father pushed aside the door to go outside, the early light pierced the gloom of the cottage, falling on Andrew's young sisters, Catherine and Mariota, cuddled up together still fast asleep.

Rising at his father's bidding, Andrew felt the mud floor cold beneath his feet as he went outside. The boy scratched himself and shivered. Though it was late April, the ground was chilly and last night's rain lay in puddles. Not for the first time he wished he was old enough to have shoes like his father instead of going barefoot like the women and other children.

John Kerr's voice broke through his thoughts. "We'll be finishin the ploughin the day. I'll see to the oxen. Efter ye hae eaten ye'll gang down to the smith's to collect the coulter he's been mendin."

"Am I allowed to drive the team the day?" Andrew asked.

"We'll see," was all the answer that his father would give and with that the lad had to be content.

Inside the cottage, his mother had finished the morning milking and was letting the cow and her calf out into the yard. Then she turned back to the hearth where flat bannocks had been slowly baking overnight. Lifting one from the circle of stones, Mistress Kerr broke it into pieces and gave some to the children. They bit into the coarse bread, a mixture of ground peas and barley, and washed it down with milk, creamy and fresh and still warm from the cow.

Breakfast over, Andrew was off with the wooden plough over his shoulder. Down the loan he went to the smithy where John McNair was busy sharpening the repaired blade.

"There ye are, Andra! Yer faither will be in need o this the day. See the coulter's guid as new, fine and shairp. Tell yer faither he could use it for cuttin the claith for my next pair o breeks!"

Andrew laughed, "He'll want it shairpened again afore he'll be back at his stitchin. There's muckle outside work the now. The tailorin will hae to wait."

The smith fixed the iron blade to the Kerrs' plough while he replied, "Aye, efter our ain ploughin's past, we'll doubtless hae our turn of the laird's fields to dae. Right, that's it done now. Run alang, I hae mair to dae than stand here bletherin!"

Back at the cottage, Andrew found his father still struggling with the oxen. One was standing quietly in the yard, but John Kerr was looking grim as he pulled at the other animal and grunted at his son.

"This thrawn beast will nae stand still! Put the coulter down and come ower here. Lift the oxen-bow till I steady the brute."

Andrew took the curved wooden collar from its wall-hook and held it in front of the ox in readiness. His father renewed his grip on the horns of the beast's lowered head. The ox glared at man and boy and suddenly jerked its head up twisting its horns in Andrew's direction. The lad dodged the danger while his father stood firm.

"Now! Put it ower its head. Quick!"

With the collar safely in place, the ox gave up the game and quietened down as they made their way to the fields. When his father had his breath back, Andrew ventured to speak to him.

"Where are the lassies and my mither?"

The question seemed to annoy John Kerr.

"You might ask! Just when I need them all, the laird's officer is wantin a day's work frae the women. So yer mother and the bairns are awa spreadin muck on the Laird's fields at Cromlix. I ken we hae to dae our darg, but it's aye at our busy time that he wants his due!"

Andrew kept quiet, not wanting to irritate his father further, but inwardly he sighed, thinking, 'That's my chance gone for drivin the team. I'll hae to clear the stanes frae the rig wi nae lassies here to dae it.'

He kept his thoughts to himself as he helped his father to put the harness on the oxen and yoke the pair together. Together with their neighbours' two pairs, they made up a team of six draught beasts. With all three pairs together they attached the chain that linked all the yokes to the plough and they were set to begin.

While John Kerr lined the team up at the head of the long strip of land, Andrew went ahead picking up the stones from the surface and tossing them in the weedy pathway at the side, knowing that the way had to be cleared. He would be in trouble if the coulter got spoiled again on a hidden boulder! Then behind him he heard his father greet their neighbours, James Gillespie and William Wright who would help the Kerrs in exchange for using the plough later on their own rigs.

"My lassies can lift the wee stanes while Andra looks out for ony that's buried," one of the men suggested and so at last they were underway.

It was tiring work, levering out half hidden obstructions to the plough and rolling them into the narrow waste strip between the rigs, but Andrew was pleased to be doing a man's work.

"Mind that your stanes are nae fallin on my rig," another neighbour warned them, "Or I'll gie them back and mair!"

Andrew's father was quick to retort, "Maist likely, it's frae your rig that half of thae stanes came! My lad kens what he's daein'."

The oxen, still thin from their sparse winter-feeding, strained at their task and James Gillespie had to stay by their heads, coaxing them to pull their weight.

With a sharp stick in his hand, William Wright moved up and down the team prodding the reluctant animals to keep moving. Once or twice a weary animal's legs gave way under it as it slipped on the heavy clay. Then Andrew had to hold the head of the fallen ox while the men stretched their arms under the animal's belly and heaved it back on to its feet, ready to start again.

Sometimes the coulter, sharp though it was, slipped off the surface of the solid clay, unable to cut into it. Then Andrew had to stand balancing on the wooden ploughshare forcing the blade down with his weight, biting into the soil while John Kerr drove the oxen forward. The skill was in knowing when to jump off, before the extra weight became more of a hindrance than a help, and Andrew had the knack of it. As the morning wore on, the lad felt tired but pleased with himself too, knowing that he was doing a good day's work and that his father was satisfied.

Over the oatcakes and ale that Mistress Gillespie brought for the mid-day break, the conversation centred on the tasks on hand.

"We can mak a start on your rig the day, James, and finish wi yours the morn's morn, Will. We're on my last furrow now."

Sleepy after the morning's exertions and a mouthful of ale, Andrew was suddenly alert again. His father saw the unspoken question in the lad's expression. John Kerr smiled.

"Aye, Andra, ye can tak the next furrow. Now haud awa! Hearken to what I tell ye. We'll lead the beasts. Ye'll guide the plough. Mind to keep the ploughshare straight and steady!"

Andrew was back on his feet, keen to get back to work. The other men grumbled but rose too, taking their places. Through his excitement, Andrew could hear his father's repeated instructions. "Steady! Look ahead. Keep the coulter pointin down. Mind now, ye're pullin ower to the side!"

Trying to follow all these directions at once, the lad made his way unsteadily along the rig, doing his best to keep his furrow parallel to his father's. He frowned, finding the task harder than it looked when his father did it. The ploughshare seemed to have a will of its own, and then just as his father had warned the coulter veered to the right and off the cultivated strip towards the stones between the rigs. His shout of consternation brought the leaders to a halt and John Kerr hurried to take charge of the plough.

"I tauld ye to watch. We'll hae to gang back a bit," he said while Andrew looked on anxiously.

The neighbour they'd had words with earlier couldn't resist a sarcastic comment as men and oxen tried awkwardly to reverse.

"Is that the Kerrs tryin to widen their rig?" he shouted.

Again John Kerr rose to the bait. "Talk sense, man. Dae ye think I want to break my coulter again on thae stanes? The lad's just learnin!"

Andrew squirmed with embarrassment but at least their neighbour had deflected his father's annoyance.

"We all hae to learn," his father repeated as he finished the furrow and turned to survey the rig. "See, yer row is nae bad, Andra. Indeed, it's weel turned for a first attempt," he added loudly for his neighbour to hear.

So the lad who made his way home later was tired, but fairly pleased with his day. His mother and sisters were back home from the muck spreading and he told them about his first ploughing, exaggerating both the length and the straightness of his furrow. Catherine and Mariota looked at him admiringly while his mother glanced at his father and smiled quietly.

"Our laddie's growin!" she said, stirring the black pot on the fire. "Now, Catherine, tell what you and Mariota did the day."

"We gathered the nettles for the broth. There was plenty growin round the edge o the field we were spreadin. That's them in the pot," the small girl said proudly.

"There's barley as weel," added Mariota.

Mistress Kerr ladled the broth into wooden bowl and handed them around the family. While they supped she spoke to John Kerr.

"Dae ye mind Jonet Murriach?" she asked him.

"Aye, I mind o her a while back. Was she nae in trouble for charming some kye that were sick?"

"Aye, that's her," Andrew's mother continued. "It was seven summers past when ane o the elders at Inverallan cut the heid frae a sick stirk and buried it. He thought to mend the rest o his beasts, and Jonet went ower and splashed charmed water on them. Weel, she's been tryin out her charms again!"

"Again! She maun hae nae sense! What happened last time? Was she nae punished alang wi the kirk elder?"

"Weel, he had to repent in the Kirk o Lecropt but she didna. But now there's talk o her bein' arrested! She'll find hersel in the Tolbooth!"

The rest of the talk went over Andrew's head as fatigue got the better of him and he curled up fast asleep beside the fire.

The next thing the lad knew was his mother shaking his shoulder. Morning had broken and his father was issuing instructions again.

"Andra, the laird has sent word that the common is open again. Ye can tak the milk coo and the wee calf up to graze on the moor the day."

"But what about the oxen?" the boy asked. "Ye can see their ribs stickin out!"

"They hae twa mair days ploughin mind, for the Wrights and Gillespies. They'll be out efter that. The coo's mair important. Yer mother will be wantin rich milk for makin the cheese. Ye can bring back some fresh grass for the oxen, but nae mair than ye can cairry under yer oxter. We dinnae want reports to the laird about takin mair than our fair share!"

"Will ye nae want me for the ploughin the day?" asked Andrew, knowing the answer before his father replied.

"Ye canna practise on other folk's rigs! Ye'll maybe get a turn at the harrowin later if Jamie Gillespie will trust ye wi his horse! Yer mother and the lassies can help wi clearin the stanes the day."

Andrew's mother finished the milking and gave him some with his bread. She broke off an extra piece of the warm bannock. "There's a bite for later," she said. "Now mind, Andra, if ye let it, the wee calf will suck the coo dry. Tak a rope and tether it awa frae its mother. It will get its share efter evenin milkin."

With his food tucked into his plaid and the rope wound over his shoulder, Andrew was off, prodding his charges into order. Other older lads from the cottages of Bridgend were gathering their beasts together, and his friend Jamie fell into step with him as he turned towards Allan Water.

The mud surface of the loan was churned up by the hooves of the cows wending their way downhill. At the bridge some folk were going through the city gate and crossing into Dunblane but the boys kept to the near bank, taking the path past the old ford. From the riverside path, the lads could see that the town on the opposite bank was coming to life. From low rush-thatched cottages of the Mill Row and from the High Causeway above, smoke rose thickly as women busied themselves preparing porridge over open fires. The smell of peat mingled with the meal reminding Andrew of his mother's bannock. He made sure it was still safe in his plaid for later.

Now the morning sunlight glinted on the water as it surged past the mill. Stopping to gaze across, Andrew watched the mill wheel turning, steadily driven by the river swollen by the recent spring showers. As always he was awestruck by the wheel's revolutions, the only mechanical movement in the whole village. He thought about his own folk and their Bridgend neighbours, relying on their own strength and muscle power and on their few draught animals for their round of farming tasks. Only the miller had the uncanny knowledge of how to harness the power of nature itself, the water of the river and the fire in the kiln. This set him apart from other men.

Then the lad noticed that the miller himself was mucking out the pig house beside the mill and the sour smell wafted over. His stomach heaved as the stench reached him, adding to the uneasiness he felt even at this distance from the miller and his pigs.

He started as Jamie spoke beside him.

"Clarty swine! Ane broke awa frae its tether last week. What a commotion when it got intae the haining ower yonder and trampled the new grass! The miller will be findin himsel in court payin for the damage if he's nae mair careful!"

"Weel, we hae to move on," said Andrew, somehow relieved to have his

Dunblane Cathedral from River Allan.

132

attention diverted from the mill's perpetual motion.

Now, as they moved along, the ruined remains of the bishop's palace and the cathedral behind it dominated the opposite bank. When one of Jamie's beasts stretched her neck over into the lush green grass of the Bishop's Meadow by the path the lad had to jerk her back.

"Aye! It's us that will be in court if we're nae careful," Andrew joked.

When they reached the common ground of Cromlix other tenants were already there, their beasts all marked to avoid arguments over ownership. In the past that had not always kept them safe from hungry wolves or the occasional plundering highlanders, but today, so close to Dunblane the lads were not afraid of these dangers. Still they had to keep watch over the animals, making sure that they did not wander too far and get lost. With the calves safely tethered, the herds settled in a sheltered spot.

On a day like this, herding was a task they enjoyed. The spring winds had blown the clouds away and the moor was fresh with new growth. The green of the young grass was broken by a sprinkling of yellow, where sunlight danced on the early broom. Larks sang, trilling as they spiralled high above the boys' heads. The cattle munched contentedly while the herd lads relaxed, enjoying their bannocks with clear water from a nearby burn.

Jamie wandered off and came back with two shoots from an elder tree. The soft pith was easily pushed out of the centre leaving it hollow. Andrew watched while Jamie carefully cut small holes in the tube and lifted the pipe to his lips. The sounds that came out were quite tuneful and Andrew tried to copy the older boy. The squeaks that he produced had them both laughing.

"Ye maun hae some music lessons, Andra! But it's time to gang back to Brigend. Look at the sky."

The sun was dipping towards the west as the herds gathered their charges and Andrew remembered to pull some grass for the oxen. By the time they rounded the bend in the river and could see the cathedral, the sky was beginning to darken and black clouds gathering overhead brought the bright day to a sudden close. Jamie could sense the younger boy's anxiety and mischievously added to it.

Nudging Andrew's arm as they came closer to the mill, he said, "Dae ye think the fairy folk are about yet, visitin their friend, the miller?"

Andrew shivered as he saw in his mind's eye the child-sized creatures who took wicked delight in tricking mortals. Everyone knew that the Wee Folk were responsible for many misfortunes that befell ordinary families. Andrew remembered that his own mother had kept to the cottage until Mariota's christening in case the bairn was spirited away. Everyone had heard of mothers who had found their own bonny babies replaced by wizened changelings left by the fairies. Mistress Kerr had kept some iron above her bairn's cradle to protect her from their power.

"Jamie," he asked, "Is it true that the miller is in league wi the fairies? I hae heard tell that they dance and sing on the knowe above Kilbryde Burn. Whiles on windy nights I hear their bagpipes playin."

"Weel," replied Jamie, "The fairies tak their oats to grind at the mill efter dark. Sometimes the miller gies them a hand to set the machinery movin. Since he helps them they dinna harm him. Indeed they guard the girnals where he stores the meal."

Andrew smiled nervously, "It's as weel we hae the river between us and them. I'll keep awa frae the mill and the miller."

As he spoke, Andrew quickened his pace, prodding the cattle on impatiently. It was a relief to turn into the familiar loan of Bridgend and to see the Kerrs' cottage. Ushering the cow in to be milked by his mother, the lad turned towards the fire. His eyes smarted with the smoke, but the smell of nettle kale in the pot reminded him that he was hungry. When he showed his young sisters the whistle he'd made, their smiles turned to an argument over who should try it first. Catherine won and Mariota burst into tears, but her brother's promise to make another pipe for her, soon had her smiling again. The uneasiness of the last part of his riverside walk melted in the smoky warmth of home as he sat on a stool enjoying his bowl of the steaming broth.

When his father returned from the ploughing Andrew helped with the oxen giving them their feed fresh from the moor. While John Kerr settled into the only chair to sup his soup, the talk of the day began.

"Is that you done wi the ploughin now?" Mistress Kerr asked her husband.

He shook his head. "We still hae the Wrights' to finish but the morn should see the end o it."

His wife smiled, "I believe ye like the ploughin mair than yer tailorin! Ye hae the name o bein a fine ploughman!"

"On a fine day it's grand work, a straight furrow's a thing ye can be proud o. But then," he added, "so is a straight seam on a fine piece o clathe woven by Will Wright, and he's promised he'll weave our first wool in exchange for my day's

Dairy cattle grazing, Cromlix.

ploughin."

"Aye, but there's a lot mair work to dae in the fields afore we'll get the wool aff the sheep,"

John Kerr nodded in agreement and added, "Aye, and a lot mair for Andra to be learnin if he's to dae a man's work alang wi me."

As April gave way to May, fresh breezes blew across the rigs drying out the heavy soil. Andrew was able to help with the harrowing, following James Gillespie's mare as she pulled a heavy frame to break up the ploughed soil. His task was to clear stubborn weeds and break up clods too large for the iron teeth of the harrow. It was back breaking work, but when he had a turn of leading the mare, the lad straightened up, proud to be at the front.

So between the everyday tasks of looking after the animals, milking, mucking out and herding, each spring day brought a variety of shared activities for the folk of Bridgend. And while they worked, they gossiped among themselves, passing on news and rumours.

It was Mistress Kerr who heard the most exciting gem of gossip in Dunblane that May and she shared it eagerly with her husband. "That Jonet Murriach has been arrested richt enough! She's in the Tolbooth!"

"Is there a charge against her?" asked John Kerr.

"Charming cattle again, I heard tell, but there's mair. Walter Bryce is held in the Tolbooth as weel and . . ." Mistress Kerr's voice dropped almost to a whisper, "he is to stand trial vera soon."

"That auld deivil," exclaimed Andrew's father, "sae he's been taken at last! He's been in mischief for lang anouch!"

"Aye, the word is that he's witched a woman in Logie, Margaret Duncanson, and her servant is to mak public repentance for dealing wi Wattie. She's to stand and admit her wrang-doin' in front of all the folk in the kirk."

Again the talk of the supernatural made Andrew feel ill at ease, but the conversation soon turned to lighter things. There was the call for all the men to another day's darg for the laird. This time it was to mend the haining, the turf dyke that surrounded the Bishop's Meadow.

As they chatted, Mistress Kerr rose and lifted the lid of the wooden meal kist in the corner. "Oh!" she said to her husband, "Then ye'll nae be able to tak this sack o oats to the mill the morn?"

"Nae, but ye're forgettin, Andra here is auld anouch now to tak it to the mill himsel."

Andrew stared at his father, not quite sure that he understood.

"Ye mean I hae to tak the oats to the meal mill in Dunblane?" The lad found his voice again, "Could my mother nae tak it?"

It was his father's turn to look disbelieving. "Dinna talk sic nonsense, Andra! Women and bairns dinna gang to ony mill. Only men are allowed. What's wrang wi ye?"

Out of the corner of his eye Andrew could see his mother's concerned look, but she said nothing.

He tried to smile. "Naethin's wrang. That's fine. I'll gang first thing in the morn."

But he didn't feel fine. The cold knot of fear that he'd felt earlier had returned to his stomach but he said nothing more. How could he say in front of his mother and sisters that the mill was the last place he wanted to go knowing that the miller was in league with the wee folk? He kept his thoughts to himself as he curled up in a tight ball on his bedding and fell at last into a troubled sleep.

Morning came all to soon for Andrew and with it the feeling of dread. His mother at the milking and his father sharpening his spade for the dyking, were too busy to notice how quiet their son was. The lad looked from his parents to Catherine and Mariota, sleeping snugly, arms around each other. Alone, in the midst of the family, Andrew could only nod at his parents' instructions and envy his slumbering sisters.

"Muck out the byre efter Jamie taks the beasts, Andra. Then gang to the mill and mind that rascal the miller only taks his due for his work. Keep a close eye on him!"

So he went about his tasks, clearing the muck into the midden that stood heaped beside the cottage ready for spreading on the adjoining kale-yard. That done, the lad heaved the sack of oats on his back and slowly took the path towards the bridge. He paused, looking wistfully along the river path that the lucky Jamie had taken with the cattle, but Andrew went straight ahead across the bridge through the Netherport. Dunblane was already busy with townsfolk hurrying to and fro, but no one paid attention to the lad with the sack.

He was reluctantly turning along the Mill Row when he was overtaken by a packhorse with sacks hanging down on its sides. A packhorse was not a common sight in Dunblane and without thinking Andrew quickened his pace to have a better look at it. From the way the sacks hung, he realised that they did not hold grain and he wondered what might be in them. The driver read the lad's thoughts and grinned.

"There's silk edgins for yer sweetheart's gown, combs and bonnie ribbons for her hair, or for yersel, a purse or maybe a pen!" The chapman continued, "I see ye're goin' to the mill. I'm on my way to see what trade I can dae wi the miller."

His friendly tone cheered Andrew up and he hurried to keep up with the pedlar. Amidst the bustle of Mill Row they hardly heard the sounds coming from higher up on the High Causeway, but their attention was caught just as they were at the mill entrance. They turned towards the shouting and sounds of running feet, in time to see a group of men scrambling down the steep track towards them. The men were holding on desperately to a wooden pole that seemed to have a life of its own. Just as Andrew noticed that the pole was threaded through the centre of a large new millstone, the whole thing began careering down the bumpy slope towards them! As the men struggled to control the 'mill-wand', the boy jumped aside, almost dropping his precious sack of oats, and watched breathlessly as the millstone came to a squelching halt in the midden!

The onlookers guffawed with amusement as the red-faced men picked themselves up out of the midden, anxiously inspected the millstone and luckily found it undamaged.

"Weel, that was fine entertainment, eh lad!" said the pedlar.

Andrew chuckled and his fears forgotten, entered the mill. Inside the sound of grinding stones and rattling machinery bewildered the lad, but his companion showed him his way around the place. As expected, there were a few customers already waiting their turn with what remained of last year's good grain harvest. Andrew watched as his precious sackful of oats went in to the kiln to make sure it was completely dried out. The miller's servant turned and shifted the grain to dry it evenly without burning, while another servant hurried back and forth with empty husks from the mill to help keep the fire going.

In the warmth, with the smell of toasted grain rising sweetly, Andrew found himself relaxing and listening to the chat around him. The customers laughed at each exaggerated retelling of the dramatic arrival of the new millstone from Blackford, but the talk soon turned to the topic of Walter Bryce.

The miller began as he paused in his work for a moment. "I saw the Bailies early the morn on the road towards the Cross, and the Laird o Kippenross is in town. They maun be startin Wattie Bryce's trial the day."

"Weel, it's clear that he's a warlock," said a customer. "Just a look at his wrinkled face and lang white hair tells ye that! And wi sic a sharp tongue, he's just the type King Jamie has tauld us to root out!"

"That's as may be, but he was a poor lookin soul the other day when I saw him thrown intae the Tolbooth," replied another.

"I hae heard that he's had dealins wi the De'il himsel!" argued another. "It will all come out at the inquest!"

But the chapman had real evidence. "Last week in Logie, a servant lass admitted in the kirk that she'd been down on her knees in front o him beggin him nae to harm her mistress!"

"Weel, there ye are! What mair evidence is wanted? He should be burned for his sorceries!" interrupted another listener.

All eyes were on the pedlar as he continued, "And when I was at Lecropt, a

Millrow from the Bridge, Dunblane.

137

servant o the Laird o Keir, tauld me that auld Wattie and Jonet Murriach hae baith confessed."

Pausing for effect, he looked round his audience.

Leaning forward expectantly, one of them asked the question the pedlar was waiting for. His voice was little more than a whisper.

"What hae they confessed then?"

The chapman nodded knowingly and answered, "Everythin, witchcraft, sorcery and charmin!"

"I tauld ye! They should baith burn!" said the first customer and this time no one argued.

Throughout this exchange, Andrew sat silent, but when the talk moved on to farming matters he gave himself a shake. He remembered his father's warning about keeping his eyes on their grain and he focused on his reason for being here at the mill. The Kerrs' sack, refilled with the dried oats was slowly cooling as it waited in line with the other sacks for grinding. In a while the lad was watching the miller himself as he poured the oats out carefully, shelling the seed heads between two horizontal grinding stones, removing the husks from the grain. Setting the stones closer, the miller then ground the oats to a coarse meal. Andrew was fascinated as it fell through the stones to be caught in a big sieve. Under his watchful gaze any grain that had escaped grinding was returned to the huge circular stones while the oatmeal dropped through to the Kerrs' sack.

At last the process was over and the miller began his calculations for payment from the freshly ground meal. First taken was a share for the Laird who owned the mill, and then some for the miller himself and for his servant, 'the knave-ship', two cupped handfuls. Just as Andrew was wondering if he'd have anything left to take home, the last payment, 'bannock, one handful of meal was taken by the second servant.

"That's all then, lad. Ye can tak it hame."

It was the miller, looking down at Andrew as he handed him the sack. In the midst of all the chat and activity around them, the lad suddenly realised that he had somehow forgotten to be afraid of this man who could make machinery work like magic! He thanked the miller and hoisted the sack on his back again.

He was just leaving when an excited figure hurried through the door.

"They hae let him gang free!" the man shouted.

"What are ye bletherin about?" asked the miller.

"What dae ye think? Wattie Bryce! They hae discharged him!"

The miller and his customers were astonished.

"But we thocht he had confessed!"

"Aye, but there was only ane witness against him, an auld woman wha blamed her ain foolishness on him. And the lairds found out that the bailies had kept Wattie awake for three days and nichts! And nae just that, he was stabbit wi swords and dirks to mak him confess that he had witched folk. When ane o the gentlemen said that he had kent Wattie for near forty years as a hard workin, honest man, the court broke up and Wattie was discharged!" the speaker finished breathlessly.

His listeners still looked disbelieving.

"Weel, he's the lucky man!" said one, disappointed at the outcome.

"We'll hear mair of Wattie Bryce. Mark my words!" said the miller.

"And what o Jonet Murriach? What's happenin wi her?"

"There's nae word o her trial yet," their informant told them.

"Ah weel, that micht be mair satisfactory! Mair news to tak on my travels. Now miller, hae ye seen my wares?" The chapman traveller was opening his pack as he spoke.

And so Andrew Kerr left his new acquaintances, the chapman, the miller and all his gossiping customers. He walked along Mill Row and crossed the River Allan on his way home to Bridgend, but this time there was a spring in his step and he was whistling happily as he strode along.

What stories he had to tell the family tonight, about meeting the chapman, about the runaway millstone, and best of all, the trial of Wattie Bryce!

Only one thing would be his own secret – the feeling of pride deep inside him, from having faced up to the place and person that he had dreaded. That was a feeling that he could not share with anyone, but now he could look his mother in the eye, now that he had been in the mill that was closed to her.

And now when they started sowing the bere barley, he would take his place with the men. Not for him the bairns' tasks like scaring the birds. Catherine and Mariota could be the watchcorns this year. Yes, now he was ready for a man's life!

Still he was glad to be leaving the mill in broad daylight . . . . when there was little chance of an encounter with any of these nasty wee fairy folk!

BAIRNS OF BRIDGEND
DUNBLANE

ANDREW KERR 1615

NOTES

The Kerr family's names have been taken from the Register of Testaments (Wills) which shows that a John Kerr of Bridgend died in 1629 while an Andrew Kerr died in 1665. The other named adults were their contemporaries, John McNair being the Bridgend blacksmith and William Wright, 'wobster', one of a long line of Bridgend weavers.

In the seventeenth century Bridgend was a separate settlement from the main town of Dunblane. The Meal Mill of Dunblane stood where the Millrow car park is now and it was the oldest of the many mills on Allan Water. As tenants of the Laird of Cromlix the Kerrs would have been obliged to have their grain ground there. Thus they were thirled to that mill.

As a child, Andrew would not have been alone in his fears of the wee folk and witches or warlocks. The old superstitions of pre-Reformation Scotland were no longer acceptable in the eyes of the church. The fairy folk could no longer be appeased with a bowl of milk left out for them, but for many people old pagan habits died hard.

Witchcraft became a statutory crime in 1563. Witch-hunts took place mainly in Lowland Scotland from around 1550 to 1700 during which time well over a thousand 'witches' were executed. In 1597 King James VI lent weight to the movement by attending the trial of a *'prickat wiche'* at Linlithgow and by writing the treatise, *Daemonologie*.

In 1615 the Privy Council gave permission by letter for the trial of both *'Waty Bryis ... and Jonnet Murriache, now in the tolbooth of Dunblane'.* Although Walter, Wattie or Watty seems to have been freed, he was dead by November 1615. (Logie Parish History), while Jonnet Murriache's fate is unrecorded.

Only three years later in 1618, Sir Archibald Stirling of Keir was holding captive a widow, Bessie Finlayson, whom he wanted to have put on trial, *'as suspect of witchcraft'*. Most witch-hunters were local lairds or kirk sessions but in this case the ministers of Dunblane Presbytery questioned the woman and decided against further action.

BAIRNS OF BRIDGEND
DUNBLANE

ANDREW KERR 1615

SOURCES AND BIBLIOGRAPHY

Advice on seventeenth century farming methods; Gavin Sprott formerly of the Scottish Agricultural Museum, Ingliston. (The museum has relocated to East Kilbryde).

The Register of the Privy Council of Scotland. Vol X 1613-1616

P. HUME BROWN. Editor; *Scotland before 1700 from Contemporary Documents*
    Edinburgh, 1893.
GAULDIE, Enid. *The Scottish Country Miller 1700-1900*
    John Donald Ltd., Edinburgh, 1981.
LARNER, Christina. *Enemies of God. The Witch-hunt in Scotland.*
    Chatto and Windus.1971
McNEIL, F Marian *The Silver Bough. Vol I. Scottish Folk Lore and Folk Belief*
        Wm. McLennan, Glasgow 1957.
MENZIES-FERGUSON, R., *Alexander Home, Pastor Poet of Logie.*
    Alexander Gardiner. Paisley. 1899.
SHAW, John. *Water Power in Scotland, 1550-1870.* John Donald Ltd., Edinburgh, 1984.
WHYTE, Ian. *Agriculture and Society in Seventeenth Century Scotland*
    John Donald Ltd., Edinburgh, 1979.

BAIRNS OF BRIDGEND DUNBLANE

BESSIE BROUN 1558

All kinds of ill that ever may be,
In Christ's name I conjure ye.
I conjure ye, baith mair and less,
By all the virtues of the messe,...   (Mass)

Furth of the flesh and of the bane,
And in the eard and in the stane,
I conjure ye in God's name.

Extract from 16th Century rhyme for healing.

BAIRNS OF BRIDGEND
DUNBLANE

BESSIE BROUN 1558

"Haud on, Rab, or ye'll hae the creel ower!"

Bessie spoke sharply to her young brother while he shifted impatiently from one foot to another, wanting to be off, back home to Bridgend in the heavy summer afternoon.

"There's a withie jaggin me!" protested the boy, wriggling to escape the prickling of the woven willow basket on his back.

"Sic a girn!" Bessie's unsympathetic retort came as she hoisted her own creel full of peat on to her shoulders. "That's as much as we can carry. Now tak care. Keep wi me."

Side by side, the children made their way down the sloping moor of Cromlix. They struggled through the sea of heather, placing their feet with care, for even in summer there were unexpected patches of bog where short legs could sink completely into oozing mud. Twisted stems of heather tore at their bare legs and feet. Ignoring the scratches, Bessie snapped off clusters of the tiny purple bells and tied a bunch round with bracken.

It was easier going on the well-trampled riverside path that took them south towards Dunblane. Below the oak trees that lined the river, Bessie spied some delicate bluebells. She plucked them carefully and added them to her posy. Allan Water sparkled in the afternoon sunlight as the pair reached the narrow wooden bridge. Bessie turned to cross it.

"Why are we crossin the brig? It's quicker this road!" Rab called.

Bessie hesitated. It was true that by keeping on this side they would follow the wide loops of the river and be back home in Bridgend faster, but the bridge led to the town, a more interesting prospect. She cast an experienced glance upwards. The sun was still high in a clear sky. That decided her.

"Come on, Rab. There's plenty time afore dark."

With that they were over the bridge and going up again through the Laighills towards the town. Ahead of them the landscape was dotted with tiny bent figures hoeing in the yards behind the long line of low thatched cottages. The children splashed across the Scouring Burn and clambered up the pathway into the narrow main street of Ramoyle. Following the hard beaten track between the houses they passed the Bishop's barn on the slope of Braeport, and reached the Overport, the gate to Dunblane.

The gatekeeper stepped forward smartly to challenge the children. "Wha hae we here?"

"Bessie and Rab Broun wi peat for our mother."

"I'll tak a look then," said the gatekeeper, inspecting the creels.

"It's only what we're due frae the moor. Our faither cut it a while back," explained Bessie anxiously, while Rab muttered at her.

"I tauld ye we should gang the ither way hame!"

The gatekeeper ignored the small boy. "That's fine, I ken yer father, Sandy, the skinner frae Brigend. Naethin to pay. Ye'll pay yer dues soon anouch come

Martinmas when ye're helpin to fill yon muckle granary of our Lord Bishop William."

While he spoke, the gatekeeper jerked his head back towards the Bishop's barn up the brae. Then with a wave of his hand he sent the children on their way downhill past the stone houses of the kirk dignitaries around the cathedral.

"Whaur's all the folk?" Rab wondered as they cut through the deserted yard of the cathedral.

Bessie too was disappointed by the silence. "Nae music the day. The choirboys maun be at the hairvist like the rest o the folk. Wait a minute, Rab, till I tak my flowers to Our Lady."

She lowered the creel from her back and slipped through an arched entrance way into the nave of the cathedral. The lass shivered at the sudden coolness and took a few seconds to see in the darkness after the warmth of the bright sunlight outside. When her eyes adjusted to the gloomy interior, she made her way between the soaring pillars to the corner that she loved. There, behind wooden screens, was the little chapel with the altar of Saint Mary.

Daylight filtering through the aisle window bathed the statue of the Virgin Mary, and flickering candles illuminated her gently smiling face. Bessie knelt and gazed up at the placid expression, smiling and yet sad too, as if hiding a secret sorrow. Sometimes Bessie caught a look like that on her mother's face.

Perhaps that was why of all the saints in the cathedral, Mary, mother of Lord Jesus, was Bessie's favourite.

"I hae brought ye some heather, My Lady," she whispered. "And some of yer ain Lady's Thimbles. They're sic a bonnie blue, just the same as yer cloak."

She laid the posy at the feet of the statue, closed her eyes and murmured an 'Ave Maria'. Her prayer finished, she noticed with sadness that the fragile bluebells were already drooping.

Rab's voice from the doorway interrupted her thoughts.

"Come away, Bessie. We maun get back to Brigend. Father will flay us alive if we're nae back soon to give a haund wi the work!"

As she scrambled to her feet, Bessie hurriedly crossed herself and whispered a farewell to the statue. The Madonna's calm smile was unchanged.

Blinking in the sunlight again, Bessie and Rab hurried downhill past the Bishop's palace till the track took them down to the river again and past the meal mill. Out through Dunblane's Netherport and across the fine stone bridge, they were in Bridgend in minutes. There was still a dearth of folk on the streets but glimpses between the cottages showed folk hard at work in their yards, tending their crops or livestock.

It was then that Bessie suddenly remembered that her mother had told her to be back in time to milk the cow, and it was past milking time already. The beast would be irritable, still missing the calf that had been taken from her. The cow was waiting, tethered outside the cottage after a day out on rich summer pastures with the old grass-woman of Bridgend. Bessie left Rab to stack the peats while she spoke soothingly to the beast. As she had feared, the animal was skittish and the lass kept out of range of its back legs, knowing that a sharp backward kick could send her sprawling and leave her bruised for days. Gradually, the cow quietened down and Bessie began milking. Under her practised hands the white jets of liquid spurted rhythmically into the wooden bucket.

She was still crouched beside the animal when her parents and the bairns, John and Helene, returned from the fields.

"Still milkin, Bessie? Ye're late frae the moor then!"

Bessie had no time to reply before Rab burst out, "We'd hae been hame afore this if Bessie hadnae stopped at the cathedral!"

Still half hidden by the cow's broad side, Bessie glared at her brother and muttered between clenched teeth, "I'll learn you to carry tales, Rab Broun!"

But her father was shaking his head. "We hae anouch to dae at hairvist without spendin time at the kirk. Why did ye gang there? It's nae a feast day!"

Bessie found it hard to explain. "It's sae peaceful . . And then when it's High Mass I like the singin when the choir's full wi the vicar and the chaplains . . ."

"Huh," her father interrupted, "the last Sabbath I was there, we couldna hear the Mass for the tradin goin' on around the door and in the kirkyard! Folk shoutin out the price o their wares, lauchin and jestin ower their bargains. They dinna heed the prayers and the priests dinna seem to care!"

"There's nae harm in the lass goin to the kirk for a while. The bairns hae worked weel. Look at the stack o peats frae the moor," her mother said.

Bessie heaved a sigh of relief. Her mother as always took her father's mind off whatever was annoying him, but he was not finished.

"Weel, weel," he said, "The morrow we'll all be together on the corn rig, me cuttin, mother and Bessie bindin and the bairns stookin. It will be a lang day!"

And so it was a long day, the first of many that started early and finished late, for the whole community, men, women and children were hard at work in the rigs around Bridgend. The men with their sickles rhythmically slashing at the corn while behind them the women and bairns gathered up the fallen grain and bound it into sheaves. Lastly ten or so sheaves were stooked upright leaning inwards to support each other and let the drying breezes through. Backs ached and fingers were calloused as they worked against time, fearful that a late summer storm might ruin the crop before it was harvested and safely dried.

Later as days shortened towards autumn, the dried grain was threshed ready for storing and Bessie like everyone else was so busy that she had no time to think about even a quick visit to the cathedral. But it seemed that the harvest was no sooner in than the folk of Bridgend were reminded that whether they attended services or not, the cathedral was central to all their lives.

In October a rider came trotting through Bridgend and clattered to a halt near the Brouns' cottage. Gathering round, Bessie's family and neighbours heard the all too familiar reminders from the Bishop's officer who remained loftily in the saddle. Obviously relishing the importance of his position, the horseman made his announcement.

"The Chancellor of the bishopric of Dunblane gives warning that the tenants of each and every one of the twelve merk lands of Brigend and of the pendicle thereof called Smith Land are due to supply their marts and teinds . . ."

"That's him here again lookin for our beasts and grain for the Bishop's larder," thought Bessie. She wondered if their milk cow would be among the beasts slaughtered . . . Her mind was brought back sharply to the officer's words when she heard her father's name.

"Alexander Broun, ane hog sheep, twa hens, ane boll of bere barley, twa bolls ane firlot of oats, ane mart hide."

The officer went on to name other Bridgend tenants and to list what they had to supply at the beginning of November for the Martinmas part of their rental. If his listeners were less than delighted they had more sense than to voice their feelings. It was only when the Bishop's officer wheeled his horse round and rode off, that the usual complaints were made.

"As if we needed remindin!"

"There will be little grain left in Brigend efter the Bishop's chancellor gets his due."

Someone added sarcastically, "We hae to remember that the bishop has a big family to feed!"

There was some laughter at that but Bessie's father's voice had no mirth in it. "Hae mind o the privilege we share o bein' allowed to buy back our ain corn frae the chancellor!"

"Now, Sandy. We'll hae nae need o that this comin winter." It was Bessie's mother, Christian, as always making her guidman see reason and she continued, "But we hae little time to lose if all is to be ready before Martinmas."

So again the Broun family was fully occupied preparing the winter store. First the stirk that had been fattened on the summer pastures was slaughtered and bled carefully into tubs. Alexander Broun expertly skinned the beast while Bessie began to help her mother with the preservation of the meat. The cutting up was skilled work and Bessie watched her mother closely while she jointed the stirk's carcase. It was gory work and their hands and arms were soon red and sticky. But Bessie was not at all squeamish till later when she noticed the fresh blood trickling down her mother's right arm.

"Look, mother," she exclaimed, "Yer airm is cut!"

The woman looked startled and then said quickly, "Och, It's naethin, just a scratch. The knife slipped."

But the trickle of blood was increasing to a flow, and then Bessie saw that there was more damage. The fingertips of her mother's left hand were almost severed and from each one the blood was pumping steadily. The colour was draining from her mother's face and Bessie knew that she had to act quickly.

"Haud yer airm up. I'll gang for Mistress Wricht to come and help."

"Nae, Bessie, nae. Gang for yer father. Naebody else."

There was a look of such fear on her mother's face that Bessie's heart all but stopped, but somehow she managed to think straight. Tearing a strip from her petticoat, she wrapped it round her mother's bleeding hand.

To John and Helene, she hissed, "Bide here you twa. Keep yer mother's airm up for her. And stop yer greetin!" she added as the bairns began to cry.

Christian Shearer was a ghastly white. There was no time to waste. Bessie continued, "I'll nae be lang. Just bide here or I'll thrash ye baith!"

With this mixture of reassurance and threat, Bessie was away from the cottage and down through Bridgend to the edge of Allan Water where her father and Rab were working at the tan pit. Under the man's instructions, the lad was tossing oak bark into the pool. They stopped stirring when they saw Bessie's breathless approach.

The expression on his daughter's face told Alexander Broun that something serious had happened.

"What's wrang, lass?"

Bessie's voice trembled. "Mother's cut hersel. All her fingers are pourin blood!"

"Whaur's Mistress Wricht or Mistress Danskine then?" Her father was puzzled as he asked the question.

"Mother said to gang for you, nane other!"

Even as Bessie answered, her father was starting back up the slope with her and calling hurried instructions back to Rab.

"That's anouch bark in the water, son. Just give it a good stir and put the skin intae it."

Back in the cottage the frightened bairns were still holding their mother's arm upright. To Bessie's intense relief, Christian Shearer managed a pale smile. Alexander Broun was gruff in his concern for her.

"What's this ye hae done to yersel, wife?"

As he spoke he was removing the bloodstained cloth from her hand. "I hae seen worse, but it's nae like you to be sae careless wi a knife!"

Her reply was a whisper. "I hae nae feelin in my fingers, Sandy."

His response was quiet and deliberate. "What dae ye mean, nae feelin?"

"It was Bessie that noticed the cuts on my fingers. There's nae feelin there."

There was a slight tremor in his voice as he asked the next question.

"And what about the haund that was haudin the knife?"

Her reply was weary. "It's nae guid. The feelin's nae there either." Bessie's mother hesitated and then continued, her voice trembling.

"But there's mair than that, Sandy. See my richt airm."

She pushed back her wide sleeve, and now tears spilled as she looked from her arm to her husband.

Bessie heard her father gasp and saw a look of horrified understanding on her father's face. She heard him say tonelessly, "Tak the bairns out, Bessie and say naethin about what yer mother just said. Gang to Mistress Wricht and see if she has any salve for yer mother. If she speirs, tell her it's nae a muckle cut. There's nae need for her to come. Tell her that."

The bewildered bairns were glad to follow Bessie into the fresh air and all three approached their near neighbour. Bessie tried to sound casual as she made her request.

"Dae ye hae any salve for a cut, Mistress Wricht?"

"Wha's cut then? I'll be alang in a wee while. I'm up to my oxters in salt water the now!"

Bessie remembered her father's warning. "My mother – but there's nae need for you to come, Mistress Wricht. I can put the salve on, and my father's there to help."

"Indeed that's nae man's work. I'll be alang soon."

Bessie grew desperate. "Please, Mistress, if I could just hae the salve the now!"

Reluctantly, the woman dried her arms and reached up to a shelf. She took down a wooden bowl and looked at the dried daisies in it.

"Ye're lucky. I hae some banewort here ready dried. Infuse it in warm water. Then I'll be alang to bathe the cut and bind the pulp ower it."

There was no arguing with her so Bessie did as she was bid and hurried back to the cottage. Her father had already bathed the cut fingers in the brine that was prepared for the mart salting and the bleeding was easing off a bit.

"Mistress Wricht is comin ower soon. She wouldnae be put aff."

While she spoke Bessie was already busy by the fire, pouring warm water over the daisies. Her mother watched her and smiled wanly.

"That's as I expected," she said, "She wants to see to her ain medicine."

"Richt, Bessie," her father said, "That's fine. Just act natural. Mind what I tauld ye."

The question that Bessie wanted to ask remained unspoken. The arm that had made her father gasp was covered up and she hadn't seen it. With the bairns huddled in the corner, she knew better than to talk about it.

It was not until Mistress Wricht had come and gone leaving the patient's fingers wrapped in the comforting daisy pulp, that Bessie brought herself to broach the subject. The bairns and Rob, his hands stained brown from the oak bark solution, were fast asleep and their mother was dozing too, when Bessie and her father returned to the task of salting the meat.

"What is it that ails mother?" Bessie's question was direct.

Her father hesitated and looked at his eldest child.

"It's nae the cuts. They should heal . . .It's how she came to cut hersel." He stopped again.

Bessie prompted him. "Mother said she couldnae feel her fingers."

"That's richt, Bessie." Still her father hesitated. "Can I trust ye, lass? Can ye keep what I tell ye to yersel?"

She nodded silently, fearing to hear the rest. Her father turned to where her mother slept now and pulled back her sleeve. Now Bessie could see what had made him gasp. Her mother's arm was covered with large blotches. The child stared at the discoloured patches and then at Alexander Broun in complete bewilderment.

"What is it, father?" she whispered.

His reply was hesitant. "Just this, lass . . . Thae blotches, the numbness in her fingers. There's just ane reason for them . . . Yer mother is a leper."

Her father's words were slow to sink in. Bessie shook her head. She could not have heard right.

'Yer mother's a leper!' The very name was hideous. She stood dumbfounded, staring stupidly at her father. She wanted to scream. 'It's a lie, a dirty lie! Never say that about my mother!' But the desolate look on her father's face told her that he was deadly serious. Only one word came from Bessie and it sounded as if it were dragged out of her.

"Leper?"

Her father nodded slowly. "It's the end, lass, and nae just for yer mother, for all o us."

Later, lying with the bairns, but not sleeping, Bessie turned it all over in her mind. . . 'Leper! But mother doesnae look like a leper . . . Lepers are ugly and misshapen with weepin sores and fingers missin!'

As she fell into an exhausted sleep she had almost persuaded herself that her father was mistaken.

But in the cool light of day when Bessie looked at her mother's poor damaged hand and remembered the discoloured patches on her arms, she was forced to face up to the situation. 'Leper!' The secret that her mother had kept was now

Bessie's burden too. There was only one other that she could share it with.

As soon as she could escape from the Bridgend cottage Bessie was off, across the bridge and through Dunblane to her haven, St Mary's little chapel in the cathedral. The heather, now dusty and faded, still lay at the Virgin's feet, recalling for Bessie the carefree summer day on the moor. On that summer evening which seemed so long ago, the cathedral had been almost deserted but today it was filled with sounds of prayer and praise. Beside the chapel where she knelt, the chaplains were chanting a mass for the souls of the dead. They paid no attention to the wee girl who whispered the awful news of her mother, praying to the Virgin to ask God for his help. The saint's tender, caring expression reassured the child that her prayer was heard and she rose feeling that her terrible load of care was shared.

Behind the choir screen the voices of the schoolboys' song rose and fell under the precentor's direction. Their pure voices soared heavenwards in a celebration of praise. Bessie peered through the fretwork of the choir screen to see and hear them better. For a few moments, lost in the glorious music, she almost forgot why she was there. Rapt in sound she let her eyes wander idly over the rich furnishings of the choir, the carved choir stalls for the clergy to rest on and the burnished brass candlesticks of the High Altar.

It all contrasted with the simplicity of the Brouns' cottage in Bridgend and the child tore herself away reluctantly to return to the stark reality of the family's situation.

Back in Bridgend, Bessie entered a conspiracy of silence with her parents. They all knew that the fate of lepers was banishment of the family from the

15th Century Ochiltree stalls
Cathedral choir.

community or abandonment of the leper by that family. The bond between her parents was too strong for them ever to part but expulsion from Bridgend was a prospect too awful to contemplate.

Meanwhile, Rab and the bairns were not to know in case they spoke out of turn, and Bessie struggled to act normally.

Mistress Wricht came to dress the cut fingers again and scolded the patient as she worked.

"I'll ne'er ken how ye managed it! Ye came close to losin' thae finger tips!"

Bessie didn't dare to look up in case her expression betrayed her, but their neighbour prattled on. "See, now, how does that feel?"

The child sighed with relief when her mother answered, "That's better. They're no sae sair, now," because of course there was no pain, no feeling.

It was strange how deception became easier with practice as the days passed. When neighbour women wondered at the fingers taking so long to heal, Bessie was quick with a story about the bairns grabbing at their mother's sore hand and re-opening the cuts.

Still, it was a constant worry. Once any neighbour got the slightest suspicion that anything was unusual about the injury, it would only be a matter of time. Suspicion would turn to fear. That fear would lead to gossip and then to terrified demands for an official examination at the Bishop's court. It would be impossible to hide the telltale patches of discoloration on her mother's arms. Then the unthinkable ejection would follow. Cast out as lepers, left to beg!

Bessie had seen them, rattling their metal cups on the end of long poles, waiting beside the cathedral or near the bridge for whatever coins people could spare, belonging nowhere, outcasts from society!

Even thinking about it brought Bessie out in a cold sweat. Sleepless nights made it all the harder to get through her work and there was more than ever of that with her mother able to do much less than usual. Even with the meat from the mart bullock salted away, there was still a great deal of preparation of the winter store. Nothing was wasted. The animal's stomach linings, thoroughly cleaned, were stuffed with meal and blood for black puddings or with meal and suet for white puddings. Under her mother's direction, Bessie tied and boiled and pricked the puddings in case they burst, and finally hung them up to dry on the roof timbers. Then there was the remaining suet to be made into tallow for soap or candles, while horns and hooves would be traded with passing tinkers who would make spoons on winter evenings.

Working from dawn to dusk through the last days of November made Bessie so tired that at last she did sleep at night. But in those sleeps the same visions always appeared . . .the groups of lepers, silent, begging, rattling their cups, 'unclean, unclean' and every leper had the same infinitely sad face of Bessie's mother. The child would wake sweating, yet in waking there was no escaping the nightmare. There was no escaping the spectre of leprosy.

December had begun before Bessie managed back to the cathedral. What she had been dreading had happened. It had begun innocently enough when Bessie and the bairns had been fetching water. At the well they met some neighbours. Mistress Danskine had spoken first. "Whaur's yer mother the day? Wi yer father at the tan pit?"

Before Bessie could reply, Helene had blurted out, "Mother, sair haund . . ."

"Is that haund nae healed?" There was surprise in Mistress Danskine's voice.

"I doubt Mistress Wricht's banewort was nae guid," another woman remarked.

"There's naethin wrang wi the salve," said Bessie quickly. The last person she wanted to offend was her kindly neighbour, Mistress Wricht. "Mother will just nae rest her haund. She's aye duntin it on things." Bessie struggled to keep her voice normal.

151

The women looked at one another and then back at Bessie.

"I mind ye said that afore," remarked one woman slowly.

"It is a lang time healin," Mistress Danskine added, "Is it nae?"

Bessie tried to smile. "I'm sure it will nae be lang now. Come awa bairns."

But as she left the gossiping group at the well, she knew with sickening certainty that the women of Bridgend had begun to suspect that there was more to her mother's injury than met the eye. The remark that followed her confirmed her feeling.

"There's somethin that lass Broun isnae tellin us about her mother!"

Later that day Bessie made her way through the busy nave of the cathedral to the little side chapel. There she knelt once more in desperate prayer at the feet of the Virgin Mary. But the statue's sad smile, that had seemed understanding before, now looked merely resigned. The child's frantic pleas for help brought no response, and she got no feeling of being heard. The strain of the terrible secret, and the knowledge that it would soon be out, sent tears of despair coursing down her cheeks. Seen through tears, the statue's face became hazy and Bessie turned and left the chapel blindly. She tripped and stumbled and fell headlong on to the flagstones of the nave and lay there sobbing on the cold floor.

It all seemed so hopeless, her mother still with no feeling in her fingers, her own unanswered prayers, and now their Bridgend neighbours exchanging knowing looks. She didn't hear the footsteps approaching, but the next thing she knew was that someone was lifting her by the shoulders, helping her to her feet. As she rose she saw a pair of sandaled feet below folds of rough grey cloth. Through her tears she recognised that the wearer was a man of the church. The face that looked down at her was kindly and the voice was warm with concern.

"What is the matter, child? Such greetin for a tumble!" As he spoke the man dusted Bessie down.

Gradually Bessie's sobs subsided and she wiped her face dry with her sleeve.

"It's nae the tumble, sir. It's my mother. She's nae weel. I was prayin to the Virgin for help but I doubt she's nae hearin me!"

Fresh tears began to trickle down her cheeks.

"Hush, now. Tell me about yer mother."

Bessie looked at him, longing to tell someone, yet dreading the consequences.

As if he read her thoughts, the churchman continued. "I am a friar, of the order of Saint Francis. Do ye know what we friars seek to do in this weary warld?"

"I hae heard a black friar preachin but I didnae understand him," the child ventured.

The friar smiled. "Yes, we grey friars also preach the gospel and we follow our Lord Jesus Christ in his care o the sick. We hae knowledge o curin many illnesses. Perhaps I could help yer mother. Where do ye bide so that I may visit her?"

"Nae!" Bessie exclaimed. "That wouldnae . . . I mean mother wouldnae want that, sir." Then in a whisper she added, "The folk o Brigend would bother her wi a lot o questions."

The friar, bending to catch her words, frowned a little. "Neighbours' questions? That is surely usual among neighbours."

Then as Bessie still looked uneasily around the busy cathedral, he added, "We can talk outside away from all this hubbub, though in truth these men of business hae nae interest in our discussion."

Out in the open yard, Bessie felt free to speak where no stone walls could echo her words nor stout pillars conceal hidden eavesdroppers. Now she could answer the friar's queries.

"Tell me about yer mother's infirmity. Is she fevered?"

Bessie shook her head.

"Is she vomiting?"

Again the child shook her head.

"Does she fall down in a faint?"

"Nae, nane o thae things."

"Then tell me child. What are the signs of yer mother's malady?"

Bessie spoke slowly, searching for the right words. The words that would tell enough but not all.

"Weel, mother has cut fingers that are slow to heal . . . since afore Martinmas."

"What else, child?" The speaker had a glint of understanding in his eyes.

Thoughts flashed through Bessie's mind. Could she trust the friar? Should she tell him more? Anyway, what difference would his knowing make now, when the women of Brigend had their suspicions? This could be her mother's last chance . . .

Her mind made up, she blurted it out.

"It's her airms. There are blotches on them!"

The friar nodded slowly, "And her fingers? Is there feeling in them?"

As she shook her head soundlessly, the tears slid down Bessie's cheeks again.

The friar spoke quietly. "Listen, child. I hae heard of a cure for such a malady." He scratched his tonsured head as he thought. "Ah, I hae it now! It requires oatmeal and oil of bay."

Bessie sniffed and tried to smile. "We hae oatmeal in plenty at Brigend, sir."

"Guid. But I fear that the oil of bay will be difficult to find."

"What is bay? I never heard tell of it."

"It's a kind o tree, beloved of the ancients who used its leaves for victory wreaths. Its leaves and berries have healin in them. But where may we find one in these cooler climes?" Now the friar stroked his beard thoughtfully.

"I hae heard that there's bonnie trees in the Bishop's orchard," Bessie ventured looking towards the palace.

"Weel spoken, child. That is where we will begin our search."

Bessie gasped. "Oh, naebody daurs gang near the palace grounds!"

The friar laughed, "That's where I and my brither friars hae the advantage ower ither men. A wanderin preacher is usually made welcome in such places, in the kitchen at least where he can beg a meal. I know that Bishop William is in Edinburgh attending a parliament of the Queen Regent. Come wi me, child, round to the kitchen. The Bishop's French cook Gabriel is an auld acquaintance of mine."

In spite of her worry, Bessie was excited as she trotted beside the grey hooded figure across the cathedral yard. The Bishop's servants directed the friar to the kitchen and raised no objection to the young girl being with him. It was all bustle in the kitchen but the friar was given a stool to sit on, a stoup of ale to sup and a hunk of bread to eat. He broke off a piece for Bessie. It was soft and light. Bessie had never tasted fine wheaten bread before, and that was not the only source of wonder. The kitchen with its vaulted ceiling was larger than Bessie's home and the child had never seen such an array of utensils, cauldrons and kettles, pots and pans and other things that she didn't recognise. And hurrying in and out, barking orders in a strange language to the kitchen boys, was Gabriel, the Bishop's French cook.

"What is he sayin to the lads?" Bessie whispered.

"He instructs them in their own tongue, French."

Bessie was mystified and the friar continued. "The Queen Regent, Marie of Guise, has many of her ain countrymen here in Scotland as advisers, soldiers and servants, like Monsieur Gabriel here."

He was interrupted by the French cook who grinned as he spoke. "Friar Ludovic, vous know verra weel that the Scottish barbarians have nae the art of cuisine. But perhaps, now that Scotland is fortunate to hae a new French king wed to the beautiful young Queen Marie, we may civilise les ecossais! But no the day! This day we must prepare for the return of Bishop William frae Edinburgh. He will reach Dunblane on the morrow. The parliament is ower and it is his wish to be here in his own palace for the winter. He suffers much frae gout and even the Queen's physicians cannae ease his pain."

Again the small Frenchman grinned mischievously as he added, "Perhaps you may be able to help him, Friar Ludovic!"

The friar chuckled, "My mission is to minister to the poor who do not hae physicians and cooks all the way frae France. That is ae reason why I am here. This little lass has need of somethin ye may hae in the Bishop's garden."

Bessie sat up straight and the cook raised his eyebrows as the friar continued. "We are in need of oil of bay for a poultice for her mother."

The Frenchman shook his head. "Alas, no. We have not a bay tree."

He gestured out of the window to the garden that swept down to the river's

Ruins of Bishop's Palace, Dunblane.

154

edge. Leaning forward, Bessie could see all the way to the rooftops of Bridgend, above the Bishop's meadow on the opposite bank of Allan Water.

The cook went on, "The garden has leeks, cabbages, onions and in summer, lettuce all for the bishop's table and in the orchard, pear trees and apple trees and against the wall below, plum trees, but I regret nae bay tree and nae other herbs. For these we hae supply frae the monastery of Sterling."

The friar laid his hand lightly on Bessie's shoulder.

"So that is where we will seek."

Through her disappointment, Bessie managed to say, "I hae never been to Sterling."

"Nae, child. I must return to Sterling to my friary on the morrow and I will visit the Abbey of Cambuskenneth on the way. The Augustinian monks have great knowledge of growing herbs for physic. Monsieur Gabriel, I thank ye for yer hospitality."

"De rien, Friar Ludovic. Some bread and ale and an exchange of news! But now I return to my cookin. My maister will not be content wi such modest fare as you have had! Au revoir!"

Outside the palace at the mercat cross, Bessie listened carefully when the friar outlined his plan.

"The day efter the morrow is the feast of Saint Nicholas. All will be watchin the boy bishop's procession. Bring yer mother and I will give her the oil of bay if I hae it."

"And if there's nae oil at the abbey?" the child asked.

"Then we shall try another remedy, though in truth I know of nane else for . . . such a malady."

The child who bade the friar farewell and made her way down through Dunblane had hope in her heart for the first time in weeks. It was with a lighter step that she crossed the bridge into Bridgend and began the walk up the sloping track towards her own home.

But in that street she met a strange silence. It was not the summer quietness of cottages empty when everyone was busy in the fields. This was a different silence. People seemed to melt away at the child's approach. Children playing in the street were grabbed and hustled indoors. Grown men and women slid out of sight and all Bessie could see was the flapping of leather doors, moved by unseen hands. She was uncomfortably aware of hidden eyes watching her progress all the way between the houses.

Only one neighbour could be seen outside her door. Distress was written on Mistress Wricht's face. As the child passed, she shook her head and, "Oh, Bessie!" was all she said, before she too turned inside her cottage. In that ghastly moment, Bessie realised that the women at the well that morning had lost no time in spreading their suspicions around. It took the child all her strength to keep walking erect till she reached home.

Inside it was clear from the dejection of the family that Bessie's deduction had been correct. The people of Bridgend had already turned their backs on the Brouns with the diseased person in their midst, her own mother. Her parents and the bairns huddled together as if to draw comfort from one another. Bessie's mother was protesting weakly, "Nae, Sandy, let me gang alane. I can join up wi some others . . ."

Alexander Broun was beside himself. "Nae, Christian, ye're nae like them. There's nae a mark on yer face. I'll ne'er let ye gang!"

Before Bessie had time to speak, Rab burst into the cottage. "What's wrang wi the folk o Brigend? Why are they all glowerin and sneakin aff like I was a leper?"

It was the first time the word 'leper' had been used since the day her mother had cut herself. In the stunned silence that followed Bessie's mother began to weep, but she put out her good hand and restrained her husband who would have struck Rab in his anger and grief. Bessie was the first to recover and she hurriedly outlined the afternoon's events in and around the cathedral, finishing with the friar's plan to meet them at the procession for the feast of Saint Nicholas.

Her father was sceptical. "Thae friars wi their miracle cures, bones o the saints and . . ."

To her own surprise, Bessie interrupted her father, shouting angrily, "Sae, what will we dae? Wait for the court officials to examine mother? And then just leave Brigend?"

Her mother nodded. "She's richt, Sandy. It's our only hope."

Alexander Broun looked at his wife and daughter and shrugged his shoulders in resignation.

"Ye're richt," he said slowly. "Ye're richt. We hae nae choice!"

The morning of December sixth was clear and bright and in any other year Bessie would have been excited about the feast day of Saint Nicholas, friend of sailors and little children. But today she felt only apprehension. Her father had decided that he himself and not his wife, Christian, would go to the cathedral yard with Bessie.

"I will nae let yer mother be stared at, or waur, by the folk o Brigend. Rab and the bairns will bide here wi yer mother. If yer friar keeps his promise to be at the kirkyard, he can come back here wi us."

Even with her father at her side, Bessie felt nervous as they made their way through Bridgend. Some neighbours looked away awkwardly, others stared defiantly, but no one spoke to them.

Around the cross it was difficult to move in the crowd there for the festivities and Bessie and her father were still pushing their way towards the cathedral when the singing of the choir heralded the start of the procession. Held aloft was a portrait of a white-bearded, kindly face depicting Saint Nicholas. Behind came his representative for the day, the boy bishop, proud to have been elected by his fellow choirboys. His gold mitre and jewelled crosier caught the sunlight and his white and red vestments were a brilliant splash of colour. Even so, Bessie hopped up and down impatiently while the whole procession moved along, the cross bearers, altar boys, chaplains and priests all in their best ceremonial robes. She was searching for the simple grey habit of Friar Ludovic. At last the crowd thinned and the Brouns were able to reach the cathedral yard. Bessie scanned the area anxiously, worried in case the friar would not be there, and she almost missed the quiet grey figure that waited by the cathedral door.

"There he is, father," she said at last.

The relief in her voice made her father smile as he remarked, "Weel, he's nae as kenspeckle as the chiel that just passed!"

Friar Ludovic smiled when father and daughter approached. "Guid morrow, Bessie, child. Guid morrow to ye baith."

He wasted no time in following Bessie and her father back to Bridgend where he spoke quietly to Mistress Broun.

"Guid woman, I believe I know what ails ye. Will ye show me yer airm?" He nodded when Bessie's mother pushed back her sleeve.

"It is as I feared, but the malady isnae far advanced, and I hae here a possible antidote."

Bessie broke in, "Is it the oil o bay?"

"Yes, child. The infirmarian of Cambuskenneth had some in his dispensary. Lavender, thyme, rue and other herbs thrive in the monastery garden but the bay tree is delicate. It is our guid fortune that the skill o the monks keeps ae precious bush alive."

As he spoke the friar was reaching inside his cloak for the pouch that hung on the cord at his waist. He produced a handful of shiny oval leaves.

"There are nae many but they are green and still contain their oil. Crush and mix them sparingly wi oatmeal and boiled water. Apply them to the affected parts."

Even as the Brouns thanked him, Friar Ludovic slipped quietly away. The Broun family stared at the leaves.

Bessie's father broke the silence. "Weel, he kept faith and brought us the leaves. We maun try them, wife."

And so they did. Bessie crushed and mixed them a little at a time and applied the still warm poultice to the arms and hands, binding it all carefully. But there were so many uncertainties. How long should the dressings be left? Hours? Days? They simply didn't know and they could not call on Mistress Wricht for help this time.

And all the while the whispering went on among their neighbours. Then the court officer rode to Bridgend bringing the news that they had been anticipating. After a long preamble, he drew himself up, cleared his throat and made the solemn announcement, naming Bessie's mother clearly.

"The court ordains that Christian Shearer, spouse of Alexander Broun, skinner at Brigend, to be considered by men of understanding if she be leper or nocht, and if so to put her solitary and in the meantime to forbid the market."

There was helpless anger in Alexander Broun's immediate reaction. "Forbid the market! Dae you think that I would allow my guidwife to gang to market to thole all thae folk starin at her? She will appear at the inquest and nae a moment afore!"

But Bessie knew that her father's anger was fuelled by fear and not just for his wife but for all of them. There was only a fortnight before the inquest so there was no time to lose in putting Friar Ludovic's remedy to the test. While Bessie dressed her mother's wounds, her father and Rob carried on with preparing their leather, though it remained to be seen if their usual customers, the saddlers and cordiners, would want these finished skins.

The bairns, kept close to the house, helped Bessie by bringing the peats to feed the fire, and every day when Bessie walked to the well, their company gave her courage to walk past the unseen eyes of neighbours. Somehow, even weighed down with heavy buckets, she managed to hold her head high with defiant pride.

The day before the inquest, with just enough of the precious bay left for one last dressing, Bessie set out for the cathedral again. Her father looked up from where he and Rab were finishing the tanned leather, and called out to her to wait.

"Here, lass," he whispered, pressing a tiny silver coin into her hand. "Light a candle for yer mother. At the High Altar, mind . . . yer mother will need all our prayers the morrow."

Bessie was still feeling surprised by her father's wishes when she entered the cathedral. She started towards her usual corner and then suddenly changed her mind and turned instead to the altar of Saint Nicholas. The Bishop's portrait looked even more benign close up in the little chapel and so the child addressed her prayers to the patron saint of children. Then she ventured through the nave to donate her father's offering and kneel as close as she could get to the choir. Peering through the screen she looked towards the High Altar. After lighting her candle she remained on her knees for a few moments watching its smoke spiral upwards half obscuring her view of the crucified Christ as she whispered her last desperate prayers.

Today, though, Bessie shed no tears. Instead, as she rose and crossed herself and left the cathedral, she simply felt exhausted. Tired of seeing her mother's suffering and her father's frustrated rage. Tired of shouldering all the household burdens, and above all tired of neighbours who shunned her family. 'I'm even tired o prayin,' she thought wearily as she reached home again.

After the bairns and Rab were bedded, Bessie pounded the last two precious

Dunblane Cathedral in Winter.

bay leaves and made the oatmeal poultice. She tried to persuade herself that her mother's arms were clear as she bound them but the sleep that she fell into at last was still a troubled one.

As the family group made their way through Bridgend the next morning, their curious neighbours watched silently. Father and children formed a protective ring round the woman who kept her bandaged limbs hidden under her grey plaid. Bessie felt strangely detached and she found herself thinking that banishment from Bridgend could scarcely be worse than living like this.

At the cathedral the inquest committee was already waiting and the Brouns stood around awkwardly, unsure of what to do. A clerk consulted his large record book and called out,

"Christian Shearer, spouse of Alexander Broun!"

Bessie's mother took a step forward and so did her father. The clerk held up his hand to bar the way.

"The woman alane, nane other," he said.

Bessie looked at her father's stricken face as her mother was led away out of sight. The child slipped her small hand into his large hand and felt him grip it tightly. Nothing was said. Even the bairns stayed silent, overawed. Minutes passed but it seemed like an eternity and then the clerk reappeared with Bessie's mother behind him. Under her plaid, Bessie could see that her arms were bare.

In the background the 'men of understanding' put their heads together and then one spoke to the clerk. The clerk turned to those assembled and made his solemn declaration.

"It is found by this inquest that Christian Shearer, spouse of Alexander Broun, skinner of Brigend, is nocht leper. The said Christian Shearer has the freedom of the market and of the town of Dunblane."

Whatever else he had to say was lost in the roar of joy that came from Bessie's father, a roar that echoed round the cathedral nave bouncing off pillars. Bessie felt her father's calloused fingers tightening their grip on her hand till she yelped with pain. Then he let go and charged at his wife, lifting her off her feet in a great hug while tears ran down his face.

"Hush, Sandy, ye muckle gowk! Ye'll frighten the bairns," was all she said while she clung to him in delight. The court officials looked on in offended surprise, while in the background only Bessie got a glimpse of the grey friar who slipped quietly out of the cathedral.

Later Bessie was to turn it all over in her mind, back in Bridgend feeling that now at last, this was where she and her family really belonged, for better or worse. Who was she to thank? Who had answered her prayers? Lord Jesus, his mother Mary, Saint Nicholas? She would pray to each in turn in future, and in her prayers she would always remember the kind grey hooded friar who had slipped so quietly in and out of their lives.

BAIRNS OF BRIDGEND
DUNBLANE

BESSIE BROUN 1558

NOTES

The Broun family's names were taken from Bessie Broun's testament registered at Dunblane in 1598. (CC 6/5/3:) Though she was married to Malcolm Wricht of Bridgend her 'guidis and geir' were left to John, Robert and Helene Broun. The list includes 'ane auld blak mear . . . ane zeir auld stirk . . . ane hog scheip' (one old black mare, one year old stirk, one yearling sheep) along with a quantity of corn and bere barley 'in the barne and barnzaird'.

The altar of Saint Mary was endowed by the Stirlings of Keir. Sir John Stirling entrusted the Observant Franciscan friars of Stirling with funds for a daily mass to be said for the redemption of his soul in Dunblane Cathedral after his death. (Cowan p46) All the little chapels that lined both aisles of the cathedral nave were destroyed in 1559 by reformers who set out to 'cast down altars, and purge the kirk of all kinds of idolatry'. Cuts in the pillars that supported the dividing screens mark where they were situated. The ruins of the Bishop's palace are situated between the cathedral hall and the river. In more recent times the gardens were used as washing and bleaching greens. In the middle of the sixteenth century high offices in the church were filled by royal commendation which in practice meant that great abbeys and their estates became sources of income for the illegitimate infant sons of James V, while bishoprics fell into the hands of noble families who took care to keep the benefices to themselves. Dunblane was no exception and the last three pre-reformation bishops were Chisholms of Cromlix who held office from 1487 to 1569. Other Chisholms held the offices of arch-deacon, dean and sub-dean (Dickinson p278)

Bishop William Chisholm's political career is well documented. Throughout the reign of James V and during the minority of Mary Queen of Scots, he was an able and conscientious member of the Scottish Parliament and was appointed to the Privy Council. When Mary of Guise was Queen Regent for her daughter, friction was so high between native Scots and 'occupying' French that an act of parliament had been passed against 'speaking evil of the queen's grace and of the Frenchmen' (APS II – 499-500) In 1555, the 'rich bishop' of Dunblane lent the Queen Regent £4,400. In 1557 he signed the marriage treaty between Mary Queen of Scots and the Dauphin of France.

Following the Reformation of 1560, ill health curtailed his political activities, but before his death in 1564 he had bestowed much of Dunblane Cathedral's lands upon his numerous illegitimate children. (Hutchison Cockburn, Ch. XI).

Unfortunately, the only mediaeval record extant of the activities in Dunblane Cathedral is the minute book of the court of the Official of Dunblane Cathedral, (1551–1554).

Leprosy is believed to have been brought to Britain by returning crusaders and several cases of it are recorded in the Stirling Burgh Records of the 1540s. The proceedings described in the tale of Bessie Broun regarding leprosy suspects are taken from these records, using the names of a documented case.

The disease is curable and is not of itself fatal. The disfigurement of advanced cases was the source of the abhorrence that its appearance caused but mild cases may be arrested without any treatment.

Reformation activities during 1559 and 1560 affected monastic establishments more than the cathedrals. The Abbey of Cambuskenneth and the friaries of Stirling were totally destroyed along with many others throughout Scotland. Such destruction diminished the possibility of reformation of the church from within the old Roman Catholic faith. (Cowan. Ch.2)

BAIRNS OF BRIDGEND
DUNBLANE

BESSIE BROUN 1558

SOURCES AND BIBLIOGRAPHY

Thanks to Mr. George Dixon and Mr A. Borthwick, formerly Central Region Archivists, for translation of Sixteenth Century Testaments.

Acts of Parliament of Scotland, 1124-1707. Vol. Edit T. Thomson and Cosmo Innes, 1814-1875.
Burgh of Stirling, Charters and Other Documents, 1124-1705. Glasgow,1884.
Burgh of Stirling, Extracts from the Records, 1519-1666. Glasgow, 1887.
Scottish Diaries and Memoirs, 1550-1746. Edit. J.G. Fyfe, Eneas Mackay, Stirling, 1928.
Rentale Dunkeldense, 1505-1517. Scottish History Society, Second Series, 1915.
Rentale Sanct Andree, 1538-1546. Scottish History Society, Second Series, 1915.
Statutes of the Scottish Church, 1225-1559. Scottish History Society 54, 1907.
The Scottish Correspondence of Mary of Lorraine, 1542-1560. Scottish History Society, 1927.
Testaments of the Commissariot of Dunblane. Scottish Record Office CC 6/5/2 CC 6/5/3.

ADDISON, Josephine, *Plant Lore*. Sidgwick & Jackson Ltd., 1985.
ALLAN, John, *The Days of the Monasteries and Latter Days of Stirling*. Stirling, 1907
ANDERSON, G R., *The Abbeys of Scotland*. J. Clarke & Co. London. (undated).
COCKBURN, J Hutchison, *The Mediaeval Bishops of Dunblane and their Church*. Oliver & Boyd, Edinburgh 1959.
COWAN, Ian B., *The Scottish Reformation*. Weidenfield & Nicholson, 1982.
COX, E.H.M., *A History of Gardening in Scotland*, Chatto & Windus, 1935.
DICKINSON, W.C., Revised by DUNCAN, Archd., *Scotland from Earliest Times to 1603*. Oxford University Clarendon Press, 1977
DICKINSON, W.C., DONALDSON, Gordon, and MILNE, Isabel, Edit., *A Source Book of Scottish History*, Vol II, 1424-1567. Oliver & Boyd, Edin. 1965.
DONALDSON, Gordon, SCOTLAND.Vol.III James V to James VII. *The Edinburgh History of Scotland*. Oliver & Boyd, 1965.
DONALDSON, Gordon, *Scotland, Church and Nation through the Sixteen Centuries*. Edin. 1772.
DONALDSON, Gordon, *Scottish Church History*. *Scottish Academic Press*, 1983.
DONALDSON, Gordon, *Scottish Historical Documents*, Scottish Academic Press, 1974.
FENWICK, Hubert, *Scottish Abbeys and Cathedrals*. Robert Hale Ltd., 1978.
FRASER, Antonia, *Mary Queen of Scots*. Weidenfield & Nicholson. 1979.
MARSHALL, Rosalind K., *Queen of Scots*, H.M.S.O. Edinburgh 1986.
NICHOLSON, Ranald, *SCOTLAND.Vol.II The Later Middle Ages*. The Edinburgh History of Scotland. Oliver & Boyd, 1965.
THOMPSON, Phyllis, *Mr Leprosy, Dr. Stanley Browne*, Hodder and Stoughton 1980.
VERNEY, P., *The Gardens of Scotland*. Batsford Ltd, 1976.
WORMALD, Jenny, *Court, Kirk and Community. Scotland 1470-1625*. Edward Arnold 1981.

BAIRNS OF BRIDGEND
DUNBLANE
SOURCES AND BIBLIOGRAPHY

I **GENERAL BACKGROUND**
DEVINE, T. M., *The Scottish Nation 1700-2000* Penguin Press 1999
LYNCH, Michael, *Scotland. A New History*. Century Ltd. 1991
MITCHISON, Rosalind, *A History of Scotland*. Methuen & Co. Ltd. 1970
ROBINSON, Mairi, Ed. *The Concise Scots Dictionary* Aberdeen University
   Press 1985
SMOUT, T.C., *A History of the Scottish People 1560-1830*. Fontana Press 1969

II **HISTORY OF DUNBLANE AND DISTRICT**
Commissariat of Dunblane, Register of Testaments, 1539-1800.
Dunblane Cathedral Kirk Session Accounts.
Dunblane Kirk Session Books of Discipline.

BARTY, Alexander B., *The History of Dunblane*, Eneas Mackay, 1944
NIMMO, William, *The History of Stirlingshire*. T.D. Morison, Glasgow 1880
RANDALL, C., *The History of Stirling*, 1819.

III **AGRICULTURE AND RURAL SOCIETY**
FENTON, Alexander, *Farm Servant Life in the 17th to 19th Centuries*.
Scottish Country Life Museum Trust 1975
FENTON, Alexander, *Scottish Country Life* John Donald Ltd., Edinburgh 1976.
SANDERSON, Margaret H.B., *Scottish Rural Society in the 16th Century*.
   John Donald Ltd., Edinburgh 1982

IV **DOMESTIC LIFE AND CRAFTS**
GRANT, I.F., *Highland Folkways*. Routledge and Kegan Paul 1961
LOCHHEAD, Marion, *The Scots Household in the Eighteenth Century*.
   Moray Press Edinburgh 1948
PLANT, Marjorie, *The Domestic Life of Scotland in the Eighteenth Century*.
   Edinburgh University Press 1952
WARRACK, John, *Domestic Life in Scotland, 1488-1688* Methuen & Co. Ltd., 1920